Praise for Rex Burke

[For] fans of Douglas Adams who like Sci-Fi stories with a sense of humour and a 'slice of life' feel to them.

Sue Bavey, book blogger, Sue's Musings

I completely, wholeheartedly recommend this gem of a book.

Rebecca @ Indie Book Spotlight

Did I devour this book or did it devour me? I ended up blazing through this rollicking adventure in one day.

Esmay Rosalyne, Before We Go Blog

If there is a natural successor to the likes of Pratchett, then Rex continues to hold the crown with his colourful, endearing characters and banterous dialogue.

KDS, book reviewer

SPECIAL DELIVERY

Also by Rex Burke

Odyssey Earth series

Orphan Planet

Twin Landing

Star Bound

Sci-Fi adventures

The Wrong Stop

Third Loch From the Sun

Special Delivery

SPECIAL DELIVERY

REX BURKE

ISBN: 978-1-916694-09-5

Cover design: Chris Hudson Design, chrishudsondesign.co.uk

Acknowledgements: Thank you to my fabulous, eagle-eyed beta-readers – Sue Bavey, Lisa Rose Wright, Val Poore, and BlueSmoke Bob.

I'm indebted to David Clegg for his military expertise – he cleared up all sorts of terrible blunders I'd made about rank and terminology, and doubtless saved me from a court-martial. John Pare, as ever, read an early version and provided some great insights. And, although it's not her kind of book, Elaine encouraged me to the end – I'd follow her into space battle any day.

Chapter 1

THEIR UNIT, OneSquad, had been fighting hard all day across difficult terrain. The planet was a squelching, crater-filled shithole, and Dix was covered in mud – at least, he hoped it was mud – but orders were orders.

"Take the ridge. Neutralise and pacify. Hold until relieved."

Or, as the sarge had helpfully paraphrased, "Run up that boggin' hill. Kill every bogger there. Get t' kettle on for a brew. Wait for them lazy boggers from TwoSquad to get 'ere once they've finished paintin' their nails."

The sarge was from one of those farming planets in the outer rim. Kallax, maybe? They all talked like that there, even the children.

The platoon OC had said, "Now, now, sergeant," and the sarge had said, "Sorry sir, quite right, once those lazy boggers from TwoSquad have decided if this hill will do for today or if we still 'ave time to run up another one for 'em before dinner."

This was why everyone secretly loved the sarge, even though he could be terrifying. You wouldn't tell him you loved him, not unless you wanted him to break your nose, but you would do anything he said without question.

The jury was still out on the officer, a fresh-faced second lieutenant who barely needed to shave but had a rash on his face that indicated he tried anyway.

Dix's squad had lost its usual leader to a broken ankle earlier in the day. When he'd been medevacked down the line, up had come the platoon's officer to see what the delay in the advance was all about.

He'd been interfering ever since. Platoon OC, 'officer commanding.' That was a joke. Twenty-one, twenty-two, if he was a day – younger than Dix even – and knew everything about everything.

Sure he did. All he'd done so far was talk bollocks over the comms-cube to HQ, and then issue jargon-filled orders that the sarge kept having to translate.

"Sarge," said Dix, lifting his vision-gogs and glancing meaningfully at the rocky heights above them. They were squirreled in a muddy trench, sheltered partly by fallen rubble. He could see beams and exposed wires, and, incongruously, the shattered screen of a holo-entertainment unit, half buried under fallen bricks. A house then, or what was left of it.

There were ten of them in the squad, strung out along the rough trench. The second lieutenant, the sarge, and eight troopers, Dix among them, and it was make-your-mind-up time. As in, they'd been here half an hour already, and the rebels on the ridge knew they were there and were getting their aim in.

A fairly shit aim, it had to be said. This was less a proper rebellion and more a petulant outburst by a bunch of disaffected ore miners who had decided to try and sell on the black market. But they had weapons, and they had the height advantage. They might not be trained, but it wasn't hard to rain fire down on an approaching force and wait to get lucky.

"Thoughts, trooper?"

Another good thing about the sarge. Asked your opinion, and not just in a taking-the-piss 'Oh-*that's-*what-you-think-we-should-do-is-it-trooper?' kind of way. Rarely acted on it, obviously, seeing as he was a fifteen-year Federation combat sarge and you were a third-year grunt, but even so. Felt like you were part of an actual team, and not just deployed as turbo-cannon fodder.

As it happened, Dix did have thoughts. They mostly revolved around not dying in a muddy hole on this shit-hole of a planet, thank you very much, but he had had some more constructive ones, too.

In the absence of attack drones – the officer's request had been denied earlier – Dix had been thinking about the unpromising terrain and how they might use it to their advantage.

"The gully, sarge," said Dix, pointing at a jagged cleft in the rock face that ran up to the top of the ridge.

It was concealed from the rebels on the top by the angles of the rocks and some shrubby growth. They weren't even looking in that direction. Instead, they had a clear line of sight down to the rubble in front of the trench, and were gaily hosing the open ground between the remains of the house and the foot of their defensive position.

The slope up to the ridge itself wasn't particularly steep, but without drone support only an idiot would try and attack that way – out in the open and uphill, into suppressing fire.

Right on cue, enter the idiot.

"Frontal assault, sergeant, don't you think?" barked the second lieutenant, sidling past a couple of huddled troopers to appear at the sarge's elbow. "Covering fire from the ruins, put a mortar team out, that should keep them occupied. We'll be up there in five minutes. I doubt they'll even stick around once they've taken a shell or two. They're miners, not soldiers. No match for OneSquad, eh sergeant?"

The sarge still had his vision-gogs on – enhanced optics, 2x zoom – so Dix couldn't see his eyes, but they had to be rolling. And that was a slight shake of the head, surely, but if it was, the officer didn't notice.

"Bear with, sir, still scanning." Then, out the side of his mouth, "What about the gully, trooper? Boggin' goat couldn't get up that."

"Goat, sarge, no. Me, yes. Grew up swiping eggs from nests on the sea stacks."

Long time ago now, admittedly, back on his home

planet, Calisto, but Dix had always been able to climb stuff. Didn't always fall off, either. He tapped his NavCom wrist-unit, double-checked the calculation against the mapping. Ninety-eight-foot climb. High, but do-able.

"It's on their blind side, they'll never even know I'm coming. Beats going out into that." Dix gestured over his head at the various clumps, bangs and ricochets that were successfully keeping them pinned in a mud-filled trench.

"That could work," said the sarge, taking in another sweep of the gully, touching the side of his gogs to zoom in a bit more. "I mean, I wouldn't want to do it, but you're a clever little bogger aren't you? Make a soldier of you yet."

Dix blinked. That was the nicest thing the sarge had said to him in the two-and-a-bit years he'd been in the unit. He even felt ridiculously proud – which *was* ridiculous, given that he'd just volunteered to climb a hundred feet up a rock to ambush a bunch of burly, heavily armed miners who would not be at all pleased to see him.

"Right, you two." The OC had seemingly tired of waiting, turned his back on the sarge and was talking to the troopers closest to him. Rennie. Distin. Not that the officer knew any of their names, even though he'd been with the platoon a month by now.

"Sir?"

"You're Alpha team. Up there." He pointed to a partially collapsed wall, about ten feet away, up and out of the trench. "Covering fire, all right? And you three" – he gestured at the next troopers down the line – "you're Beta team. One to cover, two on the mortar, from over there." He pointed a fair distance away, across open land, to where there was another tangled ruin of masonry. "Give 'em a bit of hellfire, and we'll come right up from under them. Bish-bosh."

Rennie and Distin popped their heads up to look at the wall the officer wanted them to take a position behind, and watched as a rake of tracer fire sparked across the stones. They quickly dropped back down and looked across at the sarge for help, with expressions that clearly said, "No, I don't think so, but thanks for the suggestion anyway."

"Sir, Dix 'ere 'as 'ad an idea. Not a totally stupid one. I know he looks like a bog-wit, but I think we should give it a go. We can always try your Alpha, Beta and hellfire if it don't work out." The sarge nodded at Dix, and Dix nodded back, accepting that "If it don't work out" translated as – if he fell off the cliff or got shot by a miner on the way up.

The second lieutenant wasn't having it. Seemed annoyed to be diverted from his cunning assault plan, which was going to get everyone killed.

"Dix?" he said, shaking his head. "Who's Dix?"

"Me, sir. Trooper Dix. I was just telling the sarge I can get up that gully, no problem. Get around the side of them. They won't even know I'm coming."

The officer looked over at the gully, gave it a brief glance. "No, no, never going to work. Far too slow. We need to clear them out now. Right, Alpha team, on my mark."

"But sir." The sarge held his hand up, requesting a pause. "Dix can do it. Like a yooman spider, he tells me. Let 'im try, no 'arm done."

"You seem to be under the impression this is a debating society, sergeant." The OC looked royally pissed off now, as more ricochets pinged off the stones. "I've run an assault like this dozens of times on the academy sims. They're not even proper soldiers for goodness' sake. Not frightened of a bit of live fire are we, chaps?"

Someone muttered "Academy sims, got to be kidding," though it was lost in another loud crump, from behind them this time. The shells were getting closer.

The sarge looked down the line and shook his head, deliberately this time, but it seemed to Dix in resignation rather than defiance.

"Get the men ready, sergeant, you've heard my orders." The OC shuffled back down the line and started briefing the remaining three members of the unit. "Gamma assault," Dix heard him say, before another loud explosion splattered more mud and stones on them.

"Sarge?" someone else said, with a rising note of concern.

"All right, maggots, you 'eard the officer. Rennie, Distin, you keep low, you 'ear me? We'll lob a coupla softeners from 'ere, buy you some time. Then you blaze away, give your muckers a chance to get set up with the mortar."

"But sarge, it's mad. He's crazy if he thinks that – "

"Trooper!" The sarge spoke firmly and fixed Dix with a glare. "You know how this works. It's the army, son. I do what he says, you do what I say. Them's the rules. Don't bog me about, and don't ever question me – or an officer – in the field. Got that?"

"Yes, sarge."

"Right, good lad, you're with his fancy Gamma team, so bog off down that end, will ya?"

Before Dix could squeeze past, the second lieutenant was back again, fuming. "What is the delay here, sergeant? Where's my covering fire? You two, Ronald, is it? Dustin? Get up there now. Move!"

The sarge clapped them both on the shoulder as they put on helmets and clipped their body armour closed, and then Rennie and Distin slithered out over the top of the trench and squirmed their way towards the collapsed wall. A flurry of tracer bullets kicked up stones all around them, while heavier fire smashed into the front of the wall that they were hauling themselves towards on their elbows.

Distin was hit almost immediately. He gave an anguished yelp – not even a scream – and then stopped moving, face down in the mud. Rennie scrambled forward in a panic, on hands and knees, and huddled against the low wall, shrinking down as far as he could. Dix could see him looking back towards Distin, briefly reaching out a hand before withdrawing it, realising he was never going to be able to get to him. Not that there was anything anyone could do for Distin now.

"Covering fire, man!" The officer was hopping about in the trench, popping his head up and down to check on Rennie's position.

Rennie was still cowering behind the wall. He had a shoulder-borne tube-blaster with him, carried in a holster on his back, which he plucked from behind his head when he heard the officer shouting. But the minute he tried to balance it on top of the wall, and sight it on the ridge, raking fire across the stones forced him back down again.

"You, Dix, get up there and help him," said the OC. "We're not going to get anywhere like this. We need that covering fire."

Typical. Knows my name now, when he's got something suicidal he'd like done. Three years in the army, and this was where Dix's luck ran out, because an idiot thought that just saying something – however idiotic – made it happen.

He felt a hand on his shoulder. "Stay here, Dix, lad. Get down t'other end, be ready to go when I get that blaster up with Rennie. OK?"

"Yes, sarge."

"Man's job, sir," said the sarge, as the OC started to say something. "They're good lads, but they know bog-all about battle ops. Leave it wi' me."

The sarge made to climb out of the trench, but as he went, he grabbed Dix by one of his webbing straps, pulled him close and whispered fiercely. "If it all goes to boggins, you get up that gully, spider boy, all right?"

And then the sarge hauled himself out, and made a fast, low run to the wall. He conferred with Rennie, and they hoisted the tube into position and started popping up suppressing blasts. Dix could see a couple of puffs against the rock face, close to the ridge, as they calibrated the distance.

There was a brief pause from the firing in both directions – Dix watched the sarge turn and give a hand signal to the OC, who in turn moved down the trench towards the mortar team.

Dix was also on the move, behind the OC, when a huge explosion rocked them on their heels, throwing mud into their faces. Just short of the trench this time. Close. And when Dix wiped mud from his face and looked up and out, the landscape had changed.

Half the collapsed wall had disappeared entirely. There was a crater where that section had been. And the other half had stopped being anything resembling a wall and was now just a carpet of heavy rubble. The half where Rennie and the sarge had been.

Dix could see the sarge's legs splayed at an unnatural angle, but the rest of him was buried further under the rocks. He couldn't see Rennie at all. He could, however, see Distin, who had been cut down before reaching the wall – in fact, Dix could see bits of Distin very clearly, now that they had been blown much closer to the trench.

Dix realised the second lieutenant was shouting at

him – his ears were still ringing from the explosion. Shouting, but not making any sense.

"The crater," he yelled. "That'll do, they won't hit it twice. In there with another blaster, and hurry." He turned to the mortar squad further down the trench. "Go, go, go! Time to give them something to worry about. The rest of you, on me."

Nobody moved.

Dix looked over to the crater and then back to the trench, seeing only the sarge's mangled legs and one of Distin's arms.

With Rennie buried under the rubble, that left seven of them cowering in the trench. Or rather, six doing the cowering. The seventh was shuffling and shouting, prodding one trooper after another in the chest to try and get them moving. The three in the mortar team were at the shallower, far edge of the trench – crouching, tensed – and the second lieutenant was screaming at them to move. He turned back to see Dix, on his haunches, and yelled at him, too.

"Trooper! Up and over now! That's an order!"

"No," said Dix.

"What did you say?" The second lieutenant was incandescent, his pimply cheeks flushed.

"No," said Dix again, adding, "sir" as an afterthought, just in case that was what he was objecting to. Never knew with these academy types, sticklers for protocol.

"It's an order! You're disobeying a direct order, trooper." He lunged forward and pushed Dix hard in the chest to try and get him moving. Punched him really, with a clenched fist.

The sarge had had plenty of occasions to chastise his squad; he'd never raised a finger to them, had never needed to. And was now lying dead out there, because of this idiot with bum-fluff on his cheek. Dix, without thinking, lashed out with his forearm, rocking the second lieutenant back against the trench.

"And you got the sarge killed. So I'm sneaking round and going up that gully, like I should have done in the first place. Before you cock anything else up."

The officer's face looked as if someone had been sick on his breakfast tray and then suggested he eat it quickly before it got cold. Filled with rage, he drew himself up to his full height and stood towering over Dix, which – in a protective trench that only came up to chest height – even the greenest of troopers could have told him was a schoolboy error.

Phht, phht.

Two sniper rounds came in – decent shooting for a miner, to be fair – the first catching the OC in the shoulder and spinning him around, which meant that the second missed. Lucky, as that probably would have killed him.

He sunk to his knees, groaning, and was turned around by troopers and sat against the back of the trench. He looked grey, his eyes rolling a little. Not so bloody shouty now, that's for sure.

"Right," said Dix. "Pressure on his wound, field dressing, and then get everyone shifted up this way into the deeper part of the trench. And keep your heads down."

He loaded a carry-bag with some flash-stuns and popped a blaster in his belt. Took a sighting to the gully, the bottom of which started twenty yards away, beyond the new crater. He'd be out of sight of the ridge once he reached it. After that, Dix didn't doubt he could climb the gully and surprise them from the side. He just didn't know if he could do it quickly enough, before the rebels levelled the trench with more shells and wiped out Dix's unit.

He looked back one last time before scrambling clear. "Sit tight, lads, all right? And if he perks up a bit" – pointing at the second lieutenant – "don't listen to him. Sit on him if you have to."

Later, Dix realised that had been the hardest part. Not ignoring the OC. No-brainer, that one, if not dying was the plan for the day. Not the climb either. He'd picked his way up enough crags as a kid not to be bothered by the height, and there had been plenty of footholds and hand grips in this narrow cleft to make it an easy ascent – at least for someone who was used to scaling the Calisto sea stacks.

But flopping up and over the side of the trench, and then zig-zagging through the mud for twenty yards, hearing the whine and whistle, and the deep whump of air sucked out of the sky, as shell after shell landed – that had been harder and more stressful than anything Dix had ever done before, though he did it gladly and quickly, seeing as the alternative was sitting in a trench with an idiot who might still get them all killed.

When he got to the top, it was all over quickly. There were only half a dozen rebels holding the ridge – the firepower they were raining down had made it seem like a whole lot more – and they didn't even see Dix.

He stepped out from behind a boulder, rolled a flash-stun into their dug-out, and stepped back again while the pyrotechnics and neurochemicals did their work. Gave it a minute or two for the air to clear, put on a filter-mask just in case, and then had a leisurely stroll around their gun emplacement, attaching wrist and ankle cuffs to convulsing rebels who, if they coughed any harder, would soon be missing bits of stomach lining.

Dix sent up a flare, though he figured his unit had probably worked it out by now, on account of the sudden lack of shooting and shelling.

He saw them emerge, gingerly, from the trench far below and make their way up the slope. He even went down halfway to meet them, to help haul the second lieutenant up to safety, carrying him over his shoulder – trying not to enjoy the groans of pain every time the officer's injured shoulder banged against Dix's back.

He had a shattered collarbone, and had lost a lot of blood, but would live. Dix dressed his wound properly and gave him some pain meds, and now the OC was sitting quietly in the dug-out, eyes closed, grimacing. Sentries had been posted, but the ridge was secure and the valley below was still. They had called in

TwoSquad, who would be there within the hour, with their nails fully painted, no doubt.

Dix gave a rueful sigh at that, remembering the sarge's jibe, and had another twinge of emotion when the kettle went on for a brew. He had the sarge's chip-tag in his hands – he'd gone down with a couple of the others once they'd taken the ridge, and had helped to dig out the bodies. Well, the sarge's body. Couldn't find Rennie, and there were only pieces of Distin left. The sealed bags would go out tomorrow morning.

Dix paired the sarge's tag with his NavCom wrist unit and tapped through the docs and images. Together with the sarge's bio-marker ID data, and medical and service records, there were a few more personal items. A picture of a homestead – geotagged as a settler prairie somewhere on Kallax, Dix had been right – and a couple of images of a young family. Man, woman, two kids. In the 'Name' field, the woman was tagged 'Sis,' and Dix couldn't figure out who the man was, with his arm cosily around the sarge's wife, Sis, until he twigged that this was the sarge's sister.

That figured. Dix had never had the sarge down as a family man of his own. But he had looked after his unit – his lads, his maggots – until he had come up against the immovable force of a direct order from a superior idiot. At which point, he had undoubtedly saved Dix's life – and given Dix permission to try and save everyone else's.

Which – looking around at lounging troopers, an

injured but alive second lieutenant, and six trussed prisoners – Dix had done.

All in all, Dix thought, he had done well.

Which was why, when TwoSquad finally arrived, to hoots of derision from lounging troopers, Dix couldn't believe it when the second lieutenant struggled to his feet, sought out the squad leader, and spluttered, "Arrest that man. Striking an officer, disobeying an order. I want him cuffed now."

Chapter 2

Dix bounced around in the back of a troop transit vehicle that was either negotiating endless muddy bomb craters or being driven without due care and attention for the welfare of its passenger.

He couldn't tell which, on account of the hood pulled over his head before he had been tossed in the back, hands secured behind him. He suspected the latter.

His squad had tried to intervene on his behalf, but the idiot second lieutenant – now wild-eyed, pharmaceutical pain relief coursing through his veins – had threatened them with the same treatment.

Dix had given them all a look, and a calm-down gesture. No one else needed to end up in the shit on this shithole of a planet. And once he was away from the officer, and someone more sane and less chemically excited reviewed the evidence, he'd be back with his squad in no time.

A hopeful theory that had been slightly dented by the confiscation of his NavCom unit – which no soldier ever gave up willingly – the appearance of the hood and cuffs, and the ferocious look on the TwoSquad corporal's face as Dix was bundled into the vehicle. And then demolished entirely when Dix was eventually dragged out at an unknown destination and manhandled into a cell.

Two military police goons uncuffed him and took the hood off, which was nice of them, and then kicked him through the door, which wasn't.

They were taking this seriously, then.

"What did they get you for, sport?"

Dix picked himself up off the floor and looked around. The questioner was a well-built man with a well-fed face, wearing a heavily stained jumpsuit and sitting on the edge of a metal bedframe. He had obvious bruises and one ragged, bloodied ear – it looked like someone, or something, had taken a bite out of it.

Dix shrugged. "Striking an officer, disobeying orders, but – "

"Oof." The man looked pained. "Oh dear. That's not good."

"You reckon?"

"Capital offence, they call that, sport. You know? Capital?" And he drew a hand across his neck in a slicing gesture.

"Cheery little buzzkill, aren't you? I'll be fine, it's all just a misunderstanding."

"Got you, sport, a misunderstanding." The man tapped his nose, knowingly. "You tell them that. They were very gracious about it, when I told them the same thing." He shifted his hand to his mangled ear and touched it gingerly. "Very gracious."

The cell was little more than a metal box with a strip light and a grille door. Two bare bedframes, no mattresses or pillows. One tin bucket, contents unknown but – from the smell – guessable.

The cell was probably a container within a larger container – Dix had heard the metal beneath his feet as they'd crossed the threshold, and he'd seen enough of them dropped on-planet when they had first deployed. Huge things, used as temporary storerooms, arsenals, field kitchens, muster stations, and the like. Lock-ups, too, apparently.

"What about you? Why are you here?"

"Bit of this and a bit of that," said the man. "Mostly that."

"Which is?"

"I like to think of it as supply and demand. Or demand and supply, really. They demand, I supply."

Ear-guy was a black-market trader then. Although what he was doing on this planet was a mystery, seeing as there was nothing to trade. Unless he did a fine line in exotic mud. Either way, it also didn't look rosy for him, given the dim view that the Federation had of freelance marketeers. It didn't fall under the category of hitting a superior officer, but it wasn't just failing to file invoices and pay sales tax either.

"OK. So, who was demanding what? And what were you supplying?"

The man looked more closely at Dix and seemed to take in his uniform properly for the first time. Admittedly mud-covered, but still recognisably army issue, with the Fed insignia visible on his shoulder.

"Ah well, bit delicate that, sport."

"Go on."

"Let's just say that I came across some projectile hardware and swapped it for some A-grade organic material, with a buyer all arranged. But then my transport was impounded, and here we are, at the Federation's pleasure, until I can come to a suitable arrangement."

"Projectile hardware?" Dix thought about that for a second or two, until light dawned. "You've been selling weapons to the miners? In exchange for the ore?"

"Trading, please. Not selling. There's a distinct difference, which I have been trying to impress upon our over-zealous military friends here. Selling weapons is a serious offence. I wouldn't want to get involved in that. No, I was merely trading some surplus stock for some surplus ore. Demand and supply, everyone's happy."

"But then you sell the ore?"

"A man's got to make a living. By then, the transaction is once removed. I don't see what everyone's getting so upset about."

Dix looked the man squarely in the face. "Those miners have been shooting at me today with your weapons. Killed three of my squad. Upset barely covers it, *sport*." Dix spat out the last word.

Ear-guy raised his hands in submission. "I said it was a bit delicate, didn't I? And look – I'm just a simple trader, meeting a demand. How was I to know what they were going to do with the guns? I thought they wanted them for hunting. I believe there's little else to do on this planet."

"Hunting? With ground-cannons, scope-snipes, and high-velocity blasters – to name just three of the items that have nearly killed me today?" Dix drew himself up and glowered.

"Yes, well, they've obviously been very naughty miners. I'm shocked, I tell you, shocked. Believe me, if I'd have known they were going to use them straight away, before the ore was even fully loaded… let's just say, lesson learned. They've certainly done me no favours, I can tell you that."

This guy. Dix shook his head in disgust. He thought briefly about slugging him, but it probably wasn't worth it. Dix didn't yet know how much trouble he was in, but he doubted it would help his case if, when they came to question him, there was one fewer breathing occupant of the cell than they were expecting.

Accordingly, ear-guy didn't acquire any additions to his collection of bruises and mangled appendages, and Dix plonked himself down on the other bedframe. Gave the guy a hard stare, though, just to remind him he was on dangerous ground.

There was a clanging noise from outside, and the

sound of footsteps on metal. A scuffle and a shout. The buzz of what sounded like a prod or a taser. A strangled cry.

"Making their rounds," said the trader. "That's two doors down."

"How do you know?"

"Next door's empty. It wasn't, until yesterday, but he never came back."

"Where are we?"

The guy looked surprised at this – like, isn't it obvious? Dix just said, "Hood, remember?"

"Right, of course. Well, sport, you're back at the DZ. Security block, holding cells."

That figured. The Drop Zone. Where Dix had come in. The most secure place on this dump of a planet. Which meant – good news – he wasn't going to get shot at by a disaffected miner for a while, or accidentally killed by a moron of a commanding officer. It was still unclear what the bad news might be.

"They'll let you stew for a while," said the guy, gesturing at the barebones cell. "Figure that you might get a bit chattier when you've had time to appreciate the surroundings."

Dix didn't know about that. He'd slept in a water-filled trench the previous night, next to filthy troopers who had dined on rip-heat beans for a week. Frankly, even with the bucket, this was an upgrade.

"Might as well make yourself comfortable." The trader sat back on the bedsprings, leaning against the metal wall. "What's your name, sport?"

"We're not friends, you know that, right? You got some of my actual friends killed."

"All right, sport, just trying to pass the time."

Dix let it sit for a moment, and then told him.

"Dix… Dix", mused the guy, then brightened. "Calisto, am I right? I bet I am. That's a Calisto name if I ever heard one."

Dix shrugged an assent.

"Well, Dix from Calisto, I'm Kantor. Milo Kantor, at your service." He reached down and slipped a finger inside one of his shoes, then leaned forward, proffering a slim, almost opaque, oblong chip-tag with a patterned logo. Not like Dix's army ID, but the sort that fancy businesspeople carried as a calling card – embedded with contact details, portfolio, permits, references, testimonials.

Dix waved it away, but Kantor raised himself off his bed and tucked the tag inside Dix's top pocket.

"Keep it. You never know."

"You're confident." Dix scoffed. "I don't like your chances any more than mine, right now."

"Ah well, sport, you've always got to have an edge in my game. You – striking an officer, was it? – are up against it, no question about that. But I've still got something they want, namely the location of all the rest of the projectile hardware that I happened to have acquired. Let's just say we're in negotiations."

"And how's that going?"

"I've still got an earlobe left, put it like that. We're just feeling each other out, but they definitely want the gear. Or rather, they want the people I acquired it from. I've been in worse spots. There's an agreement to be made, it's just a matter of time."

Dix wondered if *he* had an edge? Technically, he'd disobeyed an order, but other than that, what had he done wrong? He'd barely touched the second lieutenant – a flail of the arm, more than anything else. He'd achieved OneSquad's stated objective – take the ridge – captured the insurgents, and saved everyone else's life. Including, let's not forget, that of the stupidest officer on the Federation army's books.

Was that going to be enough? It would be hard to bear if this joker walked free while Dix faced the full force of whatever military laws he had supposedly broken.

There was another loud clang from somewhere outside. Dix stood up against the cell bars and turned his head, but the way the container was positioned meant he couldn't see very far down the larger space.

"It'll be dinner," said Kantor. "Don't get your hopes up. How do you feel about sloppy, brown food?"

Like it was an old friend by now, after a week in the field. But Dix never got to find out if the DZ bean recipe was an improvement on the platoon's version, because the two black-uniformed goons outside the cell weren't carrying plates or a tray.

"Dix," barked one. "Back up, turn round, arms behind your back."

He turned and heard the cell grille swing open. Felt

rough hands on him, and then his wrists were crossed tightly and secured.

"Out, you little turd." Dix felt a prod in the back. "Not so handy with your fists now, are you?"

"Well, they certainly seem to think you hit him," said Kantor. "That's cleared that up. Nice meeting you, and good luck."

"You want some of this?" One of the men brandished a baton at Kantor.

"No, sir."

"Well, shut up then. Or we might just bring forward your next little chat."

Dix heard the cell door bang behind him, and then he was marched down the metal gangway and out through a bigger door into a floodlit compound. He squinted against the unexpected glare, and stumbled, receiving a whack in the back for his troubles.

"Over there. Move."

Another metal door, another container. This one was smaller and painted white inside, with a single chair bolted to the floor in front of a fixed, metal table. The goons undid the ties behind his back, sat him down heavily, and fixed his wrists into restraints on the table. And then left, without a word.

Chapter 3

GROWING up on Calisto didn't present you with many life choices, once you had finished with the growing up part.

There was fishing, of course, starting out as a deckhand on the industrial trawlers, as Dix's father had done, and his father before him, and his father, etc, reaching back into an unbroken line of great-great-great-great-etc grandfathers.

If you were lucky, which meant if you didn't drown or lose an arm to a winch or a tiger-whale, you might make chief mate after twenty years. Retire after forty to a nice little bungalow overlooking the less fish-entraily part of the coastline.

Or there were the fish-processing factories, where you were unlikely to drown, but could still easily lose an arm if you weren't careful. Best you could aspire to here was supervisor, seeing as actual management was shipped in by the company from off-world. Supervisors got health benefits (excluding prosthetics) and a two-bedroom apartment in a company condo, which you had to give up at the end of your tenure.

The brightest sparks got to do an apprenticeship in R&D, which sounded more exciting (Research! Development!) but, when it came down to it, was steadfastly rooted in the industry's requirements. You might spend seven years doing grunt work on net tech or anti-barnacle paint, and still only end up as a line manager in one of the vessel sheds. As a bonus, you would probably have both arms at the end of it.

And if you didn't want a job that involved fishing, well, you shouldn't have been born on Calisto.

Dix hadn't been given a choice about that – stupid parents, stupid biology – but figured, as he got older, that there had to be more to life than fishing.

He was an adventurous boy, handy and capable. Quick mind, strong heart, sense of purpose. On another planet, he might have had a choice of careers. But Calisto refused to play ball, and when Dix was eighteen he had joined the rest of his cohort on the dockside at an improbably early hour, and given a pair of heavily stained oilskins that reeked of yesterday's fish and today's despair.

Consequently, when the Federation's army recruiters came to town a few years later, they were pushing at an open door, as far as Dix was concerned – given he was peering down the fish chute of at least another thirty years on the trawler deck. The serendipitous offer of another job seemed very tempting, and nothing his father said about the unbroken line of great-great-great grandfathers could sway him.

His mother had cried when he left, but Dix – eighteen years old, impatient, embarrassed – had hurried on board the shuttle with barely a backwards glance.

They badged it as 'Peacekeeping,' since the Federation was not currently at war with anyone – as long as you looked the other way in all the various territorial disputes, border skirmishes, contested trading zones, and planetary intrigues. Dix didn't keep up with politics anyway – peacekeeping sounded just fine, if it meant getting away from those overalls. He had signed on for the standard ten-year stretch as a trooper, at the end of which Dix would have a small pension, with the possibility of promotion and a bigger pension if things worked out.

But right now, three years into his enlistment – chained to a desk in an interrogation suite – things could not strictly be said to be working out. A pension of any size looked a long shot.

Dix shook his wrists in their restraints experimentally. Nothing doing there. Apart from the table, the chair and himself, the room was bare except for a vent grille on one wall and a small sphere fixed to the side that Dix assumed was a camera. He winked at it and leaned from side to side, to see if it tracked him, but it stayed still and silent.

The door opened behind him. Dix counted two sets of feet entering. Whoever they were, they stood out of sight, unspeaking, for a long beat and then came around the front of the desk and presented themselves.

"Dix, is it?" said one, while the other flicked through a pad, nodding to himself. They weren't your regular military-police types – something management about them, maybe? No caps. Sneakers on their feet rather than combat boots. Higher up the food chain, definitely. Dix hoped that meant they were more sensible and willing to listen to reason. Or at least less prone to kicking and shoving.

"Did your basic training at Camp Bastion?" said pad-guy, conversationally. "The full six months?"

"Yes, sir."

"Smashed the Blind Beast – record time. Impressive."

The Blind Beast – part test, part initiation for new grunts, following a course in a pitch-black, booby-trapped hangar, responding exactly to in-ear instructions. There were painful obstacles and interventions, even if you followed each instruction exactly. Any hesitation or deviation, any second-guessing, and there were other consequences – flash-bangs, electric prods, vomit-inducing noise-bombs. You didn't know whether you were coming or going. All you had was the voice in your head telling you what to do next, and to bloody do it now, trooper.

Coming out the hangar after twenty-odd minutes of that – sick, bloodied, disorientated – it was almost impossible to know if you'd been successful or not. Dix had done the course in seventeen, and then thrown up.

"High grades, I see. Kept up with all the classes. Didn't miss any through sickness? Conscientious recruit?"

"No, sir. I mean, yes sir."

"Scored very highly in comprehension tests, it says here." The man nodded approvingly. "The instructors thought you assimilated well. Not from an army background, but you embraced the discipline and understood your training. Top marks."

"Yes, sir. Thank you, sir."

"Then riddle me this, trooper," said the other man, wonderingly, leaning down to look into Dix's face. "If you never missed a day of training, and understood everything you were taught" – his voice was rising by this time – "then why the eternal fuck" – shouting now, right in front of Dix – "did you think it was all right – "

"To strike an officer in the field, you abject piece of trooper shit?" completed pad-guy, spittle spraying from his lips, face an inch from Dix's.

"Before disobeying a direct order in the fucking field? Because I don't remember any of that coming up in basic training, you dump-stain of a soldier."

Both men were now breathing heavily, looming over Dix, who stayed silent, assuming the questions were rhetorical. Turned out they weren't.

"Well?"

"Permission to speak freely, sir?"

"Doesn't look like you usually wait for permission, does it, you little fucker? We've reviewed the bodycam evidence. What was it again, remind me?"

Pad-guy made a show of acknowledging his colleague's question, straightening up, and flicking through his screen. "Let's see now… so, here's the bit where you hit a superior officer with a nice round-house." He showed the video to his colleague, who winced.

Dix thought 'roundhouse' was a bit much. A forearm smash at worst, in trying conditions.

"The audio's not bad either," said pad-guy. "Here's where you disobey a direct order, saying, 'No, you got the sarge killed.' And then this is my favourite bit, 'Sit on him if you have to.'"

Even Dix had to admit, when it was said like that, in the cold light of day, it didn't sound good.

"Sit on him if you have to!" shouted the other guy, apoplectic again. "Sit on a superior officer! In the field! During combat ops! Didn't have a problem in speaking freely there, did you?"

Both men took a step backwards, pad-guy's free hand resting on top of his holstered baton – drumming his fingers, making sure Dix saw the implied threat. Stood there, waiting for him to speak. Didn't need to say, "Well?" again, for Dix to realise that this was his one chance to explain himself.

Except any truthful explanation would only confirm what they already knew – that he had struck an officer and disobeyed an order in the field. There were no extenuating circumstances for that. That was Basic Training 101, which, as they also knew, he'd been extremely good at.

Dix had taken quickly to soldiering – had surprised himself, really. Had found his feet, fitted in, done well. Knew what was expected of him, and usually exceeded those expectations. He was no longer a raw recruit. He couldn't claim that he hadn't known what he was doing.

His choices now were simple: tell the truth, or make something up that wouldn't be supported by the bodycam footage.

Screwed if he did. Screwed if he didn't. So he did. At least by telling the truth, he'd be true to himself and to his squad-mates.

"Everyone knew the second lieutenant wasn't competent," said Dix. "He's been a liability since we deployed. No experience, doesn't listen to those who have. His idiot tactics got three of my team killed, including my sarge. I did him a favour, not to mention saved his life. He's welcome, by the way."

Pad-guy's eyebrows did a vertical take-off. The other guy turned puce. "A superior officer's competence?" he shouted. "Not yours to judge, trooper. What makes you the expert?"

"Completed the mission, didn't I?" Dix was throwing everything into the wind now. It had been a shitshow of a day. Someone was going to hear the truth, whatever it cost him. "Took the ridge. Neutralised and pacified. Held until relieved," he quoted, and then – after a pause, in which he took a deep breath – "You're also welcome."

"Except you didn't complete the mission, did you?

Those scumbag rebel miners are currently enjoying our lavish hospitality, breathing our air and eating our rations, instead of being riddled with blaster holes and piled up in a ditch. Your orders were to neutralise them, and don't tell me you don't know what that means?"

There probably was an argument to be made about the linguistic accuracy of Federation army orders, and the interpretation of such in the field, under fast-moving battle conditions, but Dix didn't think that was what his interrogators were after.

Neutralise/kill. Potato/potahto. Of course he knew what that meant – every trooper did – but he wasn't going to make it easy for them to hang another charge on him.

"Federation military law forbids the summary execution of enemy combatants," said Dix. He did his best to maintain a neutral expression, given that particular law – as interpreted in the field – was usually accompanied by a "Yeah, right" and a smiley face. The fact is, no one would have cared if he had wasted the miners. The Federation was nothing if not – pragmatic was one word, hypocritical another.

"Smart-arse lawyer, are you now?" shouted his interrogator.

"Just pointing out the legal situation," said Dix, adding a "sir," when he saw the guy taking another pre-shout deep breath.

"Legal situation? The nerve of this! The *legal* situation is, you didn't do your fucking job, trooper! Because the last time we checked, questioning orders and hitting superiors aren't in the training manual."

It was all nonsense. Dix had done his job and completed the mission, however they wanted to define it. No one could say he hadn't pacified the rebels – after chucking the flash-stun and trussing them in restraints, he'd never seen such peaceable miners, give or take the odd convulsion from the neuro-chems.

What these two very shouty gentlemen really meant was, 'Why didn't you follow orders, said and unsaid, legal or otherwise?' Not just those of the idiot CO, but those orders handed down from on high, cascading down the chain of command from operations room here at the DZ all the way into the trench where Dix and his squad had been sheltering from the rebel miners' barrage of fire.

Neutralise them. Kill them. That's what the army had told him to do, and he hadn't done it. And they wanted to know why.

"Well, trooper?" Pad-guy clearly abhorred a vacuum.

Dix had two answers, and they wouldn't like answer one, which was – the miners weren't soldiers, they weren't at war, and this was supposed to be peace-keeping.

He wasn't naïve. From the day he'd signed up, Dix had understood that whatever they said, he was joining an army and, at some point, he'd probably end up having to shoot at someone. And he had, several times over the last three years, because that was the job. Like hauling in the whale-sharks and slicing them open on the slaughter-deck. No point objecting to that if you were a deckhand – it was literally the reason you were there.

Only increasingly, the 'peacekeeping' missions didn't seem too bothered about the 'peace' part, leaning more heavily towards the shock-and-awe side of the ledger from the minute you were turfed out of the troop carrier. Or maybe it wasn't increasingly – maybe it was just that they broke you in for the first year or two with relatively violence-free missions. Guarding buildings, staff evac, supply-drop cover – Dix had done it all, and had shot at looters, rioters and local militias in the process. Killed the odd one, too – hard not to when you were fully tooled up in the Federation's finest assault kit.

And then before you knew it, you were being sent to a muddy mining planet, whose name you didn't even know, and told to neutralise the rebels.

Rebels. As if.

Dix didn't know the name of this planet, but he knew its type and he knew its rebels. Because it could just as well be Calisto and the fish factories, and those miners could be him and his mates. Brought up on a world with limited life choices – mining, not fishing – and one day making a mistake from which there was no going back.

It could have been Dix, if he'd been brought up on a different shithole. Dix on the ridge with black-market munitions acquired from a shifty type like Milo Kantor, hoping to make enough money from the illicit ore-trade to get off this crappy planet.

Killing those miners wouldn't have been killing rebels. It would have been killing people whose lives he knew, because it had once been his life.

That was answer one. But he wasn't going to give them that one, because his interrogators were practically rocking on their toes with rage by now. Probably not in the mood to meet him halfway in the empathy stakes.

Answer two wasn't much better, but it was all he had.

"I thought they might be useful," he said. "Have useful intel, anyway."

He hadn't exactly thought that at the time. At the time, he'd been thankful to have clambered up the gully unscathed. And then even more thankful that the gun-happy miners hadn't spotted him as he'd emerged onto the ridge. He'd had his finger on the trigger of his assault-blaster, and certainly would have fired if he'd had to. He hadn't been planning on dying, put it that way.

But Rennie and Distin, and the sarge, *had* died – needlessly – and Dix had thought that was probably enough for the day. You never knew, maybe these miners did have some information to spill that would mean the rest of OneSquad would live to fight another mission on another unnamed planet. Idiot officers notwithstanding.

So he'd pacified the miners, and not killed them,

and he still thought it had been the right decision. One that left him able to sleep at night, anyway.

"They had to have got the weapons from somewhere," he said – knowing now of course exactly where they'd got the weapons. "I didn't need to kill them to neutralise them. Thought someone might want to ask them some questions."

Dix didn't know if this would make any difference. They'd obviously already figured some of it out, given they had Milo Kantor banged up in a cell with half an ear missing. Would Dix get any credit for providing them with another intel source?

Apparently not, because pad-guy was already gearing up for another spittle-flecked assault.

"Didn't need to kill them, trooper? Is that right? That's what you thought, was it, in that tiny trooper brain of yours? You had it all worked out, did you, you piece of – "

"That'll do," said a female voice from the wall grille. "I've seen enough. Put him on the next shuttle and have him processed."

Chapter 4

DIX WAS glad to see the back of Mud Planet, but – handcuffed to a strut inside a troop jump-ship – didn't imagine that his day was going to get any better.

Nobody talked to him on the way from the interrogation cell to the DZ launch area, and the handling was just as rough, though at least he wasn't hooded again.

He didn't like the sound of "processed," given how freely the army used euphemisms. And especially because he still didn't know his fate. Although the handcuffs and the non-smiling, non-speaking guards gave him a clue.

He sat uncomfortably in a moulded trooper's seat, hands hitched high to one side, while they loaded the rest of the passengers. Captives, prisoners, whatever. These all did have hoods on, making it difficult to assess his companions. Not all of them were in army fatigues, though most were. Some could have been miners, he supposed, though as everyone was covered in the same mud, it was hard to tell. A couple of them were snivelling until told to shut up by a guard. They sounded young. Young and afraid.

When the last one had been seated – they were a dozen in all, including Dix – the guards took off everyone's cuffs, and the seat bars descended and locked. Dix could finally flex his arms, but his thighs were pinioned and movement restricted.

As the ramp slowly raised, and the red warning lights flashed in the cabin, the final guard jumped out.

"See ya, scumbags," he shouted, above the noise of the engines. "Wouldn't want to be ya." And, seeing Dix looking at him, the only one without a hood, gave him the finger.

He must have slept – hardly surprisingly, after the day he'd had. How long for, he didn't know. Most of those around him were still dozing and snoring. The two snivellers were talking to each other in low voices; one had his hand on the other's arm, as if trying to calm them.

When he woke again, it was to more flashing red lights and the indistinct crackle of chatter somewhere above his head from an internal comms channel.

They had taken all his kit from him when he'd been frog-marched to the first cell; didn't even have his military-issue wrist-unit, so Dix had no idea how long he'd been in the troop ship, or where they were headed. He'd find out soon enough.

No buffeting, no scream of engines fighting an atmosphere, no sudden drops, no heavy landing. Just the flashing red lights that signalled an arrival, and a slow glide.

Off-planet then. Station of some kind.

Then a whump, and a chunking noise. Airlock.

A slight drop, and then stillness. Legs down, canopy landing.

The rear door folded open in a squeal of hydraulics, and Dix looked out into a hangar. A couple of other jump-ships sat on nearby aprons, while a small squad of troopers stood off to one side, hands on baton-prods. There was a large caption on the far hangar wall, stencilled in white letters, several feet high: PH-017.

If the Federation army liked euphemisms – peace-keeping, neutralise – it loved acronyms and initials.

For example, OneSquad's instant, rip-heat, bean rations were MREs – Meals, Ready to Eat – though, according to all troopers, the only initial letter that was vaguely accurate was the R for ready, as the MREs could be consumed hot or cold. (Whether they were in fact MWEs, meals worth eating, was another matter entirely.)

There were lots more that troopers used on a daily basis. The flash-stuns, which Dix had taken out the miners with, were officially known as APIs (anti-personnel incapacitators); his missing navigation-and-communication wrist-unit was a NavCom, and so on.

And when crusty old sergeants wanted to threaten recalcitrant or wayward new recruits during basic training, they invoked the horrors of a short stay at the nearest PH. "Couldn't be arsed to clean those boggin' boots properly, trooper? How's about I arrange a trip to the PH, son? Don't need sparkling boots there, should be right up your street, you 'orrible little trooper."

PH: Prison Hulk.

The army had twenty of them, spread around Federation space. Everyone knew that. This, apparently, was number seventeen.

They were notorious among new recruits and seasoned troopers alike. Repository of deserters, thieves, persistent insubordinates, and captive rebels, not to mention the usual army roster of psychopaths, rapists and murderers who couldn't help but show their true selves during downtime on their various missions.

The hulks weren't prisons, as such. More like black-site processing centres, while the army decided what to do with whatever human flotsam had drifted to the surface. Forbidding places where the Fed army's HR department and Health and Safety Executive had no remit. It was doubtful they appeared on any inventory of army facilities.

Some PH inmates – the lucky ones – would go on to actual prisons and serve a sentence, before being dishonourably discharged. A larger proportion would end up on some hellish slave-labour planet, where luck didn't come into it at all, unless it was to die quickly before the diseases and injuries took hold. And others simply disappeared – executed, left to rot in a dungeon, thrown out of the airlock. For those types of offenders, no one ever knew what happened to them and no one cared.

Dix didn't know what type of offender he was considered to be, but the fact that he was at PH-017 for processing was emphatically not in his favour.

"Out!"

The seat bars clicked and raised, and they were ordered out of the craft and onto the apron. As each prisoner stood, their hood was whipped off, and for the first time saw the reality of their situation. A Fed army prison hulk. No hood, no handcuffs. Which meant – nothing to hide, nowhere to run, no hope.

A trooper shouted out names and offences. Theoretically, alleged offences, but by the time you were on a hulk ship, there was no alleged about it. Theft from supplies. Desertion. Taking up arms against the Federation – at this, the two that Dix had noticed on the jump-ship trembled.

They were nineteen years old, twenty at most. Dix got a good look at their faces. Young and scared, he'd been right. He didn't think they'd been among the miners he'd taken out. Doubted they were even miners, didn't look old enough or tough enough. Sons of miners, maybe – full of bravado, accompanying their dads with their black-market guns, until the army came to town to sort them out.

Dix was last. Striking an officer and disobeying an order in the field. The words echoed around the hangar, and he saw some of the others look up and take a closer interest in him. He was clearly a cut above your usual thief or deserter. These were serious, capital offences and, if he couldn't talk his way out of them, Dix was in for a very short stay at PH-017.

"Dix, on me," shouted another trooper, as the line of prisoners started to move slowly towards the hangar exit, under close guard. He peeled off from the others towards a side door, following the trooper, with another in lock step behind him.

Was that it? Had he just been 'processed'? Was that the extent of the due process afforded to him by right as a member of the Federation's armed forces? In which case, in Dix's opinion, the due process badly sucked.

They marched him down a tight corridor and through security gates into a wing where dark-grey room doors stretched out into the distance on both sides.

A door was opened with a key card and Dix was shoved through. Nice for a cell, pretty crappy for a hotel room. Scuffed white walls, bed, single ceiling light, no window. He heard it lock behind him and turned, watching as the door became transparent. Dix could see one of the troopers on the outside, his hand against the now see-through door.

"Get showered and change. You stink," said the trooper, who then removed his hand. The door turned a solid grey again.

Nice trick.

Dix saw the pile of clothes on the bed – a made bed, with sheet and pillow, be still his beating heart. T-shirt, combats and shirt, underwear, clean socks, and a pair of boots, cleaned to the exacting standards of a crusty drill sergeant. None of it standard army issue, no labels, no insignia.

A sliding, concertina door in the room opened on to a – it couldn't be, could it? It could. A compact but serviceable wet room with toilet and shower. A towel was folded on a high shelf. Not a large towel, or a fluffy towel, but a clean, dry towel, nonetheless. Dix almost cried at the sight.

On the basis that this could all be a clerical error – his real cell, the rat-infested one with a rancid bucket, awaiting somewhere down the hall – Dix undressed quickly and turned the water on in the shower. Even if he was dragged out now, he'd feel a million times better about being unceremoniously dumped out of the airlock, or whatever it was they had in store for him – doomed but clean.

Rivulets of filth poured off him, while a lighter stain emanated from his hands and lower arms as he scrubbed under the powerful jet. The sarge's blood, and Distin's too, mixed in with the dirt as he'd scrabbled in the rubble for their lifeless bodies. Bits of a body in Distin's case.

Dix bowed his head under the water, letting it pound his neck and shoulders, and watched the stain spread and circle towards the drain. Letting the sarge go, and Distin, and Rennie – poor sod Rennie, who said he'd joined up to see the galaxy, and now lay buried forever, unmarked, unfound, in a particularly horrible part of it.

Dix put on the clothes laid out on the bed. His old uniform was where he'd dropped it on the floor, muddy footprints leading from there into the shower room. It spoke loudly of a week in the field, wet, ragged and dirty, like the body it had covered. He didn't even want to touch the clothes, nudging them gingerly with a fresh boot towards the edge of the room. They left a smear. The sarge would have had kittens.

The sarge. Dix remembered something. He turned his old uniform over, with some distaste now he was Trooper Clean of Company Pristine, and delved inside his battle-tunic pocket. Fingers touched the sarge's chip-tag – his very identity, his life and record – that Dix had taken from around his neck after they'd retrieved the body.

They'd probably incinerate Dix's uniform with the prison hulk's garbage, but the sarge's tag – and the family recorded on it – deserved better than that. Even if Dix was just going to be pushed out of an airlock sometime soon, the sarge could come with him – not back to Kallax, but to the stars at least.

There was a hammering at the door, and a shout for Dix to present himself at attention. He grasped the chip-tag and pulled it out of the mud-caked pocket. Stuck to it was the second one, the oblong one Milo Kantor had given to him – forced on him, really – the businessman's calling card. He palmed them both quickly, slipping them into a pocket in his new clothes, and faced the door. Shoulders straight, chest out, arms by his side. The door faded from grey to see-through.

"Ma'am," said someone, out of sight, before a uniformed officer stepped in front of the door and looked Dix up and down. Single Federation icon on her shoulder – a major. Older than Dix, in her thirties. Close-cut hair, steely gaze. Dix found himself saluting, quick smart.

"Trooper Dix." It wasn't a question, it was an appraisal. "At ease. Do you understand why you're here?"

"Yes, ma'am."

"Do you know what the penalty is for striking an officer and disobeying an order in the field?"

"Yes, ma'am."

"And yet you did it anyway, trooper? Tell me why? You may speak freely."

"Yes, ma'am. Thank you, ma'am. It seemed like the best option at the time, ma'am. To achieve the mission objectives."

"Interesting. That's a lot of ma'ams, by the way." The major pursed her lips for a second, pondering. "I don't suppose you're keen on a court-martial, at which you *will* be found guilty?"

She seemed to be waiting for a response, but what kind of question was that?

"No, ma'am."

"Understandable. Given your previous good conduct and otherwise exemplary record, after you're found guilty you will be sent to Arcana Minor. Indentured labour, no return."

Dix understood that this was the army doing him a favour. Rather than immediate execution, he'd get to live out his days on Arcana Minor – aka Glow Planet – digging for high-grade uranium in a chain gang. Rumour was they used an actual chain. Those days would not be very many.

Dix sagged a little.

"Or." She left that hanging.

"Ma'am?"

"I'm putting together a small team for a clandestine, unsupported op in hostile terrain. Very hostile terrain. Absolutely objectionable terrain, in fact. Casualties are possible. Very possible."

"You're recruiting me, ma'am?"

"I'm giving you a choice."

"It's not a great choice, ma'am." Dix, emboldened now. Looking at the wrong end of a one-way trip to a hot planet and weighing up his options.

"So sorry to disappoint, Dix." She sounded amused. "But you do have certain attributes we're looking for."

"What are those, ma'am, if you don't mind me asking?"

She half-laughed at Dix's effrontery. "Well, let's see. You have been shown to think on your feet. Platoon records indicate you were highly thought of – your sergeant had recommended you for promotion, did you know that?"

Dix did not. His eyes pricked a little.

"But then, luckily for me, you fucked up," she said. "And now your greatest attraction is that you're both available and expendable."

At least it was honest.

"Don't tell me you're thinking about it?" She looked less impressed at Dix's lack of an immediate response. "Do I need to expound more on the charms of Arcana Minor?"

"What happens afterwards, ma'am? After the mission?"

"Assuming you're still alive, you mean?"

That was unnecessary.

"It's within my gift to commute the sentence that you are still going to receive," she said. "Come back, mission completed, and we'll talk. And now it's make-your-mind-up time. Are you in? Or shall we have you take off those nice, clean clothes, put *those* ones back on, and ask the troopers here to escort you to court?"

Chapter 5

THEY ALLOWED him one glorious night of mortar-fire-and mud-free sleep in the bed in his en-suite cell, and even brought him dinner and breakfast. Dix had never had a holiday, or been inside a hotel, but he was beginning to see why people went on about them.

Later, the door swung open without warning, and he was hurried out of the room and down several indistinguishable corridors. He was no longer accompanied by troopers, or even prison guards, but by a single, taciturn operative, dressed in all-black. No visible weapon. Almost as if they weren't too worried about him trying to escape from an ultra-high-security prison hulk with nowhere to go except deep space or, when inevitably caught, a dwarf planet that literally glowed.

Dix entered another hangar through a huge sliding door, and the operative just pointed, turned on his heels and left.

"Dix, over here."

It was the major, standing with three other people by an array of opened kit boxes. Clothing was strewn around; someone was picking through one of the boxes, tossing stuff they evidently didn't like the look of. Dix heard a "Hell, no."

"Fresh meat," said another, looking over at Dix. A woman with tight, curled hair and a red headband. Ripped, with an undeniable presence. A tone somewhere between contemptuous and challenging. "What did this one do?"

"Settle down, Vaskez." The major beckoned Dix over. "Right, everyone get what they need?"

There were some grumbles about styles and sizes, especially from a giant of a man — six-six at least, barrel chest, broad shoulders, and the emphatic suggestion of rippling muscles under a tight crewneck.

"It's not a fashion show," said the major. "You know the brief."

"Sure," said the third person, a smaller man — normal size, anyway — with a wiry frame and a pinched face. "Dress like shit in dead people's clothes."

"Wait, people died in these clothes?" That was Vaskez, suddenly looking down at her combats, vest and boots. Dix found himself doing the same.

"Not exactly *in* them, I'm guessing," said the thin man. "If you're going out the airlock, well… waste not, want not, right?"

"That's enough. Let's get to it. Dix, meet your new crew." The major indicated each one in turn.

Vaskez, still observing him with a cool detachment, a slight sneer.

Drake, the big man – raised a finger in acknowledgement.

Alard, the wiry one. Looked around, without ever catching anyone's eye.

"Everyone, this is Dix," she continued. "And that completes the team. My name is Major Galloway, and this is the last time you'll see me in person, so you better listen and listen good. First things first. This is not an officially sanctioned operation, which is why you're not wearing uniform, or anything that could identify you as a Federation soldier. Hence our dress-up boxes."

"How come Dix gets a matching set, at least?" That was Vaskez, still sore at her selection.

Galloway ignored her. "Now, I'm not big on protocol and rank. I'm big on getting things done. You don't have to salute me or call me ma'am. In fact, the more you call me ma'am, the older you make me feel" – she looked meaningfully at Dix – "and the older and more crochety I feel, the more likely I am to have you shot. This is by way of saying that this is not your usual army operation. You are going to have operational autonomy for the duration of this mission. But when I make the big calls, you do what I say, and if you don't there are no second chances. You're all here for a reason, and this is already your second chance. Is that clear?"

There were nods, and one truncated "Yes, m'– " from Vaskez.

"Good. Now that's understood, let me tell you a story. Anyone heard of Hauga?"

Shakes of the head this time. She had pronounced it How-ga. Sounded vaguely familiar to Dix – a planet somewhere in the sticks?

"Not surprising," continued Galloway. "Not much news comes out of there these days. It's a grain-and-bean planet out in ARC space."

Advance Reach Colonial. That wasn't just outer rim, like the sarge's planet, Kallax. That was outer outer rim. Even if there was news from there, it wouldn't be new by the time it reached Fed space.

ARC space was the bit of the galaxy which the Federation would like to advance into – maybe even put down colony roots, hence the name – but where there existed an uneasy agreement that it wouldn't. An uneasy agreement with the Axis, that rather nasty conglomerate of warlord planets that seemed to push the Federation's buttons just a little bit more each year.

A skirmish here, a lightning raid there, or even a full-blown invasion, followed by a quick asset-strip and then withdrawal. Nothing that could turn into a war, because the Federation wasn't at war with anyone, heaven forbid. But its 'peacekeeping' forces were a different matter, and they had occasionally been drawn into brief and violent firefights with Axis mercenaries, after which everyone backed away again into their respective corners and agreed not to escalate.

"Historically, the Haugans were a fiercely independent people," said Galloway. "Had a nice self-sufficient planet, kept themselves to themselves. Out there in ARC space, they figured they were free. Favoured neither side, Fed or Axis. But the astute among you will have heard me using the past tense. Hauga is very definitely not free anymore. It's under close Axis control, has been for years and years. The planet is blockaded, occupied, heavily taxed, oppressed. And the Axis home planets presumably have got more grain and beans than they know what to do with."

"And we care about this, because?" said Vaskez.

"We don't," said Galloway. "Or rather, we haven't until now. It's ARC space, a long, long way from anywhere. Be nice to have a foothold there, but the supply lines are insane. We'd want to be invited in – too hard to hold otherwise."

"Axis seem to have managed it."

"Yes, well, I'll come onto that. But you're right, the Axis are there, and we don't like that. But no one wants to provoke a war over a hayseed planet that doesn't want either of us. We're not in the occupation-and-oppression business."

Of course not, just the peacekeeping business. Having occupied a muddy planet recently on behalf of the Federation, and oppressed its miners, Dix wasn't sure about the difference, but he kept his counsel.

"Thought you said this was a story?" said Alard. "The Axis have got themselves a pet planet somewhere in the boonies, so what?"

Alard – running his mouth, really leaning into the not-saluting and not-calling-her-ma'am bit. Even so, he seemed nervous. Jittery, even. The quick mouth maybe over-compensating?

"Well, here's the interesting thing," said Galloway. "The Haugans also don't like it that the Axis are there, obviously. They'd like rid of them and, according to our sources, are ready to do something about it. Which, in turn, we would very much like to encourage, without getting directly involved."

"So, we're what? A saboteur team? Some shit like that?" Vaskez asked the question, but it was what Dix was thinking, too. And also thinking, that sounds dangerous and potentially non-survivable – just as Galloway had promised him.

"Not exactly," she said. "We've been building a picture of Haugan resources for a while now. They have been developing a weapon, with which we're told they can defeat the Axis and regain their independence. Now, here's the bit you've been waiting for. Nine years ago, in the face of another Axis crackdown, the weapon was moved off-planet to a secret location for continued testing and development. The subsequent blockade of Hauga means that's where it's stayed. The Haugans won't move without it. No weapon, no rebellion."

"That's our job? Delivery?"

"Turns out there's a brief window of opportunity. Two days ago, we received a back-channel communication that the Haugan weapon is primed and ready for transportation. Tucked up in its secret location, ready to be moved. The Federation can't be caught with the weapon, or even suspected of having it, as that would mean war. So, you're going to fetch it and deliver it to Hauga, undetected. And then we're going to let the rebellion play out. We've helped Hauga, they'll be grateful, everyone's happy. Well, not the Axis, but you get the drift."

Dix realised that, given his situation, his opinion about this plan would count for nothing, but even so, he still had questions. Let's pretend that the Federation and Major Galloway gave a crap about the four of them, offered up here as expendable couriers.

"Our sources, you said? Reliable, are they, about the nature of this weapon? Sure that it will make a difference?"

"We've had boots on the ground on Hauga for a long time," said Galloway. "Sleepers. Embedded. Good people. There's no doubt about it. The Haugans call the weapon Lightburst. Years of development have gone into it."

"Hell, yeah," said Vaskez. "Cool name. That's what I'm talking about." She mimed dropping a large bomb, opening her clenched fist and making an explosive sound.

"We go, we fetch, we deliver?" said Dix. "That's it?"

"That's it," said Galloway. "Only – "

She let that hang for a beat. Fond of that, Dix noticed. Liked to ramp up the drama.

Drake, the big man, took the bait. "Only what?"

"Your mission is to go and get the weapon and deliver it to Hauga. Problem one – can't be certain, but we think the Axis eavesdropped our comms, and now probably know the location of the weapon, too. So you need to get there first, and quickly, which is why we're all here, having this little chat. Problem two – Hauga itself is blockaded, locked up tight, and no one gets in or out. Certainly not a Fed army unit. Which means you're going in incognito, no tactical support, no back up. If you're caught, the Axis will persuade you to talk – they're good at that – but we'll deny your existence."

Alard laughed and deadpanned, "That seems fair."

"What did you expect?" said Galloway. "You can always choose the alternative career path I mapped out for you previously."

Presumably similar to the one explained to Dix. As she'd said, they *were* all here for a reason.

"With respect, ma'am," said Vaskez – full emphasis on ma'am, totally disrespectful – "sounds like a piece-of-shit mission with every prospect of it going wrong and us all dying?"

"Just how you like it, Vaskez, or so I'm told?"

"Hell, yeah." Vaskez beamed at Galloway. Dix could no longer tell if she was ragging on the major or not.

"Can't we just fetch it and then airdrop them this weapon, whatever it is? You know, miss out the whole getting-caught-and-tortured-by-Axis bit?" That was Alard, still looking for a silver lining.

"You want to drop something they call Lightburst?"

said Drake. "Drop it from a height? You think that's a good idea? Dumb-ass."

"I'll just hide behind you, big guy. Use *your* massive, dumb ass as a deflector shield."

Drake raised himself to his full height from the box he'd been leaning against, and stood close to Alard, toe to toe, which also meant Alard's eye to Drake's bulging neck. "You want to say that again, Run-boy?"

They bristled at each other. Dix already didn't fancy their chances on this op. How did this help? And what was 'run-boy' all about?

"Break it up, ladies," said Vaskez.

"Word is," said Galloway, "the Haugans have always been a bit grandiose about things. Society developed along quasi-clerical-military lines. High Council, lords, monks, all that. At least until the Axis arrived. Now they're just all unwilling subjects. Point is, despite the name, the weapon is not a planet-buster, as far as we can tell. To be honest, we don't know what it is or how it works. But we do know they won't move without it – and that with it, they say they can win. It's worth a shot. We can't use it ourselves, and we don't want the Axis to have it, so let's get it to Hauga and see what happens."

"And we're your best option?" said Dix. "I mean, you do have an army to choose from. Not that I'm not grateful for the opportunity" – someone, Alard probably, sniggered – "but why us?"

"Let's just say that I work on the margins of the Fed

army structure. I have a certain – shall we say, autonomy, in various matters. Need-to-know matters."

A black-ops spook, then. Probably not even a genuine major. Almost certainly not called Galloway.

"All you need to know," she continued, "is that – unbelievable as it may seem – you have all been selected for a reason." She looked around the four of them, as if she couldn't quite believe it herself. "Which we'll come onto. But your major attribute right now is that if you're caught, you don't look like army troopers. For me, it's all about deniability. You're now officially freelancers, and I don't care about freelancers, unless and until they deliver."

If you're caught. At least she'd been kind enough not to say 'when.'

Chapter 6

"WHAT THE HELL IS THAT?"

"Your ride," said Galloway. She had walked them across the hangar and through an airlock to a launch portal.

"No chance," said Alard, who looked a bit green. "Come on, look at it."

"Does it even have an engine?" Vaskez slapped the fuselage and then withdrew her hand and inspected it. It was covered in reflective flecks, like the craft was moulting.

Dix wasn't any kind of fly-boy. Strictly boots on the ground and, before that, more at home on the sea. He had been in a ton of spacecraft since – dropped here and there on Federation business – but they all at least looked like proper ships. Vessels you could be confident of getting out of at the other end.

This one looked like it had already been in a fire-fight. It was scarred and pitted – actually, make that severely dented in places. Small cargo hold, upper deck, maybe an eight-seater, max. Oil, or something – what did Dix know? – was dribbling out of a vent, which couldn't be right, and a mechanic was hammering noisily at a protruding, bent, deflector panel in the belly, trying to get it back into position.

Put it this way. Even if Dix had somehow managed to escape from the guards on the jump-ship that brought him here, and somehow evaded re-capture, and somehow found his way to this craft, where an inviting door had somehow been left open for a stow-away, he still wouldn't have got on board.

"Easy," said Drake, putting his large hand on the shaft of the mechanic's hammer, mid-swing, stopping it dead. "There's a knack to it. Like this." He spread his hands out on the panel, leaned forward, and braced with his chest and pushed. They all heard a click as the panel re-set itself, flush into the fuselage. "There, see."

"And you know that, how?" said Dix.

"A Star-Jumper X42," said Drake. "Stripped out, fully modded, an absolute beast under the hood. Very fast, very manoeuvrable. Don't judge a book by its cover."

"Sounds like you know your way around a spaceship?"

"I should. This one's mine," said Drake, trailing his hand lovingly across the side of the craft. "Hello, Star darling, how've they been treating you?"

They all looked at him. Galloway explained.

"Your classic in-system, souped-up, smuggler's ship.

For small-size, high-value items. Very difficult to catch, unless you get lucky. And, sadly for Drake, one of our patrols got lucky. After a bit of a chase and a friendly exchange of fire."

"You're a smuggler?" Alard looked surprised.

"Ex-smuggler, obviously," said Galloway. "Now a valued team member. And also, though it pains me to say, an excellent pilot. Drake here is your ticket in and out for the weapon, and then in – and hopefully out – for Hauga itself."

"How does he even fit in the pilot seat?" said Alard, moving quickly out of reach.

"You'd be surprised what I can stuff into a small space," said Drake. "Here, let me show you."

"Is it going to be like this for the whole trip? This little bro-cuddle thing you've got going on?" Vaskez looked bored of the back and forth.

"I still don't know about this," said Alard.

"What's to know?" said Vaskez, impatiently. "You get on the nice spaceship. Drake flies us to get the big bomb. You don't talk the entire way. All sounds perfectly understandable to me."

"I don't travel well," said Alard. "I get sick."

"You're sick on Star, I don't care what your special skill is, you're going out into the void." Drake flashed his eyes at Alard.

"Well, no," said Galloway. "You'll need him, unfortunately. Let's all just settle down. Drake, you want to run them through the flight procedures?"

Drake spent five minutes talking them through how

things worked on board his Star-Jumper. Basically, the rules were – they all did what he told them, when he told them, preferably without any backchat, and no one was to be sick on *anything*.

"And where exactly are we going in this rust-bucket?" said Alard.

Galloway flipped open a pad and showed them a chart. "Sending the coordinates now," she said to Drake. "This little charmer of a planet is Vitlok. It's dark and cold, and no one in their right mind would think of living there, which is why the Haugans hid their weapon on it. It's kept in a facility overseen by a cadre of researchers and scientists, who are more than ready to hand over the fruits of their labour. Once you've taken delivery, you make straight for Hauga."

It all sounded simple, but that was the army for you. Dix's experience, the simpler something sounded, the more fucked-up something became down the line. 'Take the ridge, neutralise and pacify' being a case in point.

"You said the Axis might also be onto it?"

"Could be," said Galloway. "Best to assume they are. Which is why you're going right now in Drake's zippy little Star-Jumper. Beat them to it. You should be able to get in and out without too much fanfare. Drake's used to sneaking around and picking up illicit items."

"And if we engage?"

"Let's hope you don't have to. But Vaskez is more

than capable of handling herself. She'll run security and protection."

Vaskez nodded, self-satisfied. "Yeah, baby. Don't you worry your pretty little heads about the nasty Axis mercs."

"And him?" Dix gestured at Alard. "What's he bring to the party?"

"Think of him as your scout," said Galloway. "Pathfinder. Point man."

"You're army?" Alard didn't look right for the army. Dix wasn't sure what it was, but there was something about Alard that didn't add up.

"When he wants to be," cut in Galloway as Alard was about to speak. "The thing about Alard is that he's extraordinarily good at finding his way. Technically, he shouldn't ever get lost. And yet he somehow manages to keep misplacing his platoon. Careless, aren't you, Alard?"

"What can I say?" said Alard, shrugging. "Army life's not for everyone."

"He's a runner," said Drake, disdainfully. "Abandons his mates in a heartbeat. Isn't that right, Run-boy?"

Run-boy. Dix got it now. Alard was a deserter. A serial one, by the sound of it.

"They're not my mates," said Alard. "I don't have mates."

"Imagine my surprise."

"Says the honest, trustworthy, contraband smuggler."

The pair of them bristled at each other again.

"That just leaves you, trooper," said Vaskez, breaking up the badinage and stepping back to appraise Dix. "What did you do to deserve this little excursion? What's your special skill?"

That was a good question. Dix knew why he was here – hitting an idiot, disobeying an idiot's orders. But he didn't know *why* he was here.

"Ah, yes, Dix," said Galloway. "Dix has trouble with authority, doesn't follow orders, thinks for himself. Disobeyed an officer in the field. We can't have that in the army."

"Word," said Vaskez, sucking in her lips. "No i in team, Dix, man, you should know that."

"And as this is no longer an army operation, that's why he's in charge," said Galloway.

There was a stunned silence.

"He is?" said Vaskez, wide-eyed, a disbelieving look on her face. "He's just a trooper."

"I am?" said Dix.

"Well, no, I'm in charge," said Galloway. "But Dix here is more accomplished than he looks, and is going to be my eyes and ears. This is a delicate operation. I need someone who's going to think first and shoot second, not the other way around. No offence, Vaskez."

"I'm not taking orders from a trooper," said Vaskez.

"Quite right. You're taking orders from me, via Dix."

"Come on, ma'am. I'm eight years in, special forces. He's still wet behind the ears."

"And he's still in charge," said Galloway. "Unless you want to step away from the mission? I can find someone else, if you prefer?" She fixed Vaskez with an enquiring eye. Slight amusement there, maybe.

"Hold on," said Alard. "There's a choice? How come Vaskez has a choice?"

"You've all got a choice," said Galloway. "Only, I wouldn't recommend option B. Anyway, Vaskez is different."

"How so?"

"Didn't she tell you?" Galloway was smiling openly now. "She volunteered, didn't you Vaskez?"

"Yes, ma'am!" Vaskez, snapped up straight, saluted.

"You've got to be kidding. Why would anyone do that?"

Dix was genuinely mystified. Out of all the reasons for ending up on this launch apron, in front of a seemingly clapped-out spaceship, embarking on a potentially short and terminal mission, that seemed by far the most unlikely.

"Duty, trooper," said Vaskez. "You wouldn't know about that."

Galloway looked sceptical. "Let's just say that Special Operator Vaskez has trouble making friends. She's not what you'd call collegiate."

"I have trouble with assholes," said Vaskez, firmly.

"Not everyone, in every unit you've ever been assigned to, Vaskez, is an asshole."

"Debatable."

"Which is why you're short of options," said

Galloway, "and why you're here." She looked around at the others and smiled encouragingly. "On the plus side," she said, "Vaskez really, really likes fighting. And she's very, very good at it."

"Hell, yeah," said Vaskez, adding "ma'am," as an afterthought.

"Question," said Dix.

The last couple of days had been unusual for him, to say the least. Back in the trenches on Mud Planet he'd been a common-or-garden army grunt, going about his daily duties. At which point he'd been arrested, locked up, charged, reprieved, and now given command of a special-ops unit.

He'd been told he could speak freely; what else could they possibly do to him, if he asked the question?

"Go ahead."

"What's to stop us taking Drake's ship? Not going to Vitlok or Hauga, but running instead? Alard sounds like he'd be up for it, and Drake, according to you, is some shit-hot pilot?"

"You've met Vaskez, right?" said Galloway. Vaskez, currently performing chin-ups on a girder, turned mid-action and sneered. "She's not going to let you do that, because her sunny disposition conceals a deep allegiance to the Federation. And even if you did manage it, where are you going to go? The Star-Jumper's an in-system ship, hasn't got the range you'd need to lose yourself. Of course, you can try hiding out on Vitlok itself, but I guarantee you won't like it."

Dix waited. He'd seen and heard enough of the

major, whoever she was, to know that she had another card to play. She just couldn't help herself with the drama.

"And, of course," said Galloway, "there's the last modification we've made to the ship. You want to tell him, Drake?"

"Bloody Feds," he said. "They've installed a remote-op kill-switch. My baby executes a flightpath anywhere except Vitlok and Hauga and the ship goes boom. And just so we're all clear, Star is not going boom. Not for anyone. It took me years to save up for her, and they don't make this model anymore."

"Smugglers have savings plans?" said Alard. "You learn something new every day."

"Right, now that's settled," said Galloway, "it's time for you all to sod off to Vitlok and go fetch a weapon. I want you off the station and out of here within the hour. Oh, one more thing – Dix, your chip-tag, if you please."

She held out a hand. Dix hesitated. The military tag every trooper wore around their neck. More even than the NavCom wrist-unit, which told them where they were and who was with them, the chip-tag was *who* they were. As well as personnel and admin records, it contained full bio-markers, which made you identifiable and contactable anywhere in the system. It came off only when you finished your ten-stretch. Or when you died. Without it, you weren't a soldier. You weren't anything.

"Hand it over, Dixie-boy," jeered Vaskez, pulling

down her T-shirt neckline to show she had relinquished hers. Alard did the same. Drake, as a civilian, didn't have one, but had presumably given up his civvy ID, too.

Dixie-boy. He didn't love that. If Dix really was in charge, *that* would be changing.

"There you go," said Galloway. "Lovely bunch of freelance smugglers, you all are now. Nothing to do with us. Now, get going."

Chapter 7

DRAKE BROUGHT them into Vitlok fast and low.

Low, because he was worried about an Axis presence and was trying to avoid alerting any broad-spec scanners.

Fast, because he could. "Because this is what I do," he said, as Alard groaned again from the back and questioned why the hell he had to drive like a hopped-up teenager in daddy's sport-elite Sky Rover.

Nothing pinged on the way in, which was good news. Looked like they'd beaten the Axis to it, if they even knew the whereabouts of the Hauga weapon. Maybe Galloway's intel wasn't all that.

"Not much of a welcome," said Vaskez, as Drake landed his craft on a scoured desert of grey stone and sand. A huge moon hung low in the sky, with a wash of stars beyond that was partly obscured by dark clouds. The land outside seemed dead and cold. A winking light on an overlay on the console nav-panel was the

only evidence that there was anything here to find –
those were the coordinates provided by Galloway.

Dix looked out across the harsh terrain at an inter-
locking range of low hills, somewhere in the mid-
distance. About a mile away – source of the winking
light and the secret Haugan compound.

"Didn't expect one," said Drake, "They are in hiding,
after all." He flicked down through Galloway's briefing
notes. "Says the facility's over there. They're expecting us."

"Can we get out of here?" said Alard. "I've
managed to keep it all in so far, but no guarantees. I
need fresh air."

"You're not going to find it out there," said Vaskez,
checking the Star-Jumper's bio-monitors. "We're going
to need fat suits" – she meant padded, thermal gear –
"and breathers. The atmosphere's for shit."

They suited up, donned an oxy-pack each, and
picked up the close-fit helmets. Dix had worn one just
once before and didn't like it. The faceplate restricted
some vision, and a trooper liked the wind on his face
and the tell-tale sounds that might carry. Even though
the breathers were fully wired and miked, all the bells
and whistles, Dix would still rather rely on his unob-
structed eyes and ears to warn of trouble.

"Weapons?" he said, knowing Vaskez was already
pissed off about this. "What have we got?"

Galloway had given them an arsenal becoming a
ragtag band of smugglers, which according to Vaskez,
was entirely made up of 'baby guns.'

"Nothing I can blow shit up with," she said. "A dented blaster, one careless owner. Two thrift-store assault rifles, couple of handguns. Drake, how do you ever get anything done with this sort of gear?"

"Please," said Drake, looking at the haul disdainfully. "I find it's best to avoid conflict in my game. Honour the deal, make the trade, get out quick."

"That's all very noble, big guy. But if the Axis are already here, we're stuffed if all we've got are these little pop-pops."

"Of course," said Drake, "I also find that the deals tend to go down more smoothly if I turn up with some persuasive arguments in my favour."

He laid his hand flat on a nearby bulkhead panel, fingers splayed, and then arched his hand so that just the fingertips touched the surface. A faint light pulsed under each finger, there was a soft click, and Drake took his hand away. A section of the panel slid open, revealing a recess crisscrossed with coloured wires and flexible tubes – typical, under-the-hood, life-support gubbins.

"Just in case anyone ever gets this far," said Drake. "Although they'd have to have cut my hand off, I suppose."

He ignored the so-what expressions in front of him, plunged a hand into the wire-and-tube spaghetti, up to his wrist, and twisted something. Another click and, as he withdrew his hand, the life-support unit – clearly a fake – slid one way and a much larger panel behind slid another, revealing a spacious, six-foot-high compartment.

"Hello, mama!" said Vaskez, grinning from ear to ear. "Drake, I think this is going to be the start of a beautiful friendship."

The first rack held a line of pristine, high-spec, Federation-issue assault rifles. There were ammo boxes and utility slings to the side, while a second rack supported an assortment of tube-blasters and field rocketry.

Dix noted some more specialist weaponry, too. Couple of Raptor drones, a belt of high-explosive boomerang scythes, and a small stack of the mobile Retriever munitions – known by army grunts every-where as Fuck-Me mines, because "Fuck me" was often the last thing you said as the little homing mine scampered into your foxhole.

Even Alard seemed impressed. "How d'you manage to hide all this from them? They must have gone all over your ship after they caught you."

Drake laughed. "I'm a smuggler, the clue's in the job title."

"And a very good little smuggler you are, too," said Vaskez, reaching forward for the biggest and most threatening-looking weapon.

Drake batted her away. "Fingers. Ask nicely and point. This hardware doesn't clean itself you know."

Dix bagged himself a rifle he was familiar with, and let Drake and Vaskez argue it out about the rest.

They put the helmets on, popped the main door and jumped out.

It was cold on the surface, not quite freezing, but with a nasty little wind that whipped up sand from the rocks. Dix could feel it stinging a narrow, unprotected band of skin on his neck. The thermal gear would be good enough to get them to the facility and back – wherever that was, and whatever it was, tucked into those dark hills somewhere. In the meantime, he'd have to put up with stale breather-air, foggy peripheral vision, and the crackle from the comms mike.

Drake shut up shop, arming the lower cargo door so he could open it remotely when they were on the way back with the weapon. Load it in and off they'd go, and not a moment too soon, as Vitlok was already ranking highly on shitholes Dix had been to in the service of the Federation army. Top three, easy.

"The fuck is he doing?" Dix was already on his way, but Vaskez's voice boomed in his ear, and he turned round to see.

Alard was on one knee by the ship, running the sand through his fingers. He then put his hand flat on a dark rock and leaned in slightly. Dix couldn't see his face in the helmet, just the slight interior glow that meant the comms and life-support systems were working normally.

"You're sick in that helmet, you'll regret it," said Vaskez. "Never get the smell out."

Alard looked up, gave her the finger, and got to his feet.

"Right," said Dix, "Let's go."

He might have been mistaken, but thought he heard a muttered 'Yessir.' Ignored it. Dix didn't imagine for one minute that anyone was going to follow his orders, and didn't intend to give any. It wasn't exactly a complicated mission. Fly in the nice space-ship, fetch the big bomb – Vaskez had been right, that's about all it amounted to. So far, anyway.

They struck out for the hills at a decent pace, Dix at point. He knew what Galloway had said about Alard, but it was a short, straight shot across the desert scrub to where they'd pinpointed the facility. Even in this half-light, with some whipping gusts of sand, no one was getting lost today. Alard's apparent super-special pathfinding skills could wait for Hauga.

It took them twenty minutes to cover the ground, Drake making up for lack of army fitness with surprisingly long strides. Dix had no idea if smugglers worked out, but Drake seemed pumped and full of beans. If the Hauga weapon was at all unwieldy, they were going to need him, and he looked as if he would be an asset, beyond his undoubted flying skills. Could probably carry one of them at the same time.

The hills turned out to be irregular, weathered fingers of stone, pushing out into the desert, creating a series of narrow canyons that faced them head on.

"Which is not asking for trouble at all," said Vaskez, peering down the nearest defile before scanning the heights above. "Which way, Dix?"

He consulted a rudimentary hand-nav that

Galloway had deigned to let them have. It was basic – just about did the job – but what Dix wouldn't give to have his Fed-issue NavCom now. That would have told him immediately if anyone else was in the vicinity, and what they were toting; all the hand-nav did was home in on a signal.

That was stronger here, with the facility apparently down the second canyon – no, third – in from the left. Although how there was anything down there, building or otherwise, was beyond him. The canyons were fifteen, twenty feet wide at most, and maybe sixty feet high. Visibility and sight lines were terrible. Vaskez was right again, this was asking for trouble.

He signalled to move, but Alard held them up. "Wait," he said and, for the second time that day, laid his hand on a rock. This time, the soaring walls of the canyon they were about to enter.

"What is this shit?" said Vaskez, who seemed eager to get going. Dix felt the same. Exposed outside the canyon walls, walking into who-knew-what inside? He didn't like any of it and wanted it over. In, out, away.

"Something's happened here," said Alard. "I can feel it."

Dix heard a 'woo-ooh' ghost noise in his helmet. Drake, laughing.

"Please, you're psychic now?" said Vaskez.

"Psych-sick, more like," said Drake. "He's just chicken. Like the run-boy he is."

"I'm only telling you what I know," said Alard.

"Which is?"

"I don't know. Just that something has happened."

"Very fucking useful. Care to be more precise?"

"I – can't. It's – too cold, too hard." Alard had both hands on the wall now, and Dix didn't know if he was talking about the planet, the canyon, himself? They didn't have time for this, anyway. Looked like they had got here ahead of any Axis interest, but why push it by hanging around?

"Right, we're moving," he said, and headed into the canyon. "It's not far, this way."

Vaskez let Drake go past her, and pushed Alard in front of her. "Got the six," she said, following them down, turning every few steps to sweep up and behind her.

The canyon turned an immediate corner and widened slightly, and then another corner, and widened again. Dix couldn't see the exit, which worried him, and while there was more space to move in, the higher reaches were now overhanging, so he couldn't see the hill tops. It felt – dark, overlooked, unsafe.

Something the sarge always used to say – if you're not sure, but you don't have a very good reason not to be sure, keep moving. Because the galaxy was full of dead troopers who had dithered in the wrong place for too long. So Dix moved them forward, towards the winking light. One more corner, one more turn.

The canyon came to an end. A curving, facing wall that rose for fifty feet, capped by a quarter-dome of rock that blocked out yet more light. They stood in a group while Dix consulted the hand-nav, didn't like what he saw, and shook it in frustration.

"We're here," he said. "Apparently. Though it's hard to tell."

"Just peachy," said Vaskez. "Dead end, kill zone, no visibility, only one way out."

Alard began to speak, but Vaskez cut him off. "And don't even start with the 'something happened here' bullshit."

Alard shrugged and pointed, high up on the facing wall. A light blinked, indeterminate source, and then another, twenty feet away on the same wall.

Dix took a couple of steps forward to get a closer look, and two more lights blinked, this time on the ground where canyon wall met floor. Between the two ground lights, stretching across the canyon floor, an illuminated line glowed, embedded in the rock – just behind Dix, between him and his crew.

"Nothing's gone boom yet," said Alard, after a short pause.

Dix was relieved about that, too. The lights and the line had all the hallmarks of an auto-trigger system, but if it didn't go boom, what did it do?

The answer came a second or two later. With a bare hiss, a doorway opened in the facing rock wall, the two halves sliding into hidden recesses. Lights flickered on inside a metallic chamber; a second, closed, door was visible inside, opposite the entrance.

"Told you they were expecting us," said Drake.

"And we think this is a good idea, because?" Alard

had another handful of sand, which he was running through his fingers, dropping it on the floor. Running it through shaking fingers.

"It's an airlock," said Vaskez. "Facility must be inside. No other way to manage on this planet. At last, we're getting somewhere."

The canyon door slid shut behind them, and there was another hiss as the pressure equalised. A soft chime and a green light told them they could remove their breathers and oxy-packs, and they rubbed their faces and pinched their noses as they studied the interior door. The air seemed good.

"Ready?" Dix punched the only visible button, and they stepped through another sliding door into the facility.

Chapter 8

Dɪx sᴄᴀɴɴᴇᴅ ᴛʜᴇ sᴘᴀᴄᴇ, Vaskez taking up a position to his right, Drake to his left, Alard, hanging back.

They were in a large chamber of dressed-stone blocks and pillars, like a wide corridor. High, wall-mounted fan units clicked and whirred. Other than that, the walls were bare, with no decoration, though an illuminated line in the floor showed the way. It dropped away in the distance, down stone-cut steps, leading into a lower, bigger, natural chamber – a cavern, whose heights were lost in darkness.

At the top of the steps, there were pockmarks in the wall; halfway down, a dislodged chunk of masonry and blast residue.

Vaskez moved quickly down into the larger chamber, sweeping as she went, then signalled for the others to follow – and motioned 'Eyes' at Dix with two fingers. He didn't need telling; he'd seen the aftermath of a firefight before.

The first body lay at the foot of the steps, face down, blast hole in its side. The head was covered with a cowl, while the black robe was rent and scorched where the blaster had hit.

Looked like Alard was right. Something had happened here.

There was more evidence the further they ventured into the chamber: blast marks on the walls, another crumpled body in the mid-distance, an overturned table – splintered and scarred, after it had been used as a last line of defence. Behind it lay two more bodies, in the same cowl and robes, spreadeagled on the floor, clutching a rifle each.

But it was still and quiet. Whatever had happened here had happened a while ago. Dix sniffed the air. No discharge smell. Maybe a day or so earlier?

"What are we thinking?"

"Galloway's Haugan monks, right?" said Drake. "I'm thinking they had a very bad day. Looks like they welcomed in the wrong people."

"This Axis?" said Vaskez.

"Has to be." Dix was sure of it. So much for their head-start. The weapon would be long gone. Galloway would be pissed. And he'd end up digging uranium for what would turn out to be a brief stay on Arcana Minor.

"If they're still around, we'll be having a bad day ourselves," said Vaskez. "They have really unloaded in here, and even with Drake's gear we're going to be outgunned."

"They're not here," said Alard, his hand on the upturned table.

"Let me guess," said Vaskez. "Woo-woo vibes, right?"

Alard ignored her and moved off towards a line of doors that opened onto one side of the chamber. Small grilles on each one, all slightly ajar.

"Where did they keep this weapon?" said Dix. "There's got to be something more like a research facility here. Bunker, maybe?" He didn't hold out any hope that it was still here, but definitive evidence that it was gone, and that it wasn't their fault, might sway Galloway. They would have tried, at least.

"Dix, over here. You should see this." It was Alard, calling from across the chamber. He had one hand resting on a doorframe and looked queasy again.

It was a monk's cell. Whitewashed walls, frame bed, and a simple desk scattered with blood-spattered papers. A chest had been overturned, and a rug was scrunched in one corner. And pinned to the wall, an alloy bolt through each palm, was a monk's body with his head sunk on his bloody chest. Bolt casings lay on the floor at his feet in a pool of blood – Dix recognised them, from a standard-issue bolt-gun, the sort of kit you might take with you if you thought you'd need to fix holds or ropes on a rocky deployment. The Axis fighters had come prepared.

Dix gently raised the monk's hoodless head by the chin. One eye gouged out, throat cut. He heard Alard gasp.

"You think he told them where to find it?" said Drake.

Dix doubted it, state of the body. This monk hadn't given anything up.

They worked their way down the line of cells, eight in all, bodies in each of them. Some more inventively disfigured than others; some clearly dragged back into their cells to be tortured, if the blood trails on the floor were anything to go by. Injured, overpowered, disarmed outside – but kept alive long enough to be questioned, and then brutally dispatched.

"Fucking Axis." Vaskez spat the name.

Dix knew what she meant. These weren't soldiers, they were butchers. Recruited by planetary warlords to fight under an Axis banner that meant little but self-interest. Hard-edged mercenaries who played by different rules. Alard was right to be scared – if they were caught, they could expect nothing less from these animals.

In the end, going through the chamber, they discovered twenty-six bodies, either in the cells, dead in the firefight, or killed where they had been overrun and captured. There were other side rooms – a large kitchen, walk-in freezers, storage areas, power and utility rooms, even a library. No sign of life in any of them – plenty of bodies and bloodstains.

What did they know? This was – what? A monastery? Something like that, anyway. Inhabited by monks, or at least people dressed as monks, hidden away on a desolate planet. Scientists and researchers, maybe, who had put up a fight even so, but had been no match for the brutal Axis mercs. A fight to the bitter death to protect the ultimate weapon that they had hoped to deliver to Hauga.

But if this was a weapons' research facility, there was no sign of the actual 'facility.' And still no evidence either way about the fate of the weapon itself.

"What do you think?" said Dix. "Wrap it up? Get out while we can?"

"Good plan," said Drake, with Alard nodding eagerly along.

"This can't be it," said Vaskez, and Dix was inclined to agree with her. "One more sweep," and she set off again, down the wide corridor that led off the main chamber to the kitchen and library.

They had missed it the first time and almost did again. A metallic screen, hung with a tapestry depicting a bright, flaring sun – a decorative flourish in this most utilitarian of habitats. Or rather, Dix had seen it on the first sweep, but hadn't noticed the angle it was set at – concealing a double-shoulder-wide gap between screen edge and rough corridor wall.

He backed up and peered around the screen, and down another passageway. "Vaskez," he said, and beckoned.

They entered slowly, an assault rifle each out before them. It was just a dozen steps or so, twenty feet, to an entranceway, through which was a final room. Another cavern, with a lower, domed roof, hung with more tapestries and centred on a stone dais, surmounted by a carved pillar.

Tied to this, hands behind his back, was a man – barely a man, after what they'd done to him. Wall-mounted spotlights played on the scene, picking out the dark red blood, the white bone, the vomit.

It was a chapel, or a shrine, Dix could see that. The bursting sun motif again, on the hanging cloths; carved figures on the central pillar; an offertory table nearby, with a shallow bowl and metal beakers.

There were gouges in the man's torso, and a slash across his cheek so deep that it revealed the jawbone and teeth beneath. His head was slumped again, like the others, but below his chin hung a pendant with a shining sun, obscured by dark stains. The boss man? Abbot, some word like that? Dix wasn't up on his religious orders.

"This one's still breathing," said Drake, who had leaned in close. "Just."

The man stirred at Drake's voice, turned and lifted his head slightly. His lips moved – what was left of them on one side – and they heard his slow, raspy voice.

"Federation?" he said. With his injuries, it sounded like 'Fev-ayshn.' Dix nodded.

"You're late," said the man.

Dix stifled a yelp. Not laughter. Admiration. This was one tough monk.

"The weapon?" said Dix. "Did they get it?"

"They came. They – asked their questions. They

left." Every word was forced and slurred, and Dix had to try hard to understand.

"So they didn't find it?"

The monk's head slumped down again. Vaskez took a bottle from her belt and squeezed it slowly, gently, into the good side of his mouth. Water pooled and dribbled.

"Did they get the weapon? Lightburst?" Dix tried again, dropping his head to the monk's ear, talking softly but urgently.

At the sound of the name, the monk raised his head again. Was that – a smile? It was horrific, either way. A ravaged face with more than one mouth.

"Deliver it. To my people." The voice came even more haltingly now. "It is ready. With light will come freedom."

"Where?" said Dix. "We've looked. The Axis took it."

"No," said the monk. "Never." He stopped, and his breath became more ragged. "The bowl," he finally said, and then slumped one last time. Dix checked for signs of life and shook his head.

"Bowl?" said Drake.

Dix pointed at the nearby table. "That?" He looked around the room. There was nothing else it could be.

Alard was closest and picked it up. Or tried to pick it up, but it was secured somehow to the table. Unmovable. It was inlaid with more sun motifs and had a slight, circular depression in the middle.

"Ideas?"

"Here, let me." Vaskez put down her weapon and tried to wrench the bowl off the table. She couldn't shift it either.

"You want me to have a go?" said Drake, flexing his not-insignificant muscles.

"Why are you all trying to break it?" said Dix. "The man said 'Bowl,' it was a clue."

"Well, unless there's a set of keys in it – which there isn't – maybe there's something underneath it? So let's wrench it off and see."

Maybe. Also – maybe 'key' was on the right track.

Dix picked up one of the beakers, turned it upside down, examined the base. Looked about right to him.

He turned it the right way up and placed the beaker in the depression at the bottom of the bowl. Fitted perfectly.

A click, and then the entire table rolled smoothly sideways, exposing a shallow ramp into a strip-lit room below.

They peered down to see glass-fronted chambers, banks of monitors and work-stations, stretching away under the stone dais. It was a lot more than a mere room, it was a series of labs and isolation units reaching far underground.

The research facility? It had to be – and it looked intact and undiscovered, because the man tied to the stone pillar had died in agony protecting what was hidden beneath his feet.

Which became obvious as they reached the foot of the ramp, and the space opened up before them.

"Well, would you look at that," said Drake.

Chapter 9

THE CHUNKY, metallic tube was lashed into place on the lower cargo deck of Drake's ship.

A little over six feet long, almost three feet high, slightly tapered at one end, hinged on one side, resting on wheel dollies for transport, keypad panel on the upper surface – it looked like the protective housing for an airborne missile or seaborne torpedo, and could have been either as far as Dix knew. Galloway hadn't exactly been forthcoming on the subject, other than the weapon's name – Lightburst.

They had rolled it up the ramp from its resting place in the underground research bunker – with some difficulty – and then guided it carefully down the stone corridor and through the main chamber. The wheels tracked through pools of blood from the fallen monks.

At one point, the leading edge, guided by Alard, had knocked against a protruding rock bulge with an unseemly clang, and they had all frozen, glaring at each other furiously. Dix had been around enough high-explosive ordnance to know that banging it hard was never a good idea.

The steps out of the main chamber had been the last obstacle. Even with Drake underneath at the back, and Dix and Vaskez lifting from the front, the tube was too cumbersome to raise safely and cleanly. In the end they'd had to splinter a couple of the upturned tables to make a rudimentary ramp, and then rig a cord-and-webbing harness to haul it up and along the access corridor into the airlock.

After that, the rest had been – not easy, but straight-forward. Breathers back on, it had been a straight run down the canyon and across the flat, desert scrub to the ship, pulling and pushing the weapon on its wheel dollies. Weighing the need not to jolt an engine of death unduly against the nagging sense of exposure on a hostile planet recently visited by equally hostile, psychopathic mercenaries. Even Alard had helped.

Dix hadn't felt safe until Drake had closed the cargo doors and punched the ship into drive, quickly putting distance between themselves and the merciless slaughter that had taken place on Vitlok.

Safe being a relative term, under the circumstances. But they were at least all still alive, and had achieved their first objective, as previously stated – get on the nice spaceship, fetch the big bomb.

Vaskez took another turn around the secured container, still trying to puzzle it out.

"Thermo-blast, you reckon? Tactical nuke?"

"How would I know?" said Dix.

"Thought you were in charge? Assumed you'd know shit like this?" She raised an antagonistic, 'No, I won't let it go' eyebrow at Dix.

"We're just the delivery team. I don't care what it is or what it does. All I care about is getting it where it's supposed to go, without dying."

"Yeah, well…" Vaskez chuntered a bit more under her breath and resumed her pacing, coming up hard against Alard, who was crouched on a bench with his head between his knees. "Now what's up with him?"

"I don't feel well."

To be fair, Alard did look very grey. He raised his head and belched, then swallowed and grimaced.

"Ship-sick?" said Dix. It happened. Not to him – used to the swell of the Calisto seas – but he'd seen hardened campaign soldiers coughing their guts up on interplanetary troop shuttles. Usually recovered when they eventually hit solid ground, but no consolation to the poor sod in the next seat with a lapful of trooper-vom.

"Something like that," said Alard, before swallowing hard again and putting his hand protectively across his stomach.

"Great," said Vaskez. "Couldn't shut him up down there with his 'something's wrong' shit. And when he finally does stop talking, it's because he's going to chuck."

"I was right though, wasn't I?" Alard looked up briefly and held Dix's eye.

Well, yes. Yes, he had been right. But what did that mean? Probably nothing, given that they had been on a clandestine mission on a crappy, cold planet. At the time, they'd all been thinking of the many and varied ways *that* could go wrong. Alard being the only one to say it out loud didn't make him special.

There was a gentle, hydraulic whoosh and Drake stepped off the dumb waiter which connected the ship's upper and lower decks.

"Morning, troopers. No one blown themselves up yet?"

"He's the trooper," said Vaskez, dismissively, gesturing at Dix. "I'm special forces. I don't know what he is," indicating Alard.

"Touchy," said Drake.

"I don't diss you and call you a petty thief, do I? Even though I could, *smuggler*." Vaskez put a spin on that, let it hang.

"Point taken. Tough crowd. I was only asking."

"Who's driving the ship?" Alard had raised his head again.

"Very funny."

"No, really," said Alard, a look of concern on his already washed-out face.

"You're serious? The AI, what do you think?"

"This heap has an AI?"

Drake bristled. "I've told you before, don't get hung up on looks. She's got me out of more scrapes than you've had hot dinners."

"You don't want to mention hot dinners around

Alard right now." Vaskez gunned him a half-sneer. "He's liable to spoil the upholstery." She scanned the barebones cargo deck. "Have you got any upholstery?"

Drake ignored them both and addressed Dix, which – Dix supposed – meant something. That he was nominally in charge, at least as far as the only non-military member of the unit was concerned.

"Worked out what it is yet?"

Dix heard Vaskez scoff from somewhere behind him, and chose to ignore that, too.

"Not really, it's locked down tight. Needs a code to open it, and we're definitely *not* going to start inputting random numbers just to see if we can break in." Dix looked meaningfully at Vaskez, who just shrugged.

"Could something that size win someone a war?"

"Depends what's in there. What the payload is. Where you drop it. Who you drop it on. All sorts of factors. But maybe."

Drake laid his hands on the casing. "The Axis really, really wanted to get their hands on this."

"Which suggests it is as valuable – destructive – as Galloway said." Dix could still see the scene on Vitlok in his head – the blood, the torn bodies, the sheer wanton violence. Someone had wanted this weapon very badly indeed.

"Valuable," mused Drake. "I wonder…"

"You can forget it," said Dix. "There's no angle we're going to play here. You heard Galloway. We're expendable, unless and until we get this thing to Hauga."

"Plus," said Vaskez, "if you try to steal it, I'll use one of your own fancy guns to stop you. This might be a black op but I'm still Fed army, and don't you forget it. The Axis are not getting this baby."

"All right, sheesh, you're touchy."

"Well, that's what comes of riding in a rattling shit-heap with a bunch of amateurs and a big, fucking mystery bomb that does who-knows-what. Tends to put a girl on edge."

"Star does not rattle, do you darling?" Drake stroked a nearby bulkhead. "Don't listen to the nasty lady trooper."

"Special forces, fucker," growled Vaskez. "And I ain't no lady."

"No shit. You talk to your mother with that mouth?"

"My mother would rip your face off just for a laugh, you skin-flap of a smuggler's scrotum, and then tell you to go fuck yourself."

"Really? The pair of you?" Dix stood between them, hands raised in an 'Enough' gesture. "You don't think we've got better things to do than pick fights with each other?"

Drake laughed. "Just messing, *Captain*." He gave Dix a mock salute. "That right, Vaskez?"

"Sure. Like Drake says, *Major*, just messing." She put one finger to her temple in the barest of salutes and nodded a half-amused acknowledgement at Drake.

So now they were both taking the piss out of him and his nominal command? Great. Not for the first time, Dix wondered what on earth Galloway had been thinking, putting him in charge.

The one thing he did know for sure was that they had a weapon to deliver, plus a space-worthy Star-Jumper – one very careful owner, it seemed – and, so far, no one in hot pursuit. Dix checked the last part with Drake, who was reassuring. To a point.

"Scanners are clear. There was nothing nasty lurking in orbit when we left. Whoever was there before us is long gone, and I can't see any trace of hostiles anywhere. No trace of anything, actually. Vitlok isn't exactly on the tourist or trade circuit. I mean, I'd never heard of it, and I thought I knew every rock in this sector."

"Nothing to worry about then?"

"I didn't say that. Just said I couldn't see or trace anything. Some of those Axis merc ships are stealthy little bleeders. Shield-tech on the latest models. There could be one keeping pace with us outside and we'd be none the wiser."

"That doesn't sound good."

"It's unlikely. If they were there, and knew what we had, they'd have paid us a violent visit by now, don't you think?"

"Agreed. Even so, better not to hang around. How far to Hauga?"

"Way ahead of you, Dix. I've been working on Galloway's projected flight plan. Not too shabby, as it happens. She seems to have found a Fed navigator who knows what they're doing. Parameters are fixed, of course. Pretty rigid, as she said, she doesn't want us flying the coop, but I can shave off a bit here and there without triggering anything untoward. Still haven't found the kill-switch, though there are…"

"Drake."

"Traces in the back end. Don't want to mess with them in flight, but maybe when we get into Hauga orbit…"

"Drake." Dix raised his voice, trying to stop the flow.

"What?"

"Hauga? How long?"

"Right, sure. Erm, one jump, twelve hours, give or take."

"So, what are we waiting for, let's jump."

"Ah, Dixie-boy," – that again, from Drake this time, he was going to have to say something – "you really do have a lot to learn about the ladies."

"What?"

"My little Star. You can't just jump her. She needs warming up. Wooing. Wining and dining, until she's ready to take wing and fly through the fabric of space and time."

"You've got to be kidding."

"About the wining and dining, sure. But you can't just jump a Star-Jumper out of the gate. Got to engage the core drive, which takes a while, and push a whole load of little buttons in sequence. And lock everything down nice and tight on board, including this highly dangerous, explosive weapon, because, you know, we'll be travelling blind at ludicrous speeds within a self-generated warp-bubble system so complicated that only about three people in the galaxy understand how it works."

Dix didn't want to think about the physics of interstellar space flight. Not his circus, not his monkey. If it worked, it worked, and that's all he needed to know. But he did want to get out of Dodge as soon as possible. "How long until we're ready to jump then?"

"Two, three hours." Drake clapped him on the shoulder. "Don't worry, it's all in hand, I'm on it." Drake made for the elevator, back to the nav deck. "You might want to have a word with your team, though." He smirked, pointing at Vaskez, now squinting at the keypad on the casing and tapping it, and Alard, head still between his knees. "I'd get some more straps around that bomb, as well. Can't be too careful."

Dix didn't know if Drake was winding him up or not, but he threw a couple more restraining ties around either end of the tube, just in case.

The jump, when it finally came, was surprisingly uneventful. Not so much as a bump or even a rumble, once Drake had flicked the last console switch in sequence and announced, "All right, Star baby, let's go!"

They had all done a hyperspace jump before, but Dix, Vaskez and Alard had always been in the bowels of some troop carrier or other, where there was nothing to see except two lines of strapped-in soldiers and stowed gear. Just another boring long-haul flight, as far as they were concerned.

Knowing this, Drake had invited them all into the nav cabin up front, where he'd made a big show of counting down the time and pointing out the sequence of lights as they turned green.

"That it?" said Alard, looking perkier than he had for a couple of hours. Nothing had changed – same life-support hum, same steady, undetectable motion, same view of the stars outside.

"Sure," said Drake, having flicked the last switch to send Star on her way. "Apart from, you know – " whereupon he directed their attention to the real-time observation window.

Where there had been constellations of stars – pinpricks against the deep canvas of space – there were now blinding white streaks that rolled and barrelled past the window towards a distant, narrowing hole, like an inverted whirlpool. It was like a long, drawn-out scream in visual form.

"Fucker," said Alard, dropping his head and retching. Drake was one step ahead of him, holding a barf-bag under his chin, intoning, "Please use the receptacle provided in the event of sudden illness."

Vaskez howled in delight at the window. "That's what *I'm* talking about. Nice, Drake, nice." She cheered again. "Go, Star, go!"

"Best seat in the house," said Drake, hitting another button on the console. The window slowly darkened and then the view returned to a standard star-and-space backdrop. "Screensaver," he said. "The jump view's all right for a few minutes, but sends you mad after a while – no perspective. I'll switch back to actual view once we jump out again, in – let's see – eleven hours fifty from now."

Alard mumbled something, lurched to his feet, and made for the back of the deck and the dumb-waiter elevator. A click and a whirr, and he descended to the lower cargo deck.

"I'm not saying that's not really cool," said Dix. "Never seen a jump in real time before. But do you have to wind him up so much?"

"Just a bit of fun," said Drake. "Besides, the man basically asks for it. What *is* the point of him?"

"Don't know," said Dix. "Galloway picked him."

"Yeah, well, Galloway's not here, and Run-boy is a weak link. Scared of his own shadow, seems to me."

"And any more of that spooky, 'something's happened here' shit and I'll personally make sure something happens to him," said Vaskez. "Now then, Drake. Give us another peek at that hellscape out there."

Dix left them to it, Vaskez yelping with joy as Drake altered the view one more time. She was a funny one – blowing hot and cold, prickly one minute, laughing the next. Dix could see that she'd be hard to warm to. Still, Vaskez' current mood was an improvement on earlier. A full fifty percent of the team was bonding now, which was better than nothing.

He went down to see how Alard was doing and found him standing by the weapon, facing the keypad.

"You all right there?"

Alard turned. Looked a bit grey again, not surprisingly. "Not really," he said. "I think something's happening."

Dix could see Vaskez's point. "You have to stop with this, Alard. It's freaking everyone out."

"No, not like that – not like before. That was – doesn't matter. But look." He stood aside so that Dix could see.

The keypad mounting was glowing, while the individual numbers lit up randomly, one after another in rapid succession.

"The hell did you do?"

"Nothing! It just started doing that. And come here, listen."

He beckoned to Dix and they crouched down, next to the tube. There was a faint but unmistakable whirring noise coming from inside.

"What's that? A cooling system, maybe? Power source?"

"How would I know?"

"Was it there before?"

"I didn't exactly listen out for worrying noises from a horribly dangerous weapon. I was just glad to get off that planet." Alard shuddered.

"Better tell the others," said Dix.

"What, that their new toy is just about to explode?"

"Don't say that."

"I knew this whole trip was a bad idea," said Alard. He straightened up. "I really don't want to be blown up in a wormhole, or whatever Drake's piece-of-crap ship is currently blasting through."

Dix got back to his feet too, and then they both saw and heard it.

The lit keypad screen stopped flickering through the numbers, which returned to their inert state. The surrounding glow winked out. And then there were six distinct beeps as six numbers flashed in turn.

The access code being activated.

Silence. A heavier, chunking sound. The whir of servos.

And finally a click, as an upper section of the tube popped open.

Chapter 10

Drake and Vaskez arrived side by side, summoned by Dix's frantic shout over the bulkhead comm panel.

"If that freaky dipshit has been sick on Star, he better be cleaning it up." Drake sounded annoyed as the elevator dropped into position on the cargo deck.

They stepped off and stared.

"What the fuck?" said Vaskez.

"Language," said Dix, automatically.

"But seriously, what the actual f– "

"You have got to be shitting – sorry, kidding – me." Drake was just as nonplussed as the rest of them.

The child stood by the side of the metallic tube. A boy, maybe nine years old. Dix wasn't great with kid ages – only child, no sibs. But nine seemed about right.

He'd climbed out unaided, right after the panel had popped, just like he'd got out of bed. Scooched over the side, dropped down, and stood there now with an open, yet unreadable, expression on his face. Like he was waiting for something.

"Well, that's fucked," said Vaskez.

Dix glared at her.

"Fudged. I said fudged."

"It's something, all right," said Drake, looking hard at Alard. "What did you do?"

"Me? Nothing!"

"It just opened," said Dix. "We were both here. We didn't touch anything. The keypad code pinged, and hey presto."

"The kid came out of there?" Vaskez looked like she was having a hard time processing what she was seeing.

"Just like he said," said Alard. "Weirdest thing I ever saw."

"But – "

Vaskez was stumped, but Dix got her gist – how, what, who, why, and a million other questions.

"Kid's been in there all along?" Drake stepped forward, closer to the boy, to peer inside the tube, but Dix grabbed his arm.

"Wait, let's not spook him."

"Doesn't look spooked, does he?"

He didn't. The boy stood there calmly, one hand across his chest, the other by his side. Belted, grey tunic over darker trousers, soft shoes. Untroubled eyes. He seemed entirely unconcerned by the situation, which was more than could be said for the rest of them.

Dix reached out a welcoming hand. The boy

looked at him but didn't move. Dix took another step closer, crouched down a little, and offered his hand again. Nothing doing.

"I'm Dix," he said. "What's your name, kid?"

"Hello, Dix." The boy's voice was clear and true. A confident voice.

Kid could speak and understand them, at least. That was the first normal thing that had happened in the last five minutes.

"That's Drake. Vaskez. Alard." Dix indicated each of them in turn. "You got a name?"

"Of course," said the boy. "I am Lightburst." He smiled encouragingly.

There was a snort from Alard, and a mumbled "Fuck's sake" from Vaskez.

"Lightburst?" said Dix, thinking that this was all kinds of wrong. "That's your name, are you sure?"

"Are you not sure of your own identity, Dix?" The boy looked more amused than anything else. "Names are powerful. I am Lightburst, and with light comes freedom. It is written and it will be."

Drake laughed. "That told you, Dix." He moved towards the tube. "Right then, Lightburst, let's have a look inside this little hidey-hole of yours."

The boy moved to one side and Drake peered in. "Survival pod," he said, straightening up after a few seconds. "There's life support, water tube, waste-evac, vid screen. A ton of soundproofing. Nice little bed. He's been tucked up in there all right."

"They put you in that?" said Dix. "Who? Why?"

"The fathers," said the boy. "When the forces of darkness came, the fathers concealed the light."

The forces of darkness. That would be the Axis mercs. Dix had never heard them called that before, but it was as good a description as any.

The fathers? Presumably the monks. But what had the kid been doing there? And – wait. The merc attack on the monks of Vitlok had been the best part of two days ago now. Maybe longer.

"You've been in there all this time, on your own? Since the – "

'Forces of darkness' did seem a bit over the top. Dix reached for something a bit more kid-friendly. "Since the bad men came?"

The boy nodded. Straight face. Unconcerned.

"How'd he get out?" Alard put into the words the thing that had been bothering Dix.

"Screen and keypad on the inside," said Drake, bending and pointing. "Am I right?"

The boy nodded and smiled, and held up one hand. There was a sequence of six, single-digit numbers written on his palm.

"The fathers told me that all would be well. That the light would return home. It is written and it will be."

And what if all hadn't been well? That was some risk the monks had been taking with a boy's life. The Axis might have found him anyway, if only one of the monks had talked. Or the life support could have failed. Or they might never have found the tube in the first place, hidden under the chapel. He could still be there, entombed, waiting for a rescue that never came.

"I wasn't worried, Dix," said the boy, in response. "The fathers said someone would come. It is written and – "

"Yeah, we know, it will be." Dix shook his head in exasperation. There were more questions than answers here.

"Is it just me?" said Vaskez, after a short silence all round. "Or did we not go to a shi– shocker of a planet to pick up a massive, fu– fricking weapon, and end up instead with a kid? Like, I think I would have remembered if Galloway had said, 'Oh, by the way, along with the big fricking weapon, pick up the kid on the way out.'"

She was trying her best not to curse, Dix had to give her that. And she did have a point.

"Maybe the rest of it's the weapon?" said Alard. He tapped further down the tube, past the point at where a nine-year-old's legs would stretch. There was a dull thud, no more than that, but there was plenty of unclaimed space in the container in front of them. "Could be anything packed in there. And then they just rigged up a pod and stuffed him in, when they knew the Axis goons were on their way?"

"Could be. Any way of finding out?"

"Short of dismantling it?" Drake shrugged. "Maybe, but we're not messing with it while we're jumping. In fact, we're not messing with it at all while it's on my ship."

"What do you suggest?"

"Leave it well alone until we can talk to Galloway again."

"Great, let's talk to her."

"No can do, Dix. You know what she said. No comms until Hauga. She's got us running silent until then."

That was right. Galloway hadn't wanted anything broadcast from anywhere near Vitlok, in case it linked the Federation to a black op that definitely wasn't taking place there, oh goodness me, no. "In any case," she'd said. "What's there to talk about until you get to Hauga? You're in trouble, no one's coming to help. You've either got the weapon or you haven't, and if you haven't, I repeat, what's there to talk about?"

Galloway had said that like it was black and white. Weapon, no weapon. Now, looking at the kid and the container he had climbed out of, Dix thought she was probably going to have to allow for some shade of grey. But that meant talking to her and trying to straighten it out.

"So, when can we establish comms?"

"Not until we're out of the jump." Drake shrugged. "Say another eleven hours?"

"Terrific." That was a long time to ponder a mystery, and Dix didn't much like mysteries. Unknowns got you killed – another of the sarge's little wisdoms, and one that Dix had thoroughly embraced. Unknowns were a bugger, and here was a big one. Or rather, a four-foot-six one with a gormless expression.

"Come over here, kid, have a seat." Dix patted a bench. The boy sat down next to him and looked at Dix expectantly.

"Lightburst, right?"

The boy nodded. Dix could hear Alard snorting again in disbelief.

"We were supposed to pick something up. From the – fathers." Dix checked to see if the boy understood him, but just got an open smile. "A kind of weapon. You know, a weapon? Bang-bang. Anyway, they said it was called Lightburst. But that's your name, right?"

The boy nodded.

Dix persevered. "So, do you know if that's it? The weapon?" Dix pointed at the tube. "Maybe you got confused? Or maybe the fathers said something that you overheard? It's all right, you know. You can tell us. We're friends."

The boy beamed. "We are? I've never had a friend. Just the fathers."

Alard started to say something about this being a waste of time, but Dix shushed him.

"Sure we are. Me, Alard, Drake, Vaskez. We're all your friends. Isn't that right, guys?"

There was a murmur of agreement. Vaskez even tried a smile, which Alard recoiled at, and she soon pulled her face back into her usual scowl.

"So, if you know anything about it, you could tell us. Like, why were you there, maybe? Or what's inside the tube?"

"I was inside, Dix." The boy looked momentarily puzzled. "Did you not see?"

"This is hopeless." Alard huffed, and plonked himself down on the bench. "You're telling us that we have eleven hours of babysitting ahead of us, before we can figure out what's going on?"

"One baby, two babies," said Vaskez, pointedly. "What's the difference?"

Alard thought about replying in kind, Dix could see, but settled back on the bench after a warning glance. Maybe having a kid around the place would keep them all civil for a while?

Dix tried again.

"How old are you, Lightburst?"

"I don't know. I just am. It is written and it will be."

"All right. Let's try something else. What were you doing on Vitlok?"

"Where, Dix?"

"The planet, Lightburst, the planet." Dix looked helplessly at the others. "Where we found you. In that – capsule."

"The fathers' house, you mean, Dix?"

"Sure, kid, the fathers' house. What were you doing there?"

"It's where I live," said the boy, in a tone that suggested 'duh?' "It's very cold outside, but we stay inside."

"Well, this is fun. You sure he's all right?" Drake spun a finger-circle next to his head. "You know? In the head."

"My head is all right, Drake, thank you."

"Ha! Schooled you, big guy." Alard seemed delighted. "Look, the kid's a bit weird, but I like him."

"You would."

"We're stuck with him for now, that's for sure." Vaskez made as if to ruffle his hair, then thought better of it – like someone unwilling to touch a cat or a puppy, because they didn't like the way they felt. "I say 'we.' I mean you. I'm going to get some kip. Wake me up when someone knows what the f– frick is going on."

"And I've got spaceship stuff to do," said Drake. "*Don't* fudge about with the weapon thingy, right?"

"Looks like it's me and you, skipper," said Alard. "Know any games?"

He seemed a whole lot cheerier. Dix couldn't work him out. Scaredy-cat, throwing up, one minute, totally accepting of the weirdness the next. Maybe he was just pleased the focus was no longer on him?

But Vaskez was right. Nothing to do now until they could hail Galloway, see if she could shed any light on the situation.

Light. I mean, please. But if he insisted, what else were they supposed to call him? Dix turned to the kid. "Lightburst, you hungry?"

"Yeah, we're not doing that," said Alard. "I don't care if we've only got him for the next eleven hours. What kind of name is that?"

"It's my name," said the boy. "It is written and it will be."

"I don't think so," said Alard. "You're going to be —
"

He paused. Raised his eyebrows, pursed his lips, and nodded his head from side to side, as if running through alternatives.

"Sol," he said. "That's a good name for a boy. Right, Sol, let's go and look at Uncle Drake's auto-galley menu. I wouldn't get your hopes up. Man's a heathen. But I did see a spag bol that didn't look too chemically enhanced."

Chapter 11

EXACTLY ELEVEN HOURS and twelve minutes later, Drake exited the jump and brought up the cabin lights. The observation window slowly brightened, revealing a gloomy swirl of faint stars, a couple of streaky gas giants, and a scattering of dull moons.

"Welcome to ARC space," he said. "Man, what a dump."

Dix had never been out this far before, into the part of the galaxy known as Advance Reach Colonial. Home to a handful of sparsely populated planets that kept themselves to themselves, Hauga among them, it was a long way from the bright lights and busy trade lanes of Federation space.

Quite why the Federation, or Axis come to that, wanted to put feelers out this far was a mystery to Dix – there were easier places to get your beans and grain from, for sure.

But that was politics for you. Dix had no idea why

he'd been sent to half the places he'd ended up fighting in – sorry, peacekeeping. As far as he was concerned, Galloway wanting to get Hauga on side, and give the Axis a bloody nose into the bargain, was all part of the same grubby game.

Vaskez came on deck, yawning. She'd been asleep for a lot of the jump-time, and Dix envied her. Soldiers needed to grab shut-eye whenever they could, but Dix had never mastered the out-like-a-light technique that Vaskez clearly had. He'd dozed for a while, but that was all – and if that was what the weight of command did to you, he was happier as a humble trooper.

"That it?" said Vaskez, looking at the view, and then, unprompted, "What a dump."

Dix saw Drake smile at that. He'd found a kindred spirit.

"Which one's Hauga?"

Drake flashed up an overlay and pointed at a small, insignificant, muddy dot in a bottom quadrant.

"What's up?" said Vaskez. "Got the calcs wrong? Run out of space-juice? Couldn't you get us any closer?"

"Galloway's flight plan," he said. "Holding position. There's a blockade in place on Hauga. She doesn't want to trigger any untoward attention, not until we're ready to go."

"How are you going to get us in without anyone noticing?"

"That's my job, don't you worry about that. Right,

Dix, you want to talk to the boss? Comms are back online."

Dix had had plenty of time to think through all the possible ways this might play out, while trying and failing to get much sleep over the last eleven hours.

They hadn't got any more out of the kid – they were all calling him Sol now – beyond a few more platitudes about things being written, and what will be will be. Family, background, anything to do with Vitlok and the monks – he either didn't know or wasn't saying, and Dix wasn't sure which of those was more alarming.

What *was* a kid doing on that planet? And *whose* kid was it? Some monk with a dubious past? Dix had heard about that sort of thing.

For his part, Sol seemed entirely unconcerned about his situation. Asked no questions, showed no anxiety or fear.

That couldn't be normal for a nine-year-old kid, surely? He'd eaten a meal, and then curled up for a couple of hours' sleep, but that was about as routine as it got. The rest of the time, he just sat in companionable silence, with that kind-of creepy half-smile he had.

At some point during the jump, Drake had rooted around in his stowed kit and unearthed a softball. He'd gestured at Sol, who looked blank, so Drake had hoisted him to his feet, stood him a ways down the cargo deck and thrown him a catch to pass the time.

The ball had sailed past a stationary kid, arms by his side, and rolled to a halt by a stanchion. Drake had fetched the ball and tried again, thinking the kid hadn't been ready. Same result, Sol looking amiable but blank when told to try catching it.

In the end, Drake and Alard had played catch for a few rounds to show him what to do. He had smiled more broadly and tried his hardest, maybe making one out of three of the soft, slow balls that Drake served up to him. Last time Dix had seen Sol with the ball, he'd been sitting cross-legged on the floor, bowling it carefully against a bulkhead so it bounced and returned to his hand. He'd examined the ball each time in delight, squeezing it gently before rolling it again.

That's what they had, a soft lad with a softball, while Galloway was expecting a weapon of mass destruction. She wasn't going to be happy.

"Dix?" Drake was waiting for an answer at the console.

"Sure, punch her up. And get Alard and the kid here, why don't you. I have a feeling seeing is going to be believing."

Drake set the call on the monitor and disappeared down to the cargo deck. After a minute or so of unanswered beeps, the screen went live and there was Galloway.

"Trooper Dix, glad to see you've made it this far."

"Ma'am."

She shook her head dismissively. Dix had forgotten, she didn't like being ma'amed. "No trouble on Vitlok then?"

"Well, I wouldn't say that, exactly."

"What would you say, exactly, trooper?"

"Axis knew. Their mercs got there first. Left a lot of bodies behind. It was pretty brutal."

Galloway looked to her side, exchanged a glance with someone unseen, and swore. "That was always a possibility. They got the weapon then," she said. Not a question – resigned, a statement of fact.

"Well, no, actually. It was well hidden. They all died protecting it. But we found it."

Galloway's face lit up. "Did you now? Well done, trooper. Very well done." She exchanged another off-scene glance and gave a satisfied nod.

"Only – "

"Don't say 'only' to me like that, Dix. I don't like caveats. Did you get Lightburst or not?"

"We did, but I don't think it's what you were expecting."

"What's to expect? It's a big bomb. Or a little bomb, I don't care. Can I tell my Haugan contacts that you've got their weapon or not? They're anxious to take receipt, as you might imagine."

That answered the one big question Dix had had up until now. Did Galloway know anything about the nature of the weapon, or about the kid, before she had sent them off to Vitlok? Her answer suggested not.

Drake had teed up some image files and Dix shared them with Galloway – the tube, as removed from the planet and, later, lashed into position on the cargo deck below.

"This is what we retrieved from – whatever that place was? A monastery? Took the four of us to get it on board. No issues, no one followed, and away we jumped."

Galloway peered at the images. "This is good work, Dix. In and out, just like we planned. Didn't even need to engage? Bet Vaskez was annoyed, she loves a good firefight." Galloway chuckled, pleased with her plan, which put Dix's back up, because it hadn't been that easy.

"Wasn't anyone *to* engage. The bad guys had been and gone, which was just as well for us, because they were not nice house guests. And they had proper weapons, not the sub-par stuff you gave us. We'd have been toast if they had still been there." Dix figured he'd keep Drake's secret arsenal to themselves for now.

"All right, trooper, settle down. You might want to remember who you're talking to." Galloway gave him a stern look.

"Yes, ma'am." Dix did that one on purpose.

"So, what's the problem?" said Galloway, still examining the images. "Looks all right to me. I mean, who knows what it does, but if it looks like a bomb and quacks like a bomb, the Haugans should be able to blow up a lot of Axis ducks with it."

"The problem is what came out of it," said Dix, carefully. He didn't know how else to phrase it.

"You *opened* it up?" Galloway looked incredulous. "You had no right! Your orders were very clear. Pick up, deliver, that was it."

"It opened itself." Dix knew, as he said it, that

wasn't making things any clearer. Galloway's face suggested she thought the same thing.

"If you've messed with the weapon in some way, Dix, there are going to be serious repercussions. You had one job, which by the way, is still only half done. You want your old life back, you better hope that weapon is still usable by the time it gets to Hauga."

"That's what I'm trying to tell you. We did our job, like you asked. But we don't know what this is or what's going on. We were hoping you might have some answers for us."

Dix could hear voices behind him, as Drake came back up with the others.

Galloway looked as if she was consulting off-stage again, then swivelled back. "The hell are you talking about, Dix?"

Sol bounded forward. "Hello Dix," he beamed, and then looked into the monitor. "Is this a new friend?"

There was a momentary silence. "Who the *fuck* is that?" said Galloway.

"Language," said four voices, automatically.

Chapter 12

DIX SPENT the best part of an hour being debriefed by Galloway. From arrival at Vitlok to the emergence of the child from the weapon container. He told her everything, going over some parts of the story two or three times.

On several occasions, she turned to consult with someone off-camera, killing the audio feed each time. She came back with slightly rephrased questions, or new angles, and Dix got the impression – no evidence, just a hunch – that this was a four-way conversation. Him and Galloway, Galloway to an intermediary, the intermediary to a Haugan contact or spokesperson, and then back to Galloway.

He was quizzed particularly closely about the kid – description, apparent health, state of mind. Dix didn't know what to tell her. The kid was a kid. Seemed to be in one piece. Bit weird and creepy. What else was there to tell?

"And the Haugan monks on Vitlok said nothing?"

"On account of them all being dead," said Dix. "Except the last one, who was almost dead and then very dead."

"I'm sensing an attitude, trooper."

"And I'm on a smuggler's ship with a kid who shouldn't be here. I'm in Axis-controlled space, just waiting to be picked off, and no one's telling me anything."

Galloway looked away again, and conducted another one of her mystery off-camera conversations.

"What do you reckon?" Dix said to Drake, who was running scans and checking flight paths.

"I don't love being sat out here, even at this distance. Only takes one Axis scout to spot us. I know we're not badged as Fed, but Galloway says they've got Hauga locked up tight. They won't welcome smugglers either. And we'd never be able to explain the hardware or the kid."

"Agreed," said Dix. "Ideas?"

"I can't deviate from the flight plan. Or, you know – boom. But I can retrace our steps. Not to Vitlok, but back to the prison hulk. Should be able to manage that without getting ourselves blown up."

"Should?"

Dix wasn't sure he loved that idea any more than hanging around in Axis space. Getting away from PH-017 was the reason they'd all agreed to the job in the first place. Apart from Vaskez, who was as strange as the kid if she had volunteered for all this. Took all sorts, he supposed.

But they had done the first part of the job, as required, and it wasn't their fault the weapon hadn't been there. Maybe it was time to make the kid someone else's problem and hope that it was enough to secure their freedom?

"Dix?" Galloway interrupted his thoughts. "I need you to listen up."

"Actually, we've been thinking. How about we bring the kid back to base? Figure we've done all we can, under the circumstances."

Galloway looked distinctly unimpressed. Dix even tossed in a 'ma'am,' but it didn't seem to help.

"Not a chance," she said. "Your orders are to continue with the mission. Proceed to Hauga. Apparently, the child is important. He's to be delivered to the Hauga High Council, clandestinely."

It was Dix's turn to look unimpressed. "You want us to smuggle in a kid now? Why? What's so important about him?"

"Yours not to reason why, trooper. They want him, they get him. And we can't have your ship heading back here. Axis mercs already searched Vitlok, and if they picked you up there in a scan at any point, they might see you scuttling back to an official Federation institution and put two and two together. I'm not risking it. I told you, this operation is strictly off the books."

"Well, this is bullshit," said Drake. "We get the kid to Hauga, then what?"

"Nothing's changed for you," said Galloway. "Deliver the kid, meet our operatives on the ground. They've got the codes to unscramble my little insurance policy, you get to fly your ship wherever you want. That's the deal."

"What about the rest of us?" said Dix.

"Same as before. Slate wiped clean. You all get to go back to work, with my grateful thanks for a job well done. We'll forget all about your little indiscretions."

"We just deliver the kid?"

"That's it. Piece of cake."

"Why do I get the feeling there's something you're not telling us? What happened to all the weapon business? Lightburst? You do know that's what the kid reckons he's called? There's something off here. None of it makes sense."

"Look, Dix, this is just how it goes. It's called adapting to changing circumstances. Maybe it's the kid that's the weapon, maybe the kid's just a kid. But the Haugans don't seem surprised he exists, and they want him returned to them. And the path to future Federation happiness is me giving the Haugans what they want. Which, in turn, means you doing what I tell you and continuing the mission."

"How can the kid be a weapon? You're telling me he's got powers or something?"

Drake snorted. "Special powers? Kid can't even catch a ball."

"I don't know." Galloway was exasperated. "It also doesn't matter. This is just about supply and demand. It's how it works. I do this for them, it gives us an edge. You do this for me, it gives you a way out of your situation."

Dix had heard a similar explanation before – from Milo Kantor, the dodgy dealer in his cell, back on Mud Planet. Right now, he wasn't sure there was much of a difference between the shady arms dealer and the shady Federation spook who held his life in her hands. They both dealt in trades that weren't actually about the thing being traded. It was all a game to them.

"There is one more thing, though," said Galloway, "before you head off."

"Here we go," said Drake. "There's always one more thing."

Galloway ignored that. "The tube casing," she said. "Have you checked it out?"

"How do you mean?" said Dix. "We didn't want to mess with it. You told us we were carrying a secret weapon, remember? Like we're going to poke around inside."

"I knew it," said Drake. "There's something in there, right? Something other than a spooky kid? It does contain a weapon, after all?"

"Yes and no," said Galloway. "There is something in there, but not a weapon. A book."

Dix wondered if he'd heard right. "A book?"

"That's what I'm told." She looked off-screen for

confirmation and then turned back. "You fish it out, it goes with the kid. It's crucial, apparently."

"And this – book – is what exactly?"

"Don't know, don't care. They're not forthcoming on the subject. But right now, if they wanted Drake here to tattoo a smiley face on his arse, you'd be going to fetch the ink and needles because – and let me be very clear – we're going to give them exactly what they want. The kid and his book, delivered in one piece to Hauga, where you'll receive further instructions. Understood?"

"And then we're done?"

"You're done when I say you are, trooper. But yes, special delivery to Hauga. That's your final mission. Now, let me talk to Drake, we've got a couple of tricks up our sleeve to get you in undetected."

Dix left them to it and went below, where he found Alard – his hands clasped horizontally in prayer – playing slap-hands with Sol, Vaskez watching on in amusement.

"You gotta see this, Dix," she said.

"He'll get it," said Alard. "Just needs a bit of practice. Right, Sol, you remember what I told you? Hands out, like this. Then I'm going to try and slap your hands, and you've got to pull them away before I do. OK?"

Sol held his hands together loosely, and looked genially at Alard.

"All right, here we go. One more time."

Alard moved his right hand apart, slowly, clearly

signalling his intention, and then swiped towards Sol's touching hands.

The kid never moved. Had plenty of time, just beamed at Alard as he felt the slap against his hands. Vaskez laughed.

"Come on!" said Alard. "You must get it?"

"Wait for this," said Vaskez. "Hilarious."

"You're trying to slap my hands?" said Sol.

"Yes!" said Alard.

"It's a game?"

"Exactly! Just like I told you."

"And it makes you happy? Slapping my hands?"

"Yes! Or no, not happy, but that's the game."

"I like it if you're happy, Alard," said Sol. "It means I have brought light. And if you are supposed to slap my hands, then it will be."

Alard groaned in exasperation. Vaskez guffawed and moved towards the elevator. "Told you," she said. "Kid's a riot. I'm out of here."

"It's like he's never played a game in his life," said Alard, shaking his head. "Where did you grow up?"

"With the fathers."

"Seriously? That might explain it. Don't suppose that was a laugh a minute. No brothers or sisters?"

"No, just fathers."

Alard laughed, thinking Sol had made a joke, but the boy's straight face said otherwise.

"I only have the fathers. It is written and – "

"Not that again. I give up, he's all yours." Alard gestured at Dix and headed for the galley.

"Would you like to slap my hands, Dix?"

Sol still had his own stretched out before him.

"No, mate, that's fine. Listen, you know your little bed?" Dix pointed at the tube casing, lashed into place. "Was there something in there with you? A book, maybe?"

Sol blinked in recognition. "The book the fathers gave me?"

"That's right. Can I see it?"

"Of course."

Sol jumped up and walked over to the tube. Leaning over, he delved inside, with Dix watching on, and ran his hand along to a pouch that Drake must have missed when he had had a look inside. Sol retrieved something, pulling at it with both hands, stood back upright and presented it to Dix.

It had some heft to it – a large, thick book, size of a box-file, bound all around in metal, and locked with a solid clasp. Unadorned on the cover except for the shining sun motif they had seen on Vitlok. And bearing an ornate, etched title.

The Book of Light.

"Here," said Sol. "It is written and it will be."

Chapter 13

Drake powered down the ship, killed the exterior lights and dimmed those in the cabin.

"Just in case," he said. "Don't want to announce ourselves to the wrong people."

It was dark outside, so Hauga wasn't exactly rolling out its come-hither welcome mat, but according to Drake they were in the right location. There were trees and plants, you could breathe the air, and no one was shooting at them. Not a total dump, was the considered opinion.

Galloway hadn't expounded further on what 'tricks' she had up her sleeve to get them in undetected. When they were in flight, and Dix had asked how they would know if it was working, Drake had just said, "Well, we haven't been blown out of the sky yet."

That, apparently, was an entirely plausible scenario. Hauga was locked up tight, with authorised entry only through Axis-controlled space ports. The Haugans couldn't get off-planet – not officially, in any case – and no one else was allowed in, unless they had very good reason.

And they didn't have a reason that the Axis would like. So, Galloway had done her thing, whatever it was – a bit of jamming, thought Drake, and hints of a decoy Federation fly-by to occupy their air defences. And Drake had done his, which yet again involved swooping and dipping at improbably high speeds before careering to a halt in a flat-floored valley, far from any signs of civilization.

"He's doing it on purpose," Alard had said, before retching again into a barf-bag.

Whether he had been or not, Drake had got them here in one piece, un-blown up, which meant the mission was still on.

"You're pretty good at this," said Dix, as Drake worked his fingers across the flight console. The big man shrugged a thanks. "Why not just be a pilot? What's with the smuggling?"

"You mean like a pilot for the Federation?"

"Sure. Or one of those commercial outfits."

"You know how much a pilot makes?" said Drake.

"Tell me."

"Not enough to buy and fly a ship like this. And I always wanted a ship like this, since I was a kid and saw it in the picture books. Got a maintenance crew job at a flying school, figured how hard could it be? Got my licence, did a few under-the-radar jobs, and then a few more, bought and sold a couple of space junks, and eventually traded up to a Star-Jumper. My own boss, with my own ship – go anywhere I want. If I was a Fed pilot, I'd be ferrying jokers like you around on those self-drive troop carriers. Or making freight runs to even bigger dumps than this. That's not flying."

So, younger Drake had had dreams. Dix could relate, only he never would have resorted to illegality to make them come true. Just wasn't in his make-up. If the army recruiters hadn't come calling, Dix reckoned he'd still be there on Calisto, knee deep in fish guts.

He also pointed out the flaw in Drake's reasoning. "Except right now, it's Galloway's ship, not yours."

"Occupational hazard," said Drake. "Not the first time I've had Star impounded, won't be the last."

"You're confident."

"Have to be in my game, else people take advantage."

Drake sat back in his seat, looked around the cabin. Drummed his fingers a bit, conversation over.

"What now?" said Vaskez, after a short silence.

"We wait for Galloway's contact. They know we're here."

"Anyone else feel like a sitting duck?"

Dix knew what she meant, but all he had to go on were Galloway's instructions, which were – sit tight and wait for contact.

"We'll be fine. We're a long way from the nearest town. This is the middle of nowhere, look at it."

There wasn't a single light anywhere in the

distance, to all sides. Just the creak of cooling ship panels, and the deep, dark black of night.

"What's Galloway's guy doing out here then?"

"Dunno, we'll find out. He helps us hide the ship, we deliver the kid, he cracks the codes, we fly away. That's the deal."

"And until then, we sit out here in the open, on a planet crawling with Axis mercs, all looking for the very thing we have tucked up in a blanket in the hold?"

"I'm guessing they don't know it's a kid. We didn't. But otherwise, that's about the size of it, Vaskez. We sit tight and wait."

"Yeah, well, it stinks. I don't mind being chased or shot at. I can do something about that. But this is just asking for trouble."

"Shouldn't have volunteered then, should you?" said Drake. "Still can't get my head around that."

It seemed like as good a time as any to ask the question. "Why *did* you volunteer, Vaskez?" said Dix. "Not enough excitement in your life?"

"Told you, duty."

"Sure." That wasn't it, whatever she said. And while it didn't matter – didn't change their circumstances – Dix couldn't help wondering. "How long have you been in service?" he said.

She looked him in the eye. "Why? Eight years, if you must know."

"Right. No stripes? You know, when you *were* in uniform, before we all got to play dress-up?"

Eight years was a long time to still be on the bottom

rung, whichever unit you were in. Trooper squad, special forces, didn't matter – if you were as handy as Vaskez supposedly was, you got promoted eventually, just a matter of time. And she hadn't.

"Who says?"

"Galloway, I suppose," said Dix. "Not directly, but she didn't choose you, did she? She chose me. Can't see her doing that if you outranked me."

Vaskez made a 'pah' sound. "There's always some asshole in charge, Dix. Telling you what you can and can't do. Me, I get the job done, seek forgiveness later. The assholes in charge don't always like that. *You* won't like that, if you get in my way."

She scowled and went off to polish her weapon, or whatever it was ungovernable space operatives with a disdain for authority did in their off time.

Sol, meanwhile, was asleep again in the hold. Dix found him curled up, softball in one hand, one arm around the large book that had come from the tube – one mystery clinging on tightly to another. While Dix was grateful he was no longer in a muddy trench being shot at by miners, he missed the simplicity of trooper life, where the only mystery was what was in that day's meal ration.

He woke Sol up and took him to the cabin, where he slid into the vacant co-pilot's seat and latched onto Drake, who was still running checks on the resting ship. Or "Uncle Drake," as Sol now called him, after hearing Alard say it in jest.

Drake, to his credit, had taken it in good spirits.

"Got a nephew at home," he'd said, which was the first indication that Drake had any kind of outside life. Even smugglers had a home and family, it seemed, although Drake showed no inclination to elaborate.

Dix watched them for a while – the kid occasionally reaching for a console button or switch, saying, "What does that one do?", Drake pushing his hand away, saying, "Don't touch that."

Seemed almost normal – a six-foot-six contraband dealer chatting to a small boy sprung from a secret weapon – which showed how Dix's life was going right now, thank you very much.

Alard was recovering outside the ship, standing in the dark. Dix joined him, and they stood there together, facing into the night.

"Feel better?"

"Now I do, feet on the ground," said Alard. "I hate flying. And ships, troop carriers, helos, space stations – and especially prison hulks."

"Sucks for you being a Fed soldier then."

"You're right there, bud. It's all right once I'm grounded. I know what I'm doing then. Switched on, you might say. But if I can't touch solid earth…" Alard made a retching sound, sticking out his tongue, gesturing with his hand.

"Got you. That why you keep deserting?" Dix had lost count of the number of ships and waystations he'd been on, as his platoon kept being shifted from one theatre of conflict to another. Country, continent, planet, it was always quicker by air. Fed troopers spent as much time in space as they did on the ground.

"I keep deserting because it sucks being a Fed soldier." Alard grinned.

Dix was no Federation blow-hard, but he'd been in the trenches with good men who had died. Good men who had had his back, as he had had theirs. This attitude rankled, and he made sure Alard knew it. "Sucks for your mates, you mean. Sucks for anyone relying on you. You didn't have to join up."

"Is that so?" said Alard. "I don't know where you come from, but I can guess. Someplace like where I come from. Tell me you had a real choice?"

"There's always a choice, Alard. You want people to trust you, you need to show them you can be trusted."

"They teach you that in trooper school? Anyway, who says I want people to trust me? People are mostly idiots. I know what I am and what I can do. That's good enough for me."

Alard knelt to the ground, one hand flat to the earth. Dix could see him in Hauga's moonlight, under a dense canopy of stars, leaning over his other, raised knee, head bowed to one side. "Someone's coming," he said.

Dix looked and listened. Nothing, just the ship behind them and a moonlit night that dissolved into empty darkness a hundred feet away. He held his breath for a few moments – no sounds out there either.

"Can't see anything."

"No shit, of course you can't. They're a mile away, at least." Alard was now down on both knees, both hands flat on the floor, head and nose raised, like a dog on alert. "Moving quickly. One person."

More of Alard's woo-woo crap? "Yeah, right, how do you know?"

"I can sense it."

"Sure you can, a mile out."

Alard got up, looked at Dix, shrugged. "I told you, I know what I am and what I can do."

Dix didn't know what to think. Alard was full of this sort of stuff, and Galloway had said he was some sort of super-scout. But he'd barely been of any use until now, and – super-scout or not – no one could see *that* far into the dark. He knew Galloway's contact was on the way; most likely, he was just messing with Dix.

"Ladies, enjoying the crappy night-time delights of Hauga?" Vaskez jumped down from the main door and joined them. "Kid's bonding with Uncle Drake." She emphasized the words and snorted. "I give Uncle Drake about five more minutes before he swats him." She patted her rifle and cast her eyes around. "Any bad guys I should know about?"

"Alard reckons someone's coming." Dix pointed into the gloom.

"Course he does. Let's have a look then." Vaskez reached to her side and brought up a Hawkeye night scope, Fed issue, top of the range. "Drake has all sorts of gear in there, thought I'd liberate this and have a play."

She started scanning from one side, moving slowly from left to right, checking the output screen. Alard grabbed her elbow and moved her decisively. "You're wasting your time there," he said. "That way."

"Touch me again, Alard, and I'll – hello. Well, fuck me."

"What is it?"

"Alard's mystery visitor, I reckon. The freak's right. Must be… sheesh, a thousand feet out. Coming in fast."

"Friend or foe?"

"How would I know? Only one contact, but let's expect the best and prepare for the worst."

"Which means what?"

Vaskez handed over the scope and swung her rifle round. "He looks at all gnarly, I'll waste him."

"He's friendly," said Alard. "Or, at least, not hostile. Heading straight towards us, no evasive manoeuvres. It'll be Galloway's guy."

"And you know this, how? Spook-o-vision?"

"I can just tell. The way he's moving. Vibes."

"Vibes, fuck's sake. I'll tell you this, he so much as looks at me the wrong way, his vibes will be spread all over the planet."

They stood in silence for another few minutes, Dix tracking the moving contact with the night scope. Alard went inside and grabbed himself a weapon, and brought Drake back with him, now also armed, and they set up in formation, waiting.

"Thought you said he was friendly?" said Dix. "We expecting trouble now?"

Alard just shrugged.

"You should always expect trouble," said Vaskez. "That way, when no one dies, it's a pleasant surprise."

She was joking – sort of – but she was also right. Dix needed to start treating this operation seriously. An unsupported op in hostile terrain, Galloway had said. Very hostile, objectionable terrain, in fact, with casualties highly likely – those had been her exact words. This was no time to lower their guard.

They moved slightly further apart and dropped to the ground, waiting in silence, weapons set. Dix gave it a couple more minutes and then raised himself to his knees and scanned again.

"That a light?" whispered Drake, from somewhere to his left.

Dix found the source, watched for a few seconds, put the night scope down, and let his eyes readjust. Without the Hawkeye, he could just about make out the faintest of glows in the distance. "Yup," he said. "One contact. Stay alert."

The bobbing light got closer and a man's profile emerged from the night, holding a flashlight in front of him. He was wearing boots, tucked-in trousers, rough-weave buttoned jacket – a worker's clothes, not military. No rifle, no belt, no visible holster, no gear of any kind apart from the light.

"Hold it right there, pal," said Vaskez. "Let's see your hands."

The man flicked off the flashlight, tucked it into a jacket front pocket and held both palms up. The dimmed cabin lights from the Star-Jumper behind them threw just enough light for them to see him properly. "Easy soldier," he said. "My name's Ash, I'm on your side. Galloway's crew, right?"

"That's us, unless she's got a bunch of other mugs chasing around the galaxy."

"Good. You got the package?"

"The package? Sure thing," said Dix. He and Ash locked eyes briefly, a nod of understanding from each. Right now – first meeting – no one was going to say more than they had to.

"OK, which one's Drake?"

Drake lifted a hand.

"We've got around four hours until sunrise," said Ash. "We need to get your ship out of sight before then. There are no patrols this far out, but we're not risking leaving it out in the open. We'll hide it at my place."

"You want me to take it up and set it down again?"

"No, not risking that either. Galloway says she gave you pilot-pushers?"

Dix had seen these used before in the field. Basically, boxes on tracks with a ton of torque that could push huge craft around.

"How far?" said Drake.

"Couple of miles."

"That'll work. They're in the hold. Let's get to it."

While Drake and Ash set the pilot-pushers, front and back, Dix took Alard and Vaskez to one side.

"Let's keep the kid out of sight, until we know the score. Tuck him in the cabin maybe, someone sit with him and keep him quiet? I don't want him handed over or spirited away until we've got what we want. Alard, you take the kid?"

"Sure."

"And Vaskez, eyes and ears, all right? Maybe prep some weapons and tidy away the rest before he gets on board? He's unarmed, but we don't know what we're going into."

Alard and Vaskez nodded, no smart comments for once. Now, with something to do, this was beginning to feel like a proper mission with a proper team. All they had to do was hold it together for just a little longer.

"All right, people," said Drake. "We're good to go. These little babies will drive themselves once I've locked in the signal from the cabin. Couple of miles, it'll take maybe half an hour. The rest of you, find a seat somewhere inside."

Ash inspected the pilot-pushers one more time, as green lights flashed on each one. He did a circuit of the craft, looked up to the cabin and gave Drake the thumbs-up, then followed Dix in through the door.

"By the way," he said, "Welcome to Hauga."

Chapter 14

Ash's place turned out to be a farm, reached along a wide track of packed stone – almost as if he'd had cause to haul nimble Star-Jumpers out of sight before. Sleeper agent, Galloway had said. Dix wondered how long he had been here.

The pilot-pushers manoeuvred the ship into a huge, wooden barn, and Ash and Dix closed the doors behind them. Ash lit a couple of lanterns, which barely illuminated the vast space.

Mounds of hay lined one side, tools and farming implements the other – horse-drawn plough, maybe, scythes? There was a ladder to an upper gallery, shrouded in darkness, and some distant snorts and snuffles, and a lingering, off-sweet smell, that suggested penned livestock somewhere in the gloom on the ground floor. A horse for the plough, cattle, or whatever sort of animals they had on Hauga? Unless anything down there had fins, that was about the extent of Dix's farming knowledge.

Drake powered the ship down completely and came to join them, patting a panel on his way. "Nice job, Star, sleep tight."

Ash looked at Dix.

"Don't ask."

Drake was followed by Vaskez and then Alard, with Sol tucked in behind, hanging on to the edge of Alard's shirt. For the first time, the boy looked nervous.

Ash bent his head a little and peeped round. "Lightburst, right? Galloway filled me in. Not what I was expecting."

"You and me both," said Dix.

"And we're calling him Sol," said Alard. "Isn't that right, kid?"

Sol said nothing, but regained some of his equanimity and resumed his customary neutral gaze.

"No actual weapon then?" said Ash.

"Just what you see," said Dix. "And the container he came in. Oh, and a book." Sol was still clutching that tightly, one arm against his chest.

"A kid and a book?" said Ash. "Well, ours not to reason why, I suppose."

"I'd very much like to reason why," said Vaskez. "Given that we're all risking our lives. Be good to know what's going on, wouldn't it, Mr Ash?" She gave out the honorific 'mister' in her usual with-respect fashion, featuring no actual respect.

"Just Ash. Look, I'm only a cog in the wheel, like yourselves. The Haugans want whatever this is – " – he waved a hand at Sol – "Galloway tells me you're coming with it, and here I am. That's as much as I know. Now, let's get you inside, meet the family."

He led them across a courtyard to a stone-and-timber farmhouse with a pitched roof, small windows with wooden shutters, and a heavy front door. It was a nice enough night – clear sky, not too cold – but that house spelled big, harsh winters. They could smell the smoke from the fire within as Ash opened the door.

A woman stood by a range, ladling soup into bowls. Two small girls played nearby on a rug, thrusting rag dolls at each other and giggling, which stopped as soon as they saw the strangers enter.

Invited to sit at a rough, wooden table, they all introduced themselves – the woman was Brennagh, though Dix forgot the two girls' names the minute he heard them. One kid was enough to have to keep tabs on.

"Eat," said Ash, picking up his spoon. "We'll talk later." He turned to the woman and conducted a low conversation, breaking off to chivvy the girls along with their food.

Dix took a spoonful and blanched. It was a green, astringent broth, with hard, white beans, strands of something fibrous, and unidentifiable lumps of gristle you'd hesitate to call meat. There was one bit that looked like the tip of an ear. He could hear Alard mumbling – "I've drunk better-tasting things out of Drake's underwear" – which earned him a cuff from the big man. Dix shot them a look. They were guests. It was food, and it was hot.

With the meal out of the way, Ash led them to seats by the fire and poured them each a drink. The man clearly had a still on the premises, and the hooch was as brutal in its way as the soup, but a few sips certainly put a rosier glow on the evening. Sol was sent over to sit with the girls. Dix could see him cross-legged on the edge of the rug, hands clasped, while Ash and Brennagh's children whispered to each other and sniggered.

"You can sleep in the barn tonight," said Ash. "There are cloaks and blankets. Then we'll get you away tomorrow."

Finally.

Dix didn't want to jinx anything until they were off this planet, but it looked like their work was done. Mission accomplished. He exchanged glances with Drake and Vaskez, and Ash poured another round of shots.

"What happens to the kid?" said Dix.

"I don't know," said Ash. "Guess you'll find out in a couple of days when you hand him over in town."

Vaskez jerked her head up. There was a short, uncomfortable silence.

"Hang on," she said. "*We* hand him over? In a couple of days? This is us handing him over. To you. Right now, job done."

"And you give us the codes for Star," said Drake. "And off we go, that's the deal."

"You get the codes *after* you've delivered the package. Galloway was clear about that. I'm just the halfway house."

"Yeah, well, that's not going to work for us." Vaskez was on her feet, eyes flashing, fingering her sidearm. Drake was up too, towering over the still-seated Ash. "I think you better just give those codes to Drake now, and we'll be on our way."

"I don't have them," said Ash, calmly, showing no inclination to get out of his seat.

"Bullshit."

"It's true. Who do you think is running this show? It sure ain't me. Told you, I'm a middleman. You finish the job, come back here, Galloway calls in with the codes. *That's* the deal."

"Calls in, how?" Dix looked around the room. There was something he'd been wondering about since they had arrived. Ash hadn't been carrying anything except a flashlight. No power at the farm, your basic ye-olde-worlde set-up. It wasn't even low tech, it was a no-tech environment, if you didn't count the spaceship in the barn.

"There's comms gear in an outbuilding," said Ash. "That's how we communicate."

"So, we fire it up now and get this mess straightened out," said Drake. "That's what I strongly suggest you do," and he flexed his biceps and clenched his fists to make his point.

"It doesn't work like that," said Ash. "I'm way out here in the wilds for a reason. I shouldn't have any comms gear at all, no one should. There are strict rules. If it's discovered, I'm dead, my whole family's dead."

"Boohoo, bullshit, and I think we'll take that risk." Vaskez was reaching for her sidearm. "Let's go, now."

Dix put himself between Vaskez and Ash, and gestured for Drake to back off, too. That hadn't taken long – him getting in Vaskez's way. He could see she was itching to start an argument, but that wasn't going to get them anywhere.

Ash's wife, Brennagh, was standing by the range looking fearful, though the children didn't seem to have noticed. Sol now had a straw hat on and a rag doll in his hand, and absolutely no clue what was going on, as the girls made up a story around him.

"Let's all calm down," said Dix.

"Good plan." Ash had sat back in his chair. "You listen to me and you might just make it back. You have no idea how this place works."

"Then why don't you tell us?"

Ash raised a glass to them all and took another drink. He looked over at Brennagh and smiled, and she visibly relaxed.

"I've been here, what, seven years now, love? Came in lawfully, before the blockade really bit, slipped out into the country, set up base." He gestured around the room. "It's not much, but it's home. Met Bren a year or so later, the girls came along a year or so after that."

"And you're what, a Fed spy?"

"We prefer sleeper agent. Eyes and ears, information-gathering, mostly. Nothing flashy, nothing risky. I've got papers, I can move around, see things, hear things. And then I report back, when I can. When it's safe to do so."

"To Galloway?"

"Galloway's just this year's flavour. Like I say, I've been here seven years, the Galloways of this world come and go."

Alard – quiet until now – gestured at the surroundings. "Must be a hard life? You don't have much."

"We get by."

"Just you out here? No neighbours? No friendly wave each morning?"

"No one for forty miles, safer that way. The farm keeps us going."

"Even so, why do you do it? You're not from here. Not Haugan, are you? You must have done your bit by now? Surely Galloway can get you out, send you home?"

Ash shrugged. "It's important work. I'm good at it. And it's my duty, ra-ra the Fed, and all that. I could say the same about you lot, why are you here?"

"I wouldn't go there," said Vaskez. "Touchy subject."

Dix filtered what he'd heard so far. "You're hidden away out here, a long way from anywhere. But you're worried about the comms gear – someone finds it, you're dead? Same with the ship, maybe? What's the deal?"

"Galloway didn't tell you?"

"Galloway didn't tell us anything, except that we were to go fetch a big, fancy weapon and deliver it to Hauga. And there's your weapon." Dix pointed at Sol, by now lying face upwards on the floor, unmoving, uncomplaining, as two small girls played dollies on his stomach.

"I'm as surprised by that as you."

"I doubt that," said Alard. "Kid nearly gave me a heart attack when he crept out of that tube."

"You've got to understand, information here comes in dribs and drabs. This is a closed society. The Axis have a tight grip on everything. And the Haugans themselves are not exactly a talkative bunch, not the higher-ups anyway. Clergy caste, bit full of themselves, very distrustful, probably with good reason, given what's happened to their planet. It took me years to make connections and gain some trust. And then I started hearing about this weapon they had squirreled away somewhere, about how they could use it if only they could get it back. I never knew what it was, just that it was vital to them."

"Vital? Have you met him?"

They looked across to where Sol now had an upturned soup bowl on his head. The girls were throwing nuts at him, and he was smiling amiably as they pinged off the bowl.

"Look, he's a prince's kid, or next in line to what's left of the throne, or the chosen one, or some such. Who knows? But I've got a Haugan contact in town waiting to take delivery, and then my job's done, and your job's done, and you can all go home." Ash clasped his hands together, in a done-deal gesture, and smiled again at Brennagh.

"Why can't you take him, if it's that important?"

"Because I've only just been, to set up the meet. I've got a travel permit and a trading quota, but it's just for me, and being seen there again so soon is not a good idea. Inquisitive people at the checkpoints might wonder what my business is. Nasty, inquisitive people. I've kept myself off the radar for seven years, I'm not risking it now. That's what you're for."

"All right," said Vaskez. "I still call bullshit, but how hard can this be? We tool up, drop the kid where he needs to go, and bye bye Hauga, it's been horrible knowing you."

Drake nodded in agreement. "If that's what we have to do, let's get it done. Right, Dix?"

Ash laughed at that. "Oh boy, Galloway really didn't tell you, did she?"

"Tell us what?"

"There are things you need to know about Hauga. Or at least, about Hauga under the Axis. They haven't just blockaded the planet, they've taken over everything – commerce, government, policing. Permits and passes, roadblocks everywhere, searches, roundups. They've got the Haugan population under lock and key."

"Why?"

"Good question. This has always been a largely

agricultural planet, so you wouldn't think you'd need to get too heavy with the locals. But there's evidence the Axis have started mining operations in the east. Rare-galaxy minerals, we think."

Dix whistled. "Would explain why they're so keen to maintain their foothold here, keep the Federation out."

Dix didn't know much about the minerals, but he'd heard about them. Knew wars had broken out over them. Knew that one of the extremely rare mineral planets had been vaporised – the whole damn thing – by the Federation, just to stop the Axis getting their hands on it. That was how valuable they were. If the Axis had found rare-galaxy minerals on Hauga, they weren't going to be giving those up in a hurry.

"Whatever it is they're after, you don't just wander around Hauga and you definitely don't want to attract the attention of the Axis guards." Ash looked serious. "They send their hardest, most morally challenged specimens here to maintain order. It's not a punishment posting, you understand? A spell on Hauga is considered a perk of the job, if you're an Axis badass."

"I'm fairly badass myself, if you hadn't noticed," said Vaskez, drawing in a big breath, clenching her fists. "Anyway, I've never met an Axis merc who could resist my highly explosive charms." She was almost strutting. "I think we'll be all right. Even Alard knows how to point a gun and pull the trigger."

"Really?" Ash was smiling again but shaking his

head at the same time. "Then you haven't heard the best bit. They've taken this place back centuries. Look around you. There's no tech allowed for Haugans – no power, no machines, no weapons. They find a gun on you – summary execution. Comms gear – summary execution. Spaceship – big, fat, summary execution. And don't think I'm joking or exaggerating. The town gibbets are full of locals who thought they could get away with a radio or a handgun. They find Fed weaponry, they'll stake you out in front of a furnace and cook marshmallows over you."

Bloody Galloway definitely hadn't mentioned any of this. Not surprisingly. Also, it was becoming clearer by the minute why bloody Galloway had plucked three expendable felons and a special services operator who could start an argument in an empty room, and sent them off on a mission that had one-way written all over it.

"So, no weapons or comms gear?" said Dix. "No permits or passes either, presumably?"

"That's right, you're going to have to sneak in. Luckily for you, I know some ways to do that."

"Tell me again why you're not the one doing the sneaking in? Knowing the way and all?"

"I told you, I can't afford to get caught. I have a family. They would kill us all."

"But it's all right if we get caught and killed?" Alard seemed affronted.

"You're soldiers, right? Fed army. It's your job. Like

this is mine. If you didn't like the terms, you shouldn't have joined up."

No one gave an answer to that, though Dix heard the echo in it of what he had said to Alard just a few hours previously.

"Anyway," said Ash, "handpicked team like you, should be a piece of cake. Galloway told me all about you."

There was that piece of cake again that Galloway seemed inordinately fond of. "She did? What exactly did she say?"

"A very particular set of skills, is what she said. Drake, the ace pilot, for one. Not many craft get in here undetected. That was nice flying."

"You're welcome," said Drake, doffing an imaginary hat.

"Dix – thinks before he acts, not afraid to take diffi-cult decisions, knows how to handle himself under pressure."

"Ooh, *she likes you, she likes you.*" Vaskez sang the refrain, mockingly.

Dix shook his head, thinking – was that him? Is that what the sarge had seen in him, too? Dix had previously thought those things were just part of being a good soldier – things he could control – but it seemed they had been enough to earn him a field promotion of sorts.

"And you, Vaskez. Now, what did Galloway say? Oh yes, constitutionally incapable of taking orders, excep-tionally good at close-quarters violence."

"That's what I'm talking about, maggots," crowed Vaskez, curling a bicep. "You better believe it." Then, realising who hadn't been mentioned, said, "What about Alard? Galloway tell you what his special skill is, because he sure as hell hides it. Unless it's puking, he's good at that."

"And running away," said Drake. "Might come in useful here I suppose, from what you're telling us."

"You've got it wrong, Alard is a special case, isn't that so?" said Ash.

"He's special all right. You should have seen him on Vitlok." Vaskez fluttered her hands and did a ghostly 'woo' sound.

"He really is, aren't you, Alard. Haven't you told them?"

"Told us what? I don't think I can take any more surprises today."

"Alard here is a pathfinder, an excellent one by all accounts."

Alard shrugged an acknowledgment.

"So what, every unit's got one of them. But there's only one of me, baby!" Vaskez flexed her muscles and high-fived Drake.

"Yeah, but Alard here has a rare genetic mutation. He's got what they call geographic empathy, isn't that right?"

"Sure," said Alard. "If you say so."

"Geo– what?"

"He's what's known as a geopath, for short."

"And?"

"He doesn't just track or orientate himself using natural clues. Geopaths can feel their way through the landscape. He understands the connections – listens to the earth, the trees, the roots and filaments under the ground, the noises and vibrations they make. Feels the moisture. Catches smells on the breeze. He knows what's down the track a long, long way ahead. His whole body remembers routes taken, and he never gets lost. It's fascinating, really."

"It's bullshit, is what it is," said Vaskez, looking distinctly unimpressed. "You're saying he talks to the mushrooms?"

"And you wonder why I don't tell anyone?" said Alard. "Thanks for that."

"You've got two days of unknown terrain ahead of you," said Ash. "You can't be spotted, and you can't be caught, or else it's over. Alard here is going to be the most useful member of your team. I'd take good care of him, if I were you."

"Well, doesn't that just put the tin hat on it?" said Vaskez. "You mean, I can't even sneak up on him and strangle him in his sleep?"

"Very funny."

Dix had heard enough for one day. Nothing Ash had told them made things any better – ten times worse in fact.

But they were still in business, and they still had a job to do, with the stakes now so much higher. It was time to call it a night, and hope he managed to get some rest.

"Well, boys and girls," he said, "looks like we've got a big couple of days coming up. Let's hit the hay."

"Normally," said Alard, "I'd be happy to see the back of this day and get some shut-eye, but you mean actual hay, don't you?"

Chapter 15

THEY GOT A FEW HOURS' sleep before being woken by Ash with bowls of maize porridge flecked with slivers of meat, and hunks of hard bread. He also handed over a canvas rucksack of supplies – more bread, dried meat of indeterminate origin, wizened apples, home-made cereal bars – and a couple of water carriers.

"You can drink straight from the rivers," he said. "Since the Axis put a halt to most Haugan industry. But I'd probably still boil any water, to be on the safe side." He grabbed a pannier from a hook and added a couple of lightweight metal pans, a few utensils, and some matches and kindling in a waterproof pouch.

"Why, Ambassador, with these gifts, you're spoiling us," said Alard in a mock-aristo tone, peering into the food bag.

"Take it or leave it," shrugged Ash. "And, my advice, don't eat the ground-squirrels. They're easier to catch than the rabbits but taste like shit."

"We really should have asked for more details about this mission before accepting. I feel that Major Galloway has been a bit naughty in keeping things from us."

Alard wasn't wrong there, and not just about the gourmet delights of Hauga. This whole mission, they'd had one secret after another kept from them so far, and it didn't look like things were going to improve any time soon.

Ash spread a map out on the ground and showed them the roundabout route to town – out of the valley, over the nearest range of hills, and through a forest, skirting several villages on the way.

"No bus?" said Alard, hopefully.

"Axis guards set fire to the last bus they found in service," said Ash. "With the passengers still in it. It's two days on foot, mostly out in the wilds. You'll pass close to the road at times, but don't get caught on it."

A couple of miles outside town, Ash told them, was an old power station – now disused – from where a service tunnel reached into the town proper, bypassing the road checkpoints. Last time Ash had used it – a year or so ago – there had been one blocked section of fallen masonry and tangled pipework, but nothing a careful crew on foot couldn't navigate.

"Once through the tunnel, you want Exit 47," said Ash. "Pops up one street over from the meeting place – a bar called 'The Two Globes,' your guy will be in there at noon, three days from now. They'll be back a day later, same time, but after that they're gone, so don't be late."

"How will we know it's him?"

"Him, her, them, I don't know who they're sending. Don't worry about that, they'll know it's you. Strangers aren't exactly common around here."

"I do worry about that, Ash. I worry about all of this." Dix gestured at the five of them, the map, the rucksack with inadequate provisions. The general messed-up-ness of it all.

"Keep out of sight, make the drop, get back here. You'll be fine."

The drop. Ash meant Sol – like the kid was just a package. Which, in a way, he was – a means to an end, their end being getting off this wretched planet. But that didn't mean Dix had to like it. A kid was a kid, after all. Not some kind of parcel to be passed around.

"And don't eat the squirrels, right?"

"Exactly! Don't worry, you got this."

Ash rolled up the map and tucked it in inside his jacket.

"Hey, we don't get to keep that?" said Drake.

"We don't need it," said Alard, flexing his fingers. "Trust me."

"What he said," said Ash. "You don't want to be caught with a map that you can't explain. Alard here is your human compass. Talking of which, tech check. Tell me you've understood what I told you?"

They had already had a spirited conversation about

that, with Vaskez the hardest to convince that they had to leave all their lovely gear behind.

Anything with an on/off button, a chip, a screen, a trigger, or an arming device, had to stay on the ship. That put all of Drake's weaponry out of bounds, and Galloway had already done a bang-up job of stripping them of everything else before they'd first left the prison hulk.

They had the clothes they stood up in, a rucksack full of food, a pannier with cooking gear, and a cloak and a sleeping bundle each. Sol still had the big book under his arm, but Dix took it off him and put it in a leather cross-body bag that Ash provided.

If they still looked like random smugglers, as Galloway had intended, they looked like not very good ones who hadn't smuggled anything of value for a while.

"It's not that I don't trust you," said Ash. "Only, if you're caught with anything and you give me up, we're all dead. So, allow me – "

He produced a wand with a black tip, which whined slightly as he flicked a switch.

"Oh, I see, *you're* allowed tech," said Drake, grumpily.

"Can't be too careful," said Ash, running it up and down the big man's frame – front, back, both arms, both legs. He did the same to Alard, seemed satisfied and moved on to Vaskez, who took a step backwards.

"Vaskez… " said Dix.

She opened her jacket to show two fearsome

hunting knives in sheaths at her waist. "I'm allowed knives. How else am I going to catch something edible?"

"You're allowed knives," agreed Ash, now behind her, running the wand down her back. It pinged, and Ash shook his head.

"Vaskez, give it up," said Dix.

She blew out her lips and reached around to pull a handgun out of her waistband, gave it to Ash. His wand still pinged. She sighed and fished out the Hawkeye scope, too.

"I swear, Vaskez, you'll get us all killed."

"Save your asses, you mean."

"Last chance, anything else?"

Vaskez reached down to her left leg, rolled up her trousers and unstrapped a pad of three adhesive disc-mines.

They all looked at her, while Drake just laughed.

"Oh, fuck it, pardon my Haugan," she said, also reaching around the back of her shoulder, under her jacket. She retrieved a concealed webbing pouch with a handful of small, flat-packed, five-point stars that would fit in the palm of a hand. Explosive, heat-seeking, hundred-foot range, horrible little weapons.

"Impact stars?" Drake guffawed. "I mean, seriously, Vaskez, roll over in your sleep and there'd be nothing left of you to find."

"I would like it on record that I am very un-fucking-happy about this softly-softly, wet-wipe of a mission."

"Noted," said Dix. "Now can we get on?"

"If you don't mind," said Ash, with just one more body to scan. He ran the wand over Dix and it pinged, to everyone's surprise.

"Who's a naughty little trooper?" Alard looked gleeful.

Dix was puzzled and couldn't think what was triggering Ash's scanner. The wand passed over his chest and pinged again, and then Dix knew. He tapped his chest pocket, delved inside with his fingers, and plucked out the two chip-tags he'd almost forgotten about. The sarge's army ID and the trader Milo Kantor's calling card.

He handed them to Ash. "I want those back," he said. The sarge's anyway. He still had vague ideas of returning it to his family, if they ever got off this planet alive, though that seemed like a long shot right now.

"I'll leave them with the other gear. Right, you all need to get going. See you back here in five, six days max."

"And then we'll get the codes?" Drake, just checking.

"Then you'll get the codes. Now go."

"We better," said Vaskez, not even looking at Ash, but idly using one of her knives to clean dirt from under a nail.

Dix looked around at his team, and then beckoned Sol over. The boy had been sitting patiently on a hay bale, passing his softball from one hand to another. Not tossing it, he hadn't mastered that yet, but he did finally seem to understand that he could use the ball to pass the time. "Ready, kid?"

Sol looked up. "Where are we going, Dix?"

He wondered what to tell him; wondered how much, if anything, he'd figured out; finally settled on, "Little camping trip. You ever been camping?"

"I have not, Dix. Is it a game?"

"Sort of. We're going to go out into the hills and woods, and keep very quiet and hidden. You think you can do that?"

"Of course, it was always very quiet with the fathers. Light speaks louder than words – it is written and it will be, they said."

Poor kid. What must his life have been like on Vitlok? The fathers had a lot to answer for.

"Well then," he said, smiling at Sol. "You're going to be really good at camping, I can tell."

Ash and his family walked them to the farm boundary and waved them off. When Dix looked back five minutes later, he could just about make out the two small girls, waving furiously, Ash with his arm around Brennagh.

Happy rural scene. Picture of contentment. And rather them than him, any day, under these harsh, throwback conditions on this locked-in planet. He could still remember the taste of that soup.

Where the farm track ended, the main, direct route towards the distant town turned to the right – a surfaced road that, going by the cracks and weeds, no longer saw much, if any, motorised transport. They sent a patrol jeep up here now and again, according to Ash, infrequently but unexpectedly. You just never knew. If you didn't have permits, safer by far to strike across country.

Alard called a halt and surveyed the scene. It was a mile across the width of the valley to a range of low hills backed by higher peaks. Somewhere along the stretch was a gully which would take them out of sight of the road and then bend around in the same general direction, rising onto higher ground. A day to reach the other side of the range, and then a descent through woodland to the outskirts of the town.

But first they had to find the gully, and the quicker the better, as they were exposed out here.

Alard walked up and down the road for a short way in each direction, and then dropped to his knees, hands flat on the floor. He straightened up after a minute. "This way," he said, pointing.

"The old freako-genes working?" said Drake. "Worms talking to you?"

"Funny," said Alard. "Never heard that one before. How about you try using your own senses a bit more?" He pointed at an arrangement of stones by the road-side, forming a rough arrow that pointed in the same direction he'd just indicated. "Ash told me he'd left it here early this morning, to give us a head start." Alard kicked the stones apart and strode off, giving Drake the finger as he went.

"Touchy little freak, isn't he?"

"Play nice," said Dix.

Honestly, the kid, Sol — who admittedly had got them all into this — was less trouble than the other three put together.

They reached the gully in around twenty-five minutes — it would have been quicker, except Sol kept stopping to pick up stones and examine bushes, like he'd never seen anything like them. Which — Dix was coming to understand — he probably hadn't, given that Vitlok was on the sharp, pointy and inhospitable side as far as planets went. Had he ever even been outside anywhere in the fresh air before? Dix didn't want to think about it — that would be too cruel on any kid.

In the end, Drake had scooped the boy up and sat him atop his shoulders, and then loped forward as Sol giggled, uncharacteristically, at being bounced across the terrain.

Once through and out of the gully, they were in open, rising country, with no discernible path. Just stands of heather, spreading patches of woody herbs, and occasional, stunted, spiny bushes.

Sol was still on Drake's shoulders and showed no sign of wanting to get off. Drake, for his part, didn't seem to mind, and made a game of jumping over some of the lower bushes.

Drake's nephew was a lucky kid, Dix reckoned, to have an uncle like that — willing to join in at a child's level. Although, to be fair, when he was around nine, Dix's own uncle had shown him how to ferment discarded fish by-catch by burying it in the ground for six months, so you know, horses for courses.

Alard indicated the general direction they should take, but soon made them stop again and told them to wait. "Take five," he said, unlacing his boots and removing his socks.

"Now what? Can't have blisters already? Have you ever actually done a route march before?"

"You want to know what's out there, or not?" he said, dismissing the catcalls. "Let me do my job." They watched as he stood, bare feet planted on the ground, eyes closed for a minute or two. Then he bent down and laid himself flat out on the ground, head resting on one outstretched arm, both palms flat to the surface.

"Sleepy time, Alard?"

He ignored them again, sat upright, put his socks back on and re-laced his boots. Jumped to his feet. "Safe ahead," he said to Dix, the only one who hadn't teased him. "Nothing to worry about. Nothing out of place, anyway. Keep to that bearing," and he pointed away across the heather.

Vaskez and Drake looked at each other, burst out laughing and walked off. Dix heard Sol ask them, "Is Alard all right?" The only reply was another peal of laughter.

Alard shrugged, and hoisted his pack, ready to leave.

"Do you have to take the boots off? Be barefoot?"

"Don't have to. It's just quicker. Besides – it's nice. Don't always get the chance."

"What do you – feel?" said Dix, wondering if that was the right word.

"You really want to know?"

"Sure, why not?"

"Most people just take the piss," said Alard. "Case in point, those two boof-heads. It's hard being the freaky kid. Then the freaky trooper." He rubbed some earth between his fingers, brought it up to smell, then flicked it to the floor.

Dix could see that – that being different singled you out. Alard had been the first to accept Sol at face value, and that made more sense now. One freaky kid recognising another, maybe?

"Tell me," said Dix, "I'd like to know."

"It's hard to describe. Right now, everything is as it should be. Connected, unbroken. There's a herd of something way over there – wild horses, probably – and I can sense fresh water from the moisture in the ground. We'll come to a stream in an hour or so. The bushes, the grass, it's all one. The flow just feels right to me. Like I say, difficult to describe. Harder, really, for me to imagine that you *can't* feel it."

Ash was right. It was fascinating, the whole geopath thing. Was it a burden? Dix imagined it could be, if you could understand that much about your surroundings, just by laying your hands on the ground. A sensory overload, every time you took a step or touched a tree?

In the end, they walked for around eight hours, until the lengthening shadows signalled an upcoming sunset. They were in higher country now – far from the valley and road – in a rocky landscape that dipped and rolled, alternating between open views for hundreds of yards and stretches where rock bluffs obscured the way ahead.

Alard would always check the lay of any unseen land, though after the first four hours or so it had been obvious that they were in completely uninhabited, un-travelled back-country. Eventually, even Alard stopped being so careful and they walked on freely.

As the sun shifted and lowered, they made camp between a rough circle of stones, near a brook where the water was cold and clear. Dix got a fire going, while Vaskez stomped off brandishing one of her wicked-looking knives.

"Remember, only quality meats, darling," called Alard, which Vaskez glared at.

"Are we camping, Dix?" Sol had been hopping from stone to stone, behaving like a normal kid for once, while they laid out their stuff.

"Sure, kid. This is camping. Why don't you come and sit down. Look, you can put these sticks on the fire if you want."

"Really? I can?" Sol looked more animated than at any time Dix had known him. "The fathers said that fire is a cleansing element, that light and fire together will bring freedom. Will this fire bring free-dom, Dix?"

"The fathers were talking out of their – "

"Drake!"

"Well, I know we shouldn't talk ill of the – you know?" and Drake made a cutting motion across his throat. "But they sound like a right bunch of jerks."

"The fathers are indeed righteous," said Sol, possibly mishearing. "What's a jerk, Uncle Drake?"

"Never mind that, Uncle Drake is just being silly." Dix distracted the kid by dragging over the cross-body bag he'd been carrying all day, the one with the book in it. "What can you tell me about this, Sol?"

Dix took the book out and held it up in the dying light. It was heavy in his hands. The metallic cover glinted as he turned it towards the fire, the sun motif on the front clearly visible.

"*The Book of Light*," said Sol, tracing the letters on the cover. "It is written and it will be."

"What is written, though?"

"Everything." The boy spread his hands wide, as if that was explanation enough. "Light, fire, freedom. The fathers have recorded it all."

Dix looked at Alard, who shrugged. Drake, too.

"I don't know what that means," said Dix. "Is it a story?"

"It is everything," said Sol. "I am Lightburst, and it's my story, the fathers said."

"Them again," said Drake. "Told you, jerks."

"Maybe, but can you make any sense of this?" said Dix.

"We could open it and see?"

"I've tried," said Dix. He showed Drake the metallic covers and spine, and the plate that covered the page edges, if indeed there was an actual book inside what appeared to be a solid, book-shaped box. A heavy clasp connected front and back, and if it did duty as a lock, there was no keyhole – rather a circular indentation a couple of inches in diameter, the size and depth of a large coin. Short of trying to cut the metal casing or break the clasp, there was no way to see what was inside.

"Only the fathers know of *The Book of Light*," said Sol. "It is written and it will be."

"Marvellous," said Alard. "Clear as mud. So we just need a father to explain what the hell is going on. Where are we going to find one of those?"

Dix wondered. Their Haugan contact in the bar, maybe? A secret meeting with a monk in a pub wouldn't be the weirdest thing to have happened to them so far.

"Guess we'll just have to wait and see," he said. "Sol, why don't you get your cloak and blanket, it's getting cold."

The kid snuggled down by the fire, and Alard unpacked some of the bread and cured meat. They watched the flames spark and dance, until a dark figure suddenly appeared from behind a rock bluff, scuffing stones as it approached.

"Don't *do* that!" Alard clutched his chest in mock distress.

"Dinner, ladies," said a dirty, muddy Vaskez, face lit by the fire, clutching two bloody, elongated forms by the scruff of the neck. "Little rabbit fuckers, pardon my Haugan. Like hiding in a burrow's going to save them."

Chapter 16

THEY CROSSED the range of hills during the next day and descended into the forest, camping beneath broadleaved trees that chittered with life. No one except Sol slept well that night, alive to every crack and rustle in the forest, even though Alard assured them it was only animals.

"Depends how big your 'only animals' are," Drake had said.

"It's not the ones you can hear that you want to worry about," said Alard, which didn't help at all, though the accompanying smile said he was probably joking.

Alard had lightened up, and the others had stopped ragging on him, pretty much at the same time. Without him – and without a map or any nav gear – they would have been lost in the forest within minutes. Even Vaskez grudgingly agreed that Alard was proving his worth, as they snaked through dense stands of trees and rough undergrowth that limited visibility ahead and blocked out light from above.

From tree to tree and clearing to clearing – hand on trunk or face to ground – he had led them unerringly onwards and, after initial doubts, they'd succumbed entirely to his expertise. Something to do with the way the sap rose and the lichen lay; the echo from capillaries deep in the ground; the layers of stone and earth that talked to him across miles of hidden country. At least, that was the best Dix could figure, however far-fetched it sounded.

Either way, Alard took point and the rest stayed close, always in line of sight. No one wanted to get turned around and lost, left behind.

After their night under the trees, they woke early and moved on. Alard said he could sense a thinning and a widening, whatever that meant, and a couple of hours later they discovered exactly what it was.

The edge of the forest. And the road towards town.

From what they remembered of the map, the old power station was ten miles further down the road. Hadn't been in operation for more than five years now, according to Ash, as the Axis had slowly shut off access to light, heat and everything else for the local population. Grinding them down, keeping them in their place.

If they stuck to the road, picked up the pace, they could probably be there in a couple of hours, but they hadn't come this far to be careless now.

"Let's keep to the tree cover where we can," said Dix, and he led them back into the forest, where they began to track parallel to the road. Slower but safer. Dix and Alard up front, Drake with Sol close by in the middle, and Vaskez bringing up the rear.

It was strange, seeing fleeting signs of civilization from behind the trees. After Ash's farm, the remote heights and the dense forest, here they were, following the route of a surfaced road with faded paint markings.

They passed an abandoned vehicle, and then another, tyres flat, rusted with age, pocked with what looked like bullet holes – no fuel-cells or rides for locals, on pain of death.

A distant line of pylons carried inert power lines; one line – cut – trailed to the ground and disappeared in a pile of leaf litter. At a solitary house, set back on the other side of the road, the windows were broken and boarded up, and a large red 'X' was spray-painted on the front door.

"Still a dump," said Drake. And it was, but it was different to the various dumps that Dix had fought over before. Not destroyed by mortars and drones, and swept through by troops. This was more like neglect. Abandonment. Deliberate degradation.

X for what? Nothing good.

Alard held up a hand, signalling for them to stay put. He stepped out from the trees, walked the thirty yards or so to the road, and knelt down for a moment. Then jogged back. "Something's coming," he said, pointing up the road. "Vehicle approaching."

They waited for a full two minutes – long enough for Vaskez to start mumbling about faulty bat ears –

before they heard it. A low whine and then the rush of wheels as an open-topped jeep careered past – one driver, one passenger, both wearing black, mounted gun rack, loud music blaring. Looked like military, drove like high-schoolers on a keg run. They weren't sticking to the regulation side of the road, put it like that.

"Axis," said Vaskez, with a sneer.

Had to be, heading towards town. If this was one of the patrols Ash had mentioned, maybe they didn't have too much to be worried about. These guys weren't exactly taking professional pride in their work.

The vehicle disappeared out of sight, and they were left again with birdsong and the crackle of leaves and sticks under their feet. Dix moved and the others followed. Don't get caught on the road, Ash had said, and that still seemed like good advice.

An hour later they stopped for water and Alard sank to his haunches. When the others readied to leave, he shook his head.

"What is it?"

"Something," he said. "Just wait a minute."

They stopped, listened and looked. There was nothing on the road.

"Another vehicle?"

"No." Alard wrinkled his nose, looked troubled. He'd had that look before, Dix thought. On Vitlok? "Something bad," he said, finally. He scraped a hand through the dirt and then rubbed thumb and forefingers together. "Not far."

For once, everyone took Alard at his word, even

Vaskez. Trust was being earned, whether he wanted it or not.

They slowed their walk and kept silent for the next few minutes. Drake pulled Sol closer to him, and the boy reached up for one of the big man's hands, trailing behind him like a baby elephant with an extended trunk.

As they curved around, following a bend in the road, they could see the jeep parked in front of a row of abandoned cottages, fifty feet away. Actually, 'parked' was too precise a word. It had just been left where it had come to a halt – middle of the road, slightly skew-whiff, not expecting, or bothered about, other vehicles.

There was no sign of the two men they'd seen earlier. But there was a body lying face down in the road by the jeep, one hand splayed out and a dark stain just visible.

"Ah, crap," said Vaskez.

"That body," said Dix, "not one of those two Axis mercs, right?"

"Nope, different clothes."

"Local? Lives here?"

"Houses look abandoned. Maybe not the one on the end, though?"

Dix took a closer look. Four cottages with broken windows and trashed furniture out front; a fifth with curtains of some kind in the top windows and a fenced garden. A dark shape rooting in the corner – was that a pig?

"What's gone down, you reckon?"

"I'd say yokel meets Axis goons. Two-to-one, away win. Looting to follow."

"Alard? This what you meant? This your something bad"

"Guess so. I'm not psychic, I just read the lie of the land."

"Well, look, it's bad but it's not our problem," said Vaskez. "Right?"

Dix agreed. Walking on by was exactly the correct decision here. Couple of miles to the edge of town and the power station. They should drop back a bit further into the trees and keep moving. It wasn't like there was anything they could do for the dead guy on the road.

The cottage door suddenly flung open from inside, and they all took an automatic step backwards and crouched down, taking cover. They watched as one of the Axis mercs staggered out, bottle in hand, shouting. There was a commotion at the door and two women stumbled out behind him, as if pushed. One was just a girl – mother and daughter, maybe. The older one had a bloodied face and a torn shirt.

"Ah, double crap," said Vaskez.

Following them up was the second man from the jeep, brandishing a rifle. He shouted at the other man and gestured at the jeep. "Music!" they heard him say.

The woman, the mother, turned and said something to the one with the rifle. Pleading – her voice, if not the words, carried to the trees, and they could hear the fear.

The man just laughed and stepped off the threshold into the garden. Pointed his rifle at the snuffling shape in the far corner and fired. There was a squeal and then silence, before the woman screamed at the loss of her pig. A scream that was drowned by music blaring from the jeep, as the second man danced a small jig, bottle still in hand. Then the man with the rifle grabbed the younger girl and pushed her towards the jeep. The older woman screamed again and held onto his free arm, but he backhanded her and kicked her where she lay.

"Fuck this," said Vaskez. "*Now* it's our problem." She glared at Dix.

Dix felt her anger – shared it – but wasn't sure. Shit happened on operations, he'd seen it – this and worse. But if you had one shot at a successful mission, you didn't get sidetracked. Improvise, adapt, sure. But getting involved, with no firepower, no back-up, and the potential for stuff to go very, very wrong… that was how missions failed.

"I'm not asking for permission," growled Vaskez, moving from a crouch to a hidden position behind a tree, a couple of feet closer to the road.

"We don't have weapons."

They were hissing at each other in the woods, but the music was covering them. Now a scream rose from the young girl as she was thrown against the bonnet of the jeep.

"Two assholes, two knives," said Vaskez. "No problem." And she darted out into the open without a backwards glance, with the off-side of the jeep between her and the two men.

"What's happening, Dix?" said Sol, peering out from behind Drake.

"Nothing, kid. Just a little problem." Dix caught the big man's eye. "Why don't you head back a bit further into the trees there with Uncle Drake, see if you can find some sticks for our fire later?" He saw that Sol was still waiting for an explanation. "While your Auntie Vaskez sorts things out," he added, in a reassuring tone.

He was taking a punt, admittedly. Vaskez did not seem like auntie material. She had probably eaten her own nephews and nieces.

Drake and Sol moved deeper into the woods, while Dix and Alard crept closer to the edge, trying to get eyes on the scene without showing themselves.

Vaskez had made a low run towards the jeep, covered by the sound of the music and the cries of the women.

The man with the bottle was in the driver's seat now, facing the house, with his back to Vaskez. He was conducting the music with his other hand, while his friend with the rifle laughingly held off the girl who was trying to reach her mother on the ground.

Dix thought about heading through the trees, back down the road, and trying to cross out of sight and then come up behind the cottages. But it would take far too long, and he didn't have a weapon. It was all going to be on Vaskez, unless he or Alard stepped out of the trees and tried to cause a diversion. The mercs might be sloppy or drunk, or both, but one had a rifle slung on his shoulder and the other had a gun rack at his back.

How lucky did Dix feel?

It didn't matter, because Vaskez took the decision for him.

She had reached the back of the jeep, down by a wheel, out of sight. Dix had a wider view and could see what she couldn't – namely, the man with the rifle tiring of tussling with the girl. He stepped back and punched her, so she fell again against the bonnet, dazed. Then he turned to face the woman on the ground and swung his rifle around to point it at her. The man in the jeep stood up, leaned back against the roll-bar and cheered him on.

At which, a figure bounced up from behind him, like an avenging jack-in-the-box – Vaskez, with knife raised. She reached around the man's head with one arm, and sliced sideways with the other across his neck in a practised move. He toppled against the windscreen, blood pouring from the deep cut.

The music played on. The other man hadn't noticed, still facing the woman on the ground, mouthing off at her, waving his rifle. Vaskez jumped down from the jeep – no hurry now – and killed the sounds, and all Dix could hear was the silence of the forest broken by the sobs of the woman and the groans of the concussed girl.

As the music died, the other merc finally looked around.

"Hey, shithead." Vaskez was quick – man, was she quick. Three paces and she'd halved the distance between them, while his brain tried to process what was going on. One more pace and he'd swung his rifle towards her, and that was as good as it got for him.

Vaskez closed the distance and chopped at his arm viciously with her knife, and then put her full weight into a stamp against his kneecap. Dix heard the crack from thirty feet away, and the scream of a badly injured man who'd realised too late what was happening.

Dix and Alard emerged from the trees and jogged to the jeep. Vaskez kicked the guy's rifle away from him, as he moaned on the ground, clutching his shattered leg and slashed arm.

Alard helped the girl, and Dix the mother, and they sat them on the house porch. They were bruised and in shock – torn clothes, scratches – and Dix ran inside and found a pitcher of water. The house had been turned upside down, with broken crockery and glass everywhere.

"Your man?" said Vaskez, pointing at the third body, on the ground by the jeep. The older woman nodded silently, vacant expression on her face.

"I hate asshole cowards." Vaskez grabbed the injured man by his shoulder and spun him around. "Any more of you?" she said, brandishing the knife in front of him.

"Please," said the man, whimpering. "We weren't going to do anything."

"Looks like you already did plenty."

"It's just us. Just me," said the man. "You can walk away. Put me in my vehicle, we'll call it quits."

Vaskez laughed. "This guy? Let me explain what's going to happen to you." She pushed the point of the knife into his shattered knee, and he screamed. "Got it yet?" said Vaskez, tracing the bloody knife up his thigh and chest and then resting it against his neck, jabbing the point in slightly.

"Please," he said again.

"Don't," said the woman, from the porch. "You know what they'll do."

"You should listen to her," said the man, "if you know what's – "

"This is good for me, thanks," said Vaskez, pushing the blade in and up. Blood pooled between hilt and neck, and the man gurgled. She held his head up while the light left his eyes and then dropped the man to the floor, like letting go of a bag of flour.

The woman groaned deeply, and then got gingerly to her feet, helping her daughter up. "Go," she said to them, "there's nothing for you here." They moved to the door arm in arm and closed it behind them. Dix could hear furniture being righted and broken items gathered together.

"You're welcome," called Vaskez, but there was no response.

"You shouldn't have done that," said Dix, meaning the impromptu mercy mission. "Going out there on your own."

"I didn't see anyone else jumping to the rescue. And I'm not apologising for dealing with scumbags."

Dix nodded. Fair enough. He didn't need to worry about Vaskez, she could take care of herself. "Exceptionally good at close-quarters violence" was entirely accurate, it seemed.

He could see Drake emerging from the trees with Sol, and held up his hand to stop the big man. Made a 'Keep him away' gesture. The kid didn't need to see Auntie Vaskez's handiwork.

"Come on," he said, "time to move."

"Way ahead of you, Dixie-boy." Vaskez bent to pick up the dead man's rifle. "Just as soon as I've got myself some new toys." She made towards the jeep and unclipped two more assault rifles from the gun rack, grabbed a handgun from one of the seats, and filled a bag with ammo-mags.

"We're not taking those, Vaskez. You heard what Ash said."

"Look, Dix, I respect you, I truly do. Three-year trooper, all the experience in the world." Vaskez grinned sarcastically. "But we got lucky this time. I want some guns for next time."

"We wouldn't have needed luck if you hadn't dived straight in."

Vaskez looked him in the eye. "You telling me you would have walked on past and ignored what was going on? You could have done that?"

She was right, of course. He couldn't. He might have come up with a plan, but it probably would have been too late and might not have worked. She had done the only thing they could, and she'd done it quickly and grimly efficiently. He shrugged, conceding the point.

"Don't know about you, Dix, but I joined up to fight scumbags. And to fight scumbags, you need guns, and lots of them. Now grab a rifle and let's get out of here."

Chapter 17

THEY HIT the edge of town a couple of hours later, the rest of the journey mostly conducted in silence. Drake had raised a quizzical eyebrow at the guns; in reply, Vaskez had simply wiped the blood off her hands and knives against the moss on a tree trunk. She shouldered one rifle, handed another to Alard, and gave the handgun to Drake.

"We talking about this?" Drake had said.

"Nope," said Vaskez, and Dix had just raised his hands in surrender.

As they got closer, the trees started to thin and then ran out altogether. A swirl of roads ahead indicated a major junction of suspended highway signs, slip-roads and flyovers, but it was eerily free of traffic. Electrically propelled traffic, that is – in the distance, a straggle of wheeled carts and individuals on foot were funnelling towards one of the access roads, with the towers of the town rising before them.

"Checkpoints that way, I'm guessing," said Dix.

"So, what does a Haugan power station look like?" Alard peered out from the last vestiges of tree cover.

"Chain-link fence, Ash said, five hundred yards that way." Dix pointed in the other direction.

"Across open ground," said Alard.

"Better be quick then." Drake lifted Sol onto his shoulders. "Ready for a horsey ride, kid?"

With one final check, they set off on a steady run, heading away from the entrance road to town. Broken advertising boards gave them some cover, before a wide drainage ditch hid them completely. Above them ran a security fence shrouded in weeds and climbing plants, with warning signs fixed at intervals.

As advised by Ash, they looked for the one broken sign, snapped cleanly in half, just the top half still fixed to the fence. The fencing beneath was overgrown with brambles and stinging climbers, and looked intact to a passing eye, but a careful push with a shoulder opened up a gap they could slip through. From the other side, they closed it again as best they could, and the stems and brambles combined again to hide the break.

And that was that. They were in, drama-free apart from a few nettle stings.

"Which way, Al?"

That was Vaskez, not taking the piss, but actually seeking information. And 'Al'? Maybe this crew was coming together?

Alard took a long look around an expansive forecourt, abandoned machinery left to rust here and there.

Huge metal sheds spread out to all sides, pylons and towers above, a series of heavy, unmarked doors along each façade. He knelt to the ground, placed a hand on the concrete surface, and scrabbled together some pebbles, rolling them between his fingers.

"Over there," he said, pointing to his far left. He kept his arm stretched out, grin widening as they followed the direction of his finger. To a post in the ground with an arrow sign saying, 'Service tunnel.'

"Very funny," said Drake, allowing himself a smile. "Geopath humour? Guess you freaks have to work with what you've got?"

"You know it," said Alard, giving him the finger, and then turning it ninety degrees to indicate the direction. He headed towards a distant, half-moon tunnel entrance, where a surfaced track and rail lines disappeared into the gloom.

Dix felt better once they had crossed the threshold into the tunnel and moved a little way inside. Not that he knew exactly what was ahead of them, but at least they were no longer out in the open. Provided Ash's intel held up, they had the cover of the tunnel to get them into town. Plus, they now had guns.

True fact, everything looked better when you had guns.

Alard led them further in, down a slope, until they figured they were now underground. A white-walled tunnel stretched ahead of them, lined with insulated cables and massed runs of pipework. Cable drums and crates were stacked at intervals – there was even a row of zip-up overalls hanging on pegs, left years ago by the last workers to pass through.

There was enough light filtering in from the entrance to show the way ahead, though it soon dissolved into darkness. Thankfully, Ash's last tip also paid off. A control panel on the wall with a single on/off switch lit a series of low-wattage bulkhead lamps that arrowed away down either side of the tunnel as far as they could see.

From the position of the sun as they'd entered the tunnel, Dix reckoned it was late afternoon. The first rendezvous was at noon the next day, which meant a night underground, and that was fine by all of them. It was dry, they had provisions, and they were out of sight. There wasn't any evidence of recent traffic through the tunnel – no tyre marks, no footprints. There were suspicious scurrying noises, which could only be rats, but you couldn't have everything.

Dix called it. "Camp here, all right? Head in tomorrow. It's two miles underground to Ash's exit, and he said there was a cave-in en route. If we have to make a quick getaway, I'd rather be on this side. We can be back in the forest in ten minutes from here."

There was murmured agreement, and they unshouldered packs and weapons and set to establishing an overnight camp.

Vaskez rolled out a cable drum and parked it at their backs as a defensive watch post. Alard pushed forward into the tunnel and set up a perimeter block of crates, just in case anyone approached from the town side. Fifty yards either side of their position, they smashed a few of the lights and scattered the plastic shards across the ground – maybe they'd get a warning crunch at least, and a few seconds' heads-up.

They lit the smallest of fires, more for the kid than anything else. He liked feeding twigs into it and it kept him occupied. They weren't going to cook on it, even though Vaskez reckoned she could catch a rat or two.

"That'll be a no," said Alard, and he distributed cooked strips of rabbit they'd carried with them from the last camp. Dried meat from the farm, apples, water and the last of the homespun cereal bars – virtually a feast. And, although they were now out of supplies, tomorrow was another day. Something would turn up. The trooper's refrain.

"Auntie Vaskez?" Sol piped up from beside the fire, tucked under his cloak.

"Say what?" Vaskez looked across at Dix, giving him the stink-eye, as if to say, I know you're responsible for that liberty. Drake snorted with amusement.

"Are we being chased?" Sol seemed curious, rather than afraid. Not for the first time, Dix wondered how much he knew about what was going on. He asked few, if any, questions. Just seemed to accept whatever they told him, which in turn wasn't much. Because – what did they know, really?

"Sort of," said Vaskez. Non-committal was probably best.

"By the forces of darkness?"

"You could say that." Vaskez looked again at Dix. This time a 'Help me out here' look.

"And did you sort things out? Dix said you were going to sort things out."

Vaskez looked like she didn't know how to respond, and Dix felt sorry for her. "Auntie V gave them a stern talking to, didn't you, auntie?"

Obviously, not sorry enough to pass up the chance to wind up Vaskez, who now just looked pissed off.

"And it's not a game?" Sol was persevering with his line of questioning.

"No, mate, it's not a game."

"Because the fathers chased me sometimes, in the halls. And if they caught me, they'd tickle me. I didn't understand the game, but it seemed to make them happy."

"They weren't all fuckwits then," said Drake. "Sorry. Language, I know. But the more I hear about them, the more I dislike them. What were they even doing with a kid his age anyway? It doesn't make any sense."

Who knew? No one had yet got to the bottom of that, and tomorrow they were supposed to hand him over, to person unknown, for reasons unknown. Dix wanted to know more about that, if only for his own peace of mind.

"Sol, do you have a mum? A mother?"

The kid looked blank.

"Everyone has a mum, Sol. Even gnarly specimens like Vaskez have a mum."

"Watch it," growled Vaskez.

Sol still said nothing.

"A dad then. A father?"

"They are all my fathers," said Sol, as if that was obvious. Like, dumb question.

Dix changed tack. "You lived on the planet with the fathers?"

Sol nodded.

"You've always lived there?"

The boy nodded again.

"Do you know why?"

"Yes, because it is written."

Dix hauled up the satchel with the book in it. "In this, right?"

"*The Book of Light*," agreed Sol.

"Why is this important, do you know?"

"Because light is freedom," said Sol. "That's what the fathers say."

Very circular, very unhelpful. This was getting them nowhere.

"Tomorrow," said Dix, carefully choosing his words, "we're supposed to take you to meet someone. With the book. Do you know anything about that?"

"A father?"

"I think so. We're not sure. But you're OK with that, if we leave you with them?"

"The fathers know best," said Sol. He looked a little sad, though. "You're not coming, too?"

"We're coming with you. But then we have to go. We just want to know you're going to be all right?"

"If it is written, then it will be, Dix. That is the way."

"How do you know what's written, though?" Dix gestured at the book. "We can't read it."

"No, Dix, only the fathers know of *The Book of Light*." Sol gave another look that said, 'Duh.'

"Give it here," said Vaskez, reaching around the fire. She took out one of her knives and tried to insert the blade into the book-shaped box, and swore under her breath as she found no purchase.

"Only the fathers open the book," said Sol, with a note of concern.

"But I'm sure aunties and uncles are allowed?" said Dix.

"I suppose so. I've never had an auntie or an uncle before."

"Well, there you go. We'll let Auntie V see if she can open it, I'm sure the fathers won't mind."

Oh, she better believe that 'Dixie-boy' was going to get mileage out of 'Auntie Vaskez' for some time to come.

Vaskez barely raised an eyebrow, intent on working her way around the book, trying to find an opening, but the box was sealed tight. They could hear the scratching sound as knife blade met durable metal.

"The fathers have a key," said Sol, brightly.

That was slightly more helpful, though only slightly. There was no obvious keyhole on the clasp, only the circular indentation. Although... Dix thought back to the grisly scene on Vitlok, and the secret cup-and-bowl access to the underground chamber. It seemed as if the monks were fond of the whole disguised-key business. Not that that helped them much right now.

Vaskez gave up and sheathed her knife. "I'll bet Drake's got something in his special ship's cupboard we could have used."

"I want to see what's in there, not blow it to bits."

"Who cares?" Vaskez pulled out her sleeping roll. "It's just a boring book."

"One that they really seem to want, as well as the kid. Maybe we'll get more answers tomorrow." Dix stood up. "I'll take first watch, spot me later?"

Vaskez hunkered down, and Dix set up by the defensive cable drum with a rifle, looking out down the tunnel. Over by the fire, Sol sat cross-legged and rolled his softball towards Drake, who rolled it back. Alard joined in, too, for a while, before reaching for his cloak and stretching out. Drake kept it going – a gentle roll, a soft bounce – until he ruffled Sol's hair and pointed at the ground, made a sleeping sign with his hands.

Kid was getting the hang of playing nice with people. Drake and Alard, too, come to that. Shame they had to say goodbye tomorrow, but maybe they'd given Sol something over the last few days. De-weirded him a bit, anyway – shown him a couple of games to play with his creepy father-monks.

Dix reckoned Sol could even keep the ball, Uncle Drake wouldn't mind.

Chapter 18

THE NEGOTIATIONS WENT BETTER than Dix had expected.

It was obvious that they shouldn't all go to the meet. Sol was their only insurance, and Dix did not like walking blind into unfamiliar terrain. He could hear the sarge barking at him about the value of field recon and knowing your enemy's strength. And while whoever was meeting them might not be the enemy, this mission was definitely on hostile terrain as far as they were concerned.

Dix wasn't ready to give up Sol without first scoping out the situation. He felt exposed enough already – no field armour, no tech, no comms, no gear – so an initial recce made sense. But he expected an argument about who was going to do that, because the command structure of this team was not what you'd call a done deal.

Surprisingly, Vaskez got it immediately.

"You and Drake should go," she said. "You might

need a large, horrible, smooth-talking smuggler to help deal with the locals."

"Offence taken," said Drake, looking far from offended.

"I'll stay with the kid, look after him. Close protection." Vaskez patted her rifle. "Get him away if I need to. And Al here can hide us in the woods."

Alard, for his part, looked happy to be left out of the initial scouting party, even though that was technically his job. Fine. Dix reckoned he could find a scuzzy, backstreet pub on his own – what trooper couldn't?

"We'll be in and out," said Dix. "Just a quick meet-and-greet, check it's all above board. If we're not back in a few hours, it all goes belly-up, you move. And we meet back at the farmhouse, OK?"

"Tell me you're taking a weapon?" said Vaskez.

Dix had thought about it but decided against it. They were in the town now – or would be, once they'd emerged from the tunnel. Who knew what other checkpoints there might be? What sort of surveillance or scanning might be in place? Best to continue looking local and harmless, in case they were stopped.

He was going to take the book, though. He might not want to hand over Sol without some reassurances, but *The Book of Light* would stand as a good-faith proof for their contact, so everyone knew where they stood.

They all slapped hands, and Dix and Drake moved out, heading at pace through the tunnel towards the town.

The going was straightforward until they reached the blockage Ash had warned them about.

"Shit," said Drake. "That look worse to you than he described?"

It did. A cave-in had pushed rubble across the corridor and pulled beams down across broken pipework. Maybe a year ago, when Ash had last been through, the collapse hadn't been so dramatic, but now stones, chunks of plaster, and packed earth were piled high in a mound that reached up towards the ceiling, obscuring the way ahead.

Dix didn't like the look of the bulging walls on either side, or the integrity of the remaining roof, but there was nothing to be done about it. This, unbelievably, was still the safest way into town for them, at least according to Ash.

Dix picked his way carefully up the mound of rubble, hearing creaks and thuds as things shifted unpleasantly all around him. At one point his foot slipped into empty space, as stones fell beneath his weight, and he stumbled before regaining his footing. He stood stock still and waited for a beat before continuing.

The mound topped out about eight feet up, where Dix could see a way across and through to the other side, though his head came perilously close to the curved, cracked tunnel ceiling. He turned to Drake, still standing at the foot of the obstruction.

"It's do-able, but you'll need to step carefully, big guy." Dix kept his voice low, thinking that the cave-in didn't need any further encouragement from vibrations of any kind.

"Fantastic. You should have brought the short-arse with you." He meant Alard.

"You'll be fine. Just don't – " Dix didn't know what. Move like a big person? Breathe? In the end, he gave Drake a quick salute and pushed himself through the opening as quickly as he could. It held, and he fairly scampered down the other side and waited for Drake to follow.

After a nervy minute or so, and more alarming creaking noises, Drake's head appeared at the top of the mound. Unlike Dix, he had to fully crouch to make his way through, crab-like, before he too took bigger, quicker strides down the other side and jumped clear.

"I know we don't swear anymore," said Drake, after a short pause, "but – "

"Exactly," said Dix. "Fudging horrendous."

"I'll look forward to that on the way back."

"If it's still clear," said Dix.

"Now why did you have to go and say that?"

They moved off into a much darker section of tunnel – the emergency lighting was still on here, but many of the lamps had gone, either broken or burned out. The ground at least was clear and eventually they found their exit – a spray-painted '47' on the wall ahead, with a flickering light above.

A metal door was wedged open. Through it, they could see a long flight of steps running up to another door.

"That must be the street exit," said Dix. "Ready for a Hauga sightseeing trip?"

"It's been lovely so far," said Drake. "Bone-and-nettle soup, three dead bodies, slept in a creepy forest, and survived the Tunnel of Death. Can't wait."

The door at the top of the steps needed a shoulder to it, but scraped open to reveal a small, bare room with lockers down two sides. A final door with a push-bar was marked 'EXIT.' Dix listened, ear to the metal, and then pressed down on the bar and eased open the door. Drake stooped to pick up a thin piece of plastic from the floor – part of an old, broken workplace sign – and wedged it between door and frame on their way out.

They were in an alley, flanked by tall, brick buildings. There was glass on the ground from shattered windows above, and piles of accumulated rubbish. A smell, too, that was hard to identify beyond something rotting. You had to give it to the sleeper agent, Ash – no one was going to venture down here on the off-chance, unless they knew there was a secret door into a disused tunnel.

Drake nodded at the street beyond, and they took a quick look before stepping out.

It was weird, but weirdly familiar, all at the same time. It had obviously been a normal shopping street at some point in the past, with retail units with large windows stretching away down both sides of a wide street. Printed signs and designs – now faded and scuffed, or with letters missing – advertised what used to be sold. Unfamiliar brands of clothes, kitchen equipment, electronics, home décor – even a pet supplies store.

But the windows were cracked and undressed, and handwritten signs told a different story – 'Food and Wood' said one, 'Shoes,' said another. In a third, two pinch-faced women were picking over a tray of brown apples, while a man in a threadbare jacket filled a battered canvas bag with earth-encrusted potatoes.

They kept moving to the end of the street, past an abandoned vehicle with years of grime on its paintwork and windscreen. One shop was completely burned out, while outside another hung a line of small carcasses on a rail under a sign that said, 'Fresh Meat.' The 'fresh' was debatable. If Hauga still had health-and-safety inspectors, they'd have a field day here.

One block over, as per Ash's directions, they looked along a similarly run-down street, this one with a small group of people gathered around makeshift grills under a large, decorated parasol. Dix could still make out the original design and wording – a picture of a sharply-dressed office worker, clutching a cocktail, with the slogan, 'Livin' the Haugan High Life.'

"Dear me," said Drake. "I hope that's rabbit on the grill?"

"By the looks of things around here, rabbit's the best it's going to be."

"You do bring me to some dream destinations. Tunnel World was terrific, really, but Hobo City has topped it. Five stars. Ever thought of becoming a travel agent?"

Dix ignored him and pointed up the street. "There's the bar, right?"

It had to be 'The Two Globes' – a dilapidated, blue-painted building with twin metal orbs in a frame that extended from the façade. Another group of people was loitering outside.

"I've heard the cocktails are great," said Drake. "The bar snacks, depends what you feel about deep-fried squirrel scratchings."

"Come on," said Dix. "Try not to look so large and frightening, we don't want to alarm the locals."

The people outside were blocking the door, but Dix sidled through, feeling all eyes on him. They weren't dressed entirely differently from the Haugans – Galloway's hand-me-downs from the prison hulk were surprisingly on-trend for an oppressed population living in a shabby, tech-free shithole. Even so, there was something about the two of them that shouted, 'Not from around here,' whether it was Dix's army crewcut or Drake's alarming bulk and height.

Inside, it was your standard city tavern, if one fallen on hard times. Stools and high-tops, sticky carpet, and the smell of ale, though with a back-note of soot and kerosene – there were hanging lamps on the walls, which suggested there was no longer anything to power the ceiling lights or the vid-game booth in the corner.

The bar itself was full, with people drinking and chatting in clusters, which was just dandy as far as Dix was concerned. The less attention they drew to themselves, the better.

He scanned the room, not knowing who he was looking for, but figuring he'd know them when he saw them – or vice versa, of course.

"Anything?" said Drake, in a low voice.

"Difficult to say," said Dix. "We should get a drink, blend in."

"How are we going to do that, genius?"

Good point. Dix's whole life – credit included – was on the chip-tag he'd surrendered to Galloway. And whatever stash Drake had was presumably hidden away on his Star-Jumper. No ID, no blowback for the Federation if they were caught, that had been the deal.

Plus side, this no longer looked like the kind of establishment that dealt in e-credits, given the general lack of tech and power. Some bags of produce on the bar – one leaking what looked suspiciously like blood – rather made the point. Minus side, they had nothing to barter for drinks.

"Nothing in your pockets? What kind of smuggler are you?"

"A resourceful one," said Drake, swiping two abandoned, half-empty glasses from a nearby table. "Hold this, look like you're enjoying a delicious beverage."

They stood at a high table. Dix sniffed his stale drink, which was as close as it was going to get to entering his body, and continued to survey the room.

"Gentlemen." A voice came from behind them – a man with a worn, lined face at the next table, collecting empty glasses. "Things that bad, eh?" He gestured at the drinks they were holding.

Dix kept his nerve, looked uncomprehending.

"I saw you," said the man. "My bar, my drinks. I could have recycled those."

"Really?" said Drake, looking appalled. Although on reflection, his drink smelled as if it had already been recycled at least once, potentially strained through someone's gym gear.

"Of course, not really, what do you think I am? Still, makes me wonder what you two are doing here? And don't say, 'Having a drink.'"

"Just passing through," said Dix, and gave the man what he hoped was a firm but non-threatening stare.

The guy paused for a second, then said, "Oh, relax, none of my business. But listen – word of warning. You're not from around here, that's obvious, but you better have papers because the scum-suckers are out in force. And if you don't have papers, I strongly urge you to move on. No one wants any trouble."

"Scum-suckers?"

"Axis, man, who do you think?" The bar-owner shook his head, as if dislodging a troubling thought. "Some fucking idiots took it upon themselves to waste a couple of guards yesterday, a few miles out, must have interrupted something. It's been the usual shitshow ever since – they disappeared the two women, they'll never be seen again. And now there are patrols every-where, fucking with everyone. Strung someone up, I heard, and there were shots earlier, that's why it's busy in here. No one wants to be out on the streets right now."

If the man noticed the look of alarm that passed between Dix and Drake, he didn't say. Instead, he just shook his head again. "Fucking heroes," he spat. "You think they'd have learned by now. It's never them that pays the price. Anyway, point is, if you two likely lads don't have papers – and I'm guessing you don't – I would very much appreciate you fucking off and finding some other place to hide in. After you finish your free drinks, of course."

The man gave them a sarcastic look, before carrying a tray of empty glasses back to his bar.

"That's heavy." Drake blew out his cheeks. "That's on us, right?"

Dix was horribly certain that it was. The woman had even tried to warn them what would happen. Not that Dix could have stopped Vaskez – or, if he was honest, would have wanted to. In any hostile situation, there were always consequences. It's just that, usually, as a trooper, you pulled the trigger or pressed the button, but rarely got to see how the bigger picture played out.

Well, now they knew. Ash had told them, and the woman had told them. You messed with the Axis and they messed back. Hard.

That was a tough lesson to learn.

Tougher for the two women, mother and daughter, obviously. Dix felt distraught about that.

"What do you think?" said Drake. "Maybe we should leave?"

"We can't go," said Dix. "You heard Ash, the first meet is set for today. I want to see who we're dealing with before we hand over the kid. Besides, where are we going to go? It's got to be safer in here than out on the street. Only other place is the tunnel, and we can't do anything from there."

"If it was just me here," said Drake, "on the job – "

"Job? You mean smuggling? Dealing contraband?"

"On the job," continued Drake, firmly, "I'd be out of here. Sometimes, you just know when it doesn't feel right. At which point, it's time to quit. I'm getting that feeling now."

"I hear you, but what choice do we have? Let's find the contact, see that we're happy to leave the kid with them, and then split. No drop, no ship access codes, remember?"

"How could I forget? Don't get me wrong, I really do want to get off this dump of a planet, but this has all the hallmarks of a Grade A cluster… fudge. Damn, that kid's got in my head." Drake smiled to himself. "Anyway, we got any likely targets?"

They scanned the room again together, Dix trying to tread the line between catching someone's eye and *catching* someone's eye, which was harder than it sounded.

"Could be anyone," he said. "Or they're not here yet?" He nodded over at an old-fashioned clock on the wall – the kind his granny had, back on Calisto, where something popped out of a door on the hour. On Calisto, it was usually a little sculpted fish. Here, who knew – the butchered head of a ground-squirrel? Either way, the hands were at 11:50.

The bar-owner stopped again on his way past. "You lads still here? Did you not get my memo?"

"We're waiting for someone," said Dix. "Then we'll go."

"Well, you better hope they turn up soon. Scum-suckers in the neighbourhood, remember. I told you what – "

The man broke off mid-sentence and looked across the room, to where there was another entrance from the street. The door there closed and there was a momentary silence as everyone clocked who had just walked in.

"Fuck's sake, that's all I need today. If it's not the scum-suckers, it's those clowns." The man looked at Dix in disgust. And Dix looked at Drake.

It seemed that their contact had arrived.

Chapter 19

Or maybe contacts, plural – two monks, in cowls and habits, just like the ones on Vitlok.

The younger one took up a station by the door, eyes flickering around the room and, occasionally, behind him, checking the street entrance. Muscle, reckoned Dix, if monks needed muscle? Probably wise, if they knew what had gone down recently on that monastery planet of theirs. Axis mercs certainly didn't seem to have a problem offing monks.

The other – a good few years older – walked slowly to a low window table and took a seat. The two people already there, sitting opposite, got up quickly and moved away. Dix could hear the murmurings in the bar all around him, including the odd snarl or growl.

"Fucking monks and fucking Council," said the bar-owner, under his breath. Dix looked at him, questioningly, and the man looked back at him, surprised. "What? Don't tell me you're a happy clapper?"

Dix didn't know what to make of that, and just shrugged and made a non-committal noise. That seemed to be the right response, because the bar-owner wasn't finished.

"We've all seen the lights in the palace, the air-con units, the food that goes in, the cosy chats with our Axis overlords. They do all right, the fuckers. Meanwhile, it's 'Await the light, it is written,' all that bollocks. You don't see many monks strung up on the lampposts, is all I'm saying."

"The High Council?" hazarded Dix.

"Too right, the High Council," said the landlord. "Must be nice for them, awaiting the bloody light in their fancy palace. Hot bath when they want one. Never done anything for the rest of us, that's for sure, am I right?"

Dix nodded, cautiously, playing for time, seeing if there was anything else to be gleaned. "What are they doing in here?" he said.

"No idea. Not buying drinks, I can tell you that, cheap fuckers. No offence."

He bustled off back behind the bar, leaving Dix and Drake in a quandary. "Well, this is awkward," said Drake. "You reckon that's the guy?"

"Only one way to find out."

"How did I know you were going to say that? The landlord's going to be pissed."

"He wants us out anyway," said Dix. "Let's do this quickly and arrange to meet somewhere else tomorrow, with the kid."

"And what do you make of all that High Council stuff?"

"Not sure. I mean, monks, religion. It's all nonsense, right?"

On Calisto, no one believed in anything except the power of the sea, and the bounty it contained. Fishers might sing one of the old songs for a good catch, or crack a bottle against the side of a new boat for luck, but no one seriously believed in a supernatural being conducting operations from on high. What were they, children? If the local Haugans disputed religious belief, too, Dix could hardly blame them, given the conditions they lived under.

Dix and Drake crossed the room and slipped into the seats opposite the monk, who looked up from his clasped hands. He adjusted his cowl to reveal a smooth, pale face; a hidden pendant hung around his neck, the leather cords disappearing into the folds of his robes.

The monk remained silent, and Dix realised he was waiting for them to speak. Not sure of the etiquette, he tried a tentative, "Father?"

The monk nodded. "You're Ash's men?" Gruff, almost dismissive.

Ash's men? Seemed a bit reductive, but it was as good an identifier as any, Dix supposed. "You could say that."

"I did say that." The monk stared at Dix, unblinking, and when Dix didn't respond, then said, "Well?" in a tone that had condescension stitched through it.

In the course of his training, Dix had been yelled at

and intimidated by some of the Fed army's most terrifying instructors and interrogators. People who were paid to get up into Dix's face, to try and rile him. They never succeeded, which was one of the reasons why Dix was such a good soldier. The monk had a lot to learn if he thought this approach was going to work, and Dix sat back in his chair and returned the gaze.

The monk tried again, dialling back the aggression a notch. "I understand you have something for us?"

Now they were getting somewhere. "You mean the boy? Or the book?" said Dix. "Just so we're clear?"

"Yes, the boy!" snapped the monk. "Where is he?"

"Not here, obviously," said Dix.

"It's a bar," pointed out Drake. "He's under-age, wouldn't be right."

The monk bristled. "You think this is a game? I assure you it is not."

"Why don't we start again?" said Dix. "I'm Dix, and this is Drake. Pleased to meet you."

"Your names are of no consequence."

The blatant rudeness did finally rile Dix. "Funny, that. Lightburst told us that names are extremely important."

The monk's eyes flashed at the mention of the name. He spoke in a low, hard voice. "You speak of things you can't possibly know. You are here to serve."

"We're here to see what sort of fuckwits call a boy Lightburst in the first place." Drake was clearly as aggravated by the monk's attitude as Dix. "What kind of name is that?"

"It's no business of yours."

"It is if you want us to hand him over. Kid's kind of grown on me. Can't catch a bloody ball, but he deserves a decent home. I'm not getting milk-and-cookie vibes from you, *Father*."

"The boy belongs with us, that is all you need to know. The book, too. We are wasting time here."

"We've got nowhere else to be," said Dix. "That right, Drake? And I think we need to know quite a bit more. This is a kid we're talking about."

"None of this is your concern. This is not your planet, these are not your people." The monk looked around the bar disdainfully. "The boy has a future that you cannot comprehend. Your only duty is to deliver him, take the money and leave."

"Money? You think we're doing this for money?"

"Chance would be a fine thing," muttered Drake.

"Your kind always seeks payment of one sort or another." The monk looked pained at the very thought.

"Our kind?" Dix was rapidly going off this pale streak of piss in a monk's habit.

"Brigands, outlaws, whatever you are."

"How dare you!" Drake drew his hands up in mock offence.

"To be fair, you are a smuggler," Dix pointed out.

"Time served," said Drake. "Guild registered. Not like those fly-by-night brigands and outlaws."

"Enough of this nonsense," snapped the monk. "Some things – some people – have a higher purpose.

The boy has a higher purpose. You are the dark, he is the light."

"Let me guess. 'It is written,' right?" Dix tapped the satchel and opened the flap, so the monk could see the book within.

"*The Book of Light*," gasped the monk. "Give that to me!" He leaned across the table and grabbed the satchel from beside Dix.

"Guess he wants his book back," said Drake. "Big reader, are you?"

"And the boy!" hissed the monk. "Where is he?" His attention was caught briefly by the second monk, who had left his station by the door and bent to whisper in his ear. The older monk nodded, dismissed his companion, and then snapped his fingers at Dix. "Enough prevarication," he said, "it is not safe here. Things can go badly for strangers on Hauga these days."

The snapped fingers were bad enough, but the tone was unmistakable.

"Is that a threat, Father?"

"It is the simple truth. Now, take me to the boy."

Dix had also had enough. If handing over Sol had ever seemed right, it now seemed less so by the minute.

This man, religious monk or not, was an asshole. And if he was a representative asshole – of the apparent assholery that was the Haugan High Council – then Dix wanted at least to confer with his crew. Talk to Sol, come to that, and see what he thought of it all. Maybe this was just what they were like – Asshole

Monks Incorporated? If Sol said they were all right, and was happy to go with them, then perhaps they could still seal this deal?

There was a loud noise at the rear door as a uniformed man barged in, pushing the watching monk there to one side. Hearing raised voices, Dix turned to see two more men entering through the main door. One stood sentry there while the other moved into the room. All three had the Axis insignia; all had holstered and cross-body weapons; all had stun-sticks drawn. Silence dropped.

"Papers!" shouted the one in the middle of the room. "And don't even think of moving."

Dix saw the landlord raise his hands slowly and then reach for a bottle, pouring three shots, very carefully, and laying them out along the bar. He gestured, raised his hands again and retreated. Obviously knew the routine.

Laminated squares were produced from pockets and coats, as the man moved around among the bar patrons, scanning each one with a flip-screen. A faint, high-pitched beep accompanied each scan, loud in the silence, followed by a slight nod and a sneer from the man with each successful check.

Dix turned his head slowly to look at Drake. The big man's eyes were darting to the rear door and back. Assessing. Calculating. Dix was doing the same with the front door. The numbers weren't bad, two against three, but the weaponry situation was concerning. Dix noticed the monk at their table hadn't moved, except to pull the satchel with the book closer to him.

The lead Axis guard paused at one of the proffered passes, and looked closely at the holder, a young man in work boots and a tabard. Dix would have said he looked unusually nervous, except everyone in the place looked nervous. Terrified even. Maybe not the two monks, whose faces betrayed little emotion, but everyone else. No one had yet said a word.

The silence endured while the young man's pass was scanned – like a collective breath being held – broken only by a different sound. Not the faint beep this time; instead, a lower sound.

A buzz. A rejection.

"No!" said the young man, but it was the last thing he said, as the Axis guard stepped back and thrust his stun-stick into his side. There was a crackle and the man dropped to the floor, his muscles spasming, his breath already laboured.

"How hard is it?" said the Axis guard. "No papers, no travel. Forged papers, well – ask your pal here."

He kicked the writhing man on the floor, eliciting a groan, and turned his attention back to the room, noticing the monk at the table for the first time.

"Well, well, who do we have here? Slumming it today, aren't we, Your Eminence?"

It wasn't meant to be respectful. There was a cackle from one of the other guards.

"Now, normally, I wouldn't ask to see your papers,

would I, you being a respected member of society and all?"

Another snort, and even – Dix thought – the slightest of murmurs of agreement from the bar patrons.

"But on account of certain members of your flock" – at which the guard kicked the prone man again, hard in the ribs – "having taken fatal liberties with two of our own yesterday, I'm going to have to ask you to produce some ID. Can't be too careful, can you? Anyone can put a dress on, say they're a monk. There are bad people everywhere, Father, you can appreciate that, I'm sure."

At the words 'bad people,' the guard jabbed his stun-stick downwards twice – stab, stab – into the young man's face. The crackling noise echoed around the room. A sizzle, a gurgle, and then another terrible silence, as what was left of the man's face oozed onto the carpet.

The monk rose from his seat. "You exceed your authority," he said, his voice firm and calm. He lifted his pendant from beneath his robe. A circle with the shining sun motif. "You know this symbol, it is the mark of the High Council. There is nothing else required." He fixed the Axis guard with the haughty stare that appeared to be his default expression. Dix wasn't sure how wise that was.

"Well, la-di-fucking-da, Father. Wouldn't want to upset the High Council, would we? All the good work you do in the community." The man sniggered and looked around the room. No one caught his eye, but Dix was sure the guard knew exactly which buttons he was pressing.

"Tell you what," he continued. "We'll just finish our checks, have our drinks from mine host, and we'll be on our way. Terrorists to catch, you know how it is. Right, you two, passes!"

And this was it. The moment had come.

Dix stood up, and Drake followed, needing to be upright, and with some room to move, if they were to make any kind of stand. Having seen what it could do, Dix was extremely wary of the guard's stun-stick.

"These gentlemen are with me," said the monk, moving clear of the table. "I can vouch for them."

"Good for you, Father, but no passes, pokey-sticky, you know the drill. Come on, I haven't got all day."

"There is no need for that," said the monk, placing himself between the Axis guard and Dix and Drake, and raising his hand. Despite all the evidence, the monk seemed to think he was in charge here.

"There is every fucking need. What do you think this is, a prayer meeting? Get back." The guard brandished his stun-stick at the monk, who stood his ground. The guard at the front door unholstered his sidearm and moved into the room, training his weapon on the monk as he advanced.

This was as good as it was going to get, Dix could see. Both guards had eyes on the monk – no love lost there – which meant they were momentarily distracted. The third guard, observing from the rear door, was a problem, but the older monk was currently blocking his line of sight to Dix and Drake. And maybe the other monk, the younger one by the door, would have something to contribute if things went to crap?

Actually, there was no 'if' about it. Crapness was guaranteed. Which meant moving quickly, if you wanted to get in ahead and surf the crap, rather than be submerged by it.

Dix didn't even look at Drake, trusting the big guy would kick in when the action started. If he didn't – well, no time to worry about that now. He lunged for the nearest guard's raised sidearm, wrenched it downwards and followed with a solid punch to the face. There was a satisfying thunk as the guard stumbled and his head hit the corner of the table.

As Dix moved, Drake saw his opportunity and pushed the old monk sharply forward into the lead guard. A zap from the extended stun-stick dropped the monk where he stood, and a split second of surprised inaction was all that Drake needed to grab the hilt of the stun-stick and turn it on the guard himself. He fell, twitching, on top of the monk.

A shout from the rear door meant the third guard was in play. Dix looked up to see him raising a rifle, but the guard didn't notice the younger monk behind him, who clubbed him with clenched fists and then kicked his knees out from under him. Not bad for a religious man.

Five seconds, three down, but it was now bedlam in the bar. Every person in there made for the doors, and through the melee Dix saw the third guard get trampled underfoot. Meanwhile, the monk who had taken him out was pinned to the wall by a tide of people rushing past.

There was a movement below Dix as the guard he had hit roused himself from under the table. Dix scrabbled for the dropped sidearm and pistol-whipped him, and the guy was finally out of the picture.

Drake pulled the lead guard off the monk, rolled him over, and kicked him for good measure. Dix couldn't, in all honesty, fault the move, gratuitous though it was. There was a preponderance of assholes on this planet, and a particular concentration of them now on the floor in this bar, either twitching, trampled or out cold.

"Book," said Dix, and Drake lifted the satchel from a seat and shouldered it. "Time to go?"

"Thought you'd never ask."

As the last person scrambled out of the bar, the younger monk advanced and knelt by his fallen colleague. "Father?" he said, as he cradled the stunned man's head. The monk didn't look in the best of health – grey face, saliva dribbling from his mouth.

The younger man looked up at Dix and Drake, who had edged around the fallen bodies. "You will take me to the boy," he said. "Now!" That imperious tone again – they must teach it in monk school.

"Yeah, fuck that," said Drake.

The young monk laid the older one gently to the floor and got to his feet. "He belongs to us."

"I don't think so," said Dix, pointing the handgun at him. "Back away, to the wall."

Dix was running on adrenaline now, full-on, field-op, trooper mode. Laser-focused, relying on instinct. It was what all the training was for. What he was good at. And whatever the monk saw in his eyes made him step backwards.

Dix leaned down, ripped the pendant from the older monk's neck, and then Dix and Drake retreated to the main door, Dix with his gun trained on the monk as they left.

"Let's go," said Drake, at the door, pushing it open. The street outside was empty, but in the distance they could hear the wail of a siren. There were probably surveillance drones already in the air.

The last thing Dix saw, as he turned to follow Drake, was the landlord – ashen-faced – downing the three shots he'd laid out on the bar, one after the other.

Chapter 20

THEY RAN hard through the streets, back to the alley and to the wedged door that led down to the tunnel. No one was out, though Dix saw open mouths and wide eyes as they flashed past the broken-down shops. Had they been seen by more dangerous eyes? It was impossible to tell.

Closing the alley door firmly behind them, Drake pulled at one of the storage lockers in the ante-room, flexing and grunting as he wrenched it away from the wall. Dix did the same, and they heaved the two units against the back of the door. If anyone *had* followed them, or found the entrance, that might slow them down a bit.

Back in the tunnel, they smashed each surviving light as they went, running from the darkness as far as the cave-in. This time, they didn't even stop to think – Dix went first, then Drake, picking their way up and over, treading as lightly as they could, trading care for speed. Bricks tumbled behind them, while metal groaned somewhere in the background.

On the other side, Drake paused before they set off again.

"Wouldn't take much," he said, looking at the hanging pipes and precarious masonry.

"Let's do it."

They yanked on a protruding beam, which gave a threatening creak as it see-sawed against twisted rebars. Another huge push, and chunks began to fall – slowly at first, and then faster as the collapse accelerated. They jumped clear and retreated, as the tunnel dissolved into a thundering cloud of dust and rubble. When it was quiet once more, the way behind them – to the town – was entirely blocked.

"Having fun?"

Dix whirled at the voice, to find Alard approaching from the direction of their camp at the other end of the tunnel.

"What are you doing here?"

Alard held out his hands and wiggled his fingers. "Geopath shit. You two have been giving me a headache for the last twenty minutes. Smashing things. Breaking tunnels. Not gone well, I take it?"

"You could say that. Where's Sol?"

"Don't worry, he's fine. Vaskez is teaching him how to field-strip a Cougar-X assault rifle."

Dix thought he was probably joking, but then again, it was Vaskez, so perhaps not.

"Do we need to move?" said Alard. "Trouble?"

Well, yes. Although what form it would take, and when it might arrive, were unclear.

"Lots. On account of it being a shithole up there, full of assholes," said Drake.

"I'm getting that impression," said Alard as he led them back to camp.

"Dix!" Sol bounded forward, a smile on his face. The kid seemed ridiculously pleased to see them. Vaskez, meanwhile, was locking the last piece of her rifle back into place, and gave Dix a 'What?' look.

"Did you see the fathers?" said the boy. "Are they coming?"

Those were tough questions to answer. "Yes" to the first. "Hope not" to the second. Dix needed more time before knowing whether or not he'd be happy to sit down and talk to one of the fathers again. Although as he'd just destroyed the only undercover access back into town, he thought he'd probably already made up his mind about that.

"It's not safe there right now," is all he said. And then, to Vaskez, pulling her to one side, "We need to talk."

She listened impassively to Dix and Drake's account of what had gone down, and asked a few perceptive questions. Whatever else she was – brash, impulsive, extremely violent on occasion – she was a good soldier. Knew the right, strategic things to concentrate on.

She was also – Dix could see – affected by what they had to tell her the Axis reprisals, and about the two assaulted women who had been taken away to an unknown fate.

"Bastards," she said.

"It's not your fault," said Dix, misunderstanding her reaction. "You did what had to be done at the time."

Vaskez looked Dix squarely in the eye. "You think I'm feeling guilty?"

"No, but… "

"But nothing. If Axis scumbags need killing, I kill them. Anything that happens after that is on them. Not me. Got it?"

"Got it."

Black-white. No grey in Vaskez's moral code. She got angry with assholes and sorted things out. Dix admired that clarity, though he didn't think life was that simple. Probably not the time to discuss it, though.

"So, what are you thinking?' she said.

"I'm thinking we get out of here," said Dix. He could see Drake nodding in agreement, no argument there. "We get caught with the kid, we're all dead, and maybe him, too – or he ends up with one set of goons or another. I don't like those monks – they didn't have a straight answer in them. And the Axis guards won't even stop to ask questions, they'll just shoot, or worse. There's nothing for Sol out there. It's brutal."

"Say you're right… "

"I am right."

"Just thinking it through," said Vaskez. "You forgotten our little predicament? No completed mission, no ship codes. No ship codes, no bye bye shit-hole. Not to mention now the whole Axis force will be on our tail. Plus, you've pissed off the monks. Probably got one killed, by the sound of it. You've managed to hack off the entire planet in a matter of hours. Nice going."

"I have a plan," said Dix.

"I'm waiting."

"Well, the germ of a plan. It ends with us having a getaway spaceship."

"Which we can't drive without the access codes. Which Galloway won't give us until we finish her mission. My mission, too, as it happens."

Vaskez looked serious. It was easy to forget that she had a different stake in all this. She was still army, through and through. So, what Dix had to say next was crucial, because if Vaskez didn't go for it, they were stuffed.

"How will Galloway know?" he said, choosing his words carefully. "About how the mission plays out, I mean. Look, you volunteered to help deliver a weapon to the Haugan resistance. So far, none of what we were told turns out to be true. Instead of a weapon, we've got a clueless nine-year-old kid. Instead of a resistance, we've got a bunch of annoying monks, and a whole planet overrun by psychopaths. I don't want to leave the kid here, it doesn't seem right."

"I'm still waiting for the plan."

"We head back to Ash's place and tuck the kid away out of sight. Job done, as far as Ash and Galloway are concerned, how would they know otherwise? We get the codes and off we go. Mission complete."

"And the kid?"

"We'll figure it out. Leave him with Ash, maybe. He's kept his family safe all this time. Or we sneak him on board, take him with us. Drop him somewhere. Orphanage, I don't know, it's what you might call a fluid plan. The important thing is, we get out of here and live to fight another day."

Vaskez looked unconvinced, but she didn't object – not yet, anyway – and Dix took that as a good sign.

They packed up their gear and headed for the main entrance, slowing as it sloped upwards towards the surface. The tunnel brightened, and if Dix had been wary about breaking for the woods during daylight, his fears were confirmed once he and Alard had scouted ahead. They crept across the abandoned forecourt to the overgrown fence, and even at this distance they could tell things had changed since they had entered the previous day.

From a hidden vantage point on a rusting crane, Dix could see a long line of people stretching from the nearby checkpoint. The Axis had clearly tightened security, and no one was getting in or out in a hurry.

Jeeps swept past on the nearby road, and there was an armoured vehicle parked on the central reservation. Black-clad Axis guards lolled around outside it, heading off in ones and twos on patrol. Alard could sense much more movement – unseen feet and vehicles – from the direction of the town centre. And sense other things, too, that he couldn't articulate, other than saying, "It's bad."

Dix couldn't help thinking of Ash's stories of swinging gibbets and summary executions. And partly, that had to be down to them – though Vaskez was right about one thing. It didn't help to feel guilty. They weren't responsible for the Axis' grisly reprisals.

"We're staying until nightfall," said Dix, back in the tunnel. "It's safe enough here for now. We'll make a break for it then."

They hunkered down against the side of the tunnel with their bedrolls and cloaks. Dix had located the control panel again, near the entrance, and killed what was left of the tunnel lighting. That left them in the natural light filtering down from the main entrance, and with several hours to wait until dark.

Vaskez – annoyingly – was asleep within minutes. Drake and Alard were talking in low voices with Sol – they were telling him riddles, and Dix could only hope they were keeping them clean. He heard the boy laugh – a delighted peal – and turned to shush them with a finger to his lips. The laugh became a strangled giggle.

What *were* they going to do with him? The answer was no clearer to Dix, and he hoped he had a better idea next time Vaskez asked, as she surely would.

He reached for the leather satchel, pulled out the book, and studied the front cover again.

The Book of Light. The title was still all he knew about its contents.

He could have left the book with the surviving

monk, but it had seemed important to take it – to keep it with Sol, anyway. The two went together in a way that he didn't yet understand. A lot of dead bodies had piled up since Sol and the book had come into their keeping. Maybe now was the time for some answers?

"Only the fathers open the book," Sol had said. And Dix had the next best thing to a father – the pendant he had taken from the neck of the older monk.

The pendant he'd like to bet fitted the circular depression on the book cover.

Chapter 21

There was a soft click and whirr. The cover of the book came loose, and Dix lifted it clear. Although it looked like a large, bound book from the outside, encased in a metallic cover, inside it was something entirely different.

It was more like a strong box for documents, with a touchscreen inset to the rear side of the front cover. With the cover and screen raised away from the body of the box, a thick pile of papers was revealed. Haphazardly stacked, rucked and scrunched, corners folded, there was nothing orderly about them – as if they had been hurriedly thrown together.

Those at the bottom were handwritten and yellowed with age; others were far more recent, lined with print and interspersed with graphs and financial records. Extraordinarily, the papers went back a century or more – the oldest written in an archaic style that, at first, Dix struggled to follow. Eventually, though, the story they told was clear, as Dix leafed through testimonies, clippings, images, and contemporaneous reports.

Hauga, it seemed, had once been plagued by rains, its abundant crops threatened, the people faced with flooding and starvation. The religious elders of the High Council counselled patience – and faith – until such times that the clouds would lift and the sun reappear. "And lo, the light did burst from the leaden skies, and the people were saved."

With this vindication, the High Council of Hauga acquired greater status and power, building a palace from which they issued edicts and guided lives. The monks had promised light and it had come, and if ever needed, it would come again.

Dix turned over a page to find a beautifully drawn illustration of the familiar flaming sun – the one on the front of the book and on the monks' pendants. And in a floral caption that framed the image were the words, "It is written and it will be."

Dix flicked back through the pile of papers; this was the earliest mention he could find of the phrase that Sol had repeated in one form or another ever since they had met him.

When times were good, it appeared that tributes and donations flowed; when they were bad, the High Council doubled down, demanding faith and patience once more. Things usually resolved themselves. Weather patterns had a habit of repeating, and the High Council had a crack team of meteorologists, if the annual charts and yield projections were anything to go by. The records dated back decades.

But as Federation space expanded, even secluded outposts like Hauga couldn't remain unnoticed forever. The Axis apparently wasn't the first force to nibble away at Hauga's resources, but it was the latest and the nastiest, and the High Council had had no response. Or at least none that had worked. The planet was strangled, its trade appropriated, the people oppressed – and the promised light that had saved them before, that would save them all again, never came.

Dix felt a tap on his shoulder. It was Alard, who pointed over at Drake, now also asleep, with Sol curled up under one of his enormous arms.

"You got it open?" he said.

"I did. What do you make of this?" Dix showed Alard the papers.

He leafed through them, looking at those Dix had pulled out for particular attention. "Dunno. Typical old-world religious justification bullshit, looks like."

"Says the man who can listen to the trees and rocks talking."

"There's nothing supernatural about me. It's just genetics. And high-performance skill and innate intelligence, obviously."

"I don't get it," said Dix. "What's so special about all this? And what does it have to do with the kid, if anything?"

Alard took another sheaf of papers from the box and flicked through them. "These are different," he said, handing them one by one to Dix. "More recent, too." He pointed at the date stamps. "They're lab reports. Let's see – we've got density scans, enzyme markers, sequencing analysis, you name it."

Dix looked at the array of lines, codes, acronyms, numbers and letters. "How do you know all that?"

"When you've got weird DNA, you get used to tests like these. Had them since I was a kid. I used to freak the other kids out sometimes, going barefoot, smelling earth, shit like that, and then they'd take me out of school. I was forever in and out of labs – got to be best friends with the medics, they let me play Battlestars on their terminals. And after all the tests, turned out there was nothing wrong with me, I'm just a mutant." He grinned at Dix.

"These are medical reports about a person?"

"Not just one person, look." Alard pointed at the title line on various papers, where there was no name attached, save for the notation, 'Subject A,' 'Subject B,' down to 'Subject F.' "Six different subjects, people, whatever," said Alard. "And all pretty fucked-up, by the looks of it."

"How do you mean?"

"All these records go on for a few months, but then these end numbers – lowball readings – they basically mean you're dead. I think these are failed experiments."

"Experiments? What kind?"

"Can't tell from these. I'd need to see more background."

Alard turned over one last document, with the same densely plotted graphs and numerical read-outs. This was 'Subject G,' though that title had been lightly crossed out and 'Subject LB' written in instead. "This one isn't dead," he said. "I mean, don't get me wrong, if it's a person, they're freakier than me, but they're still breathing. Or they were when these records were taken."

"LB?" said Dix. "You don't think...?" Actually, he didn't know what to think. None of this made sense.

"What's with the screen?" said Alard, sidetracked, tapping it.

"Don't know, hadn't got there yet."

There was a slight hum, during which the screen lit up and then filled with circle-dumps, each with a different title and containing a hierarchy of enveloped information. Alard leaned over and touched a couple of the circles experimentally, and connecting lines appeared, opening folders as the lines moved, stacking document upon document – agreement upon agreement – lab report upon lab report – blueprint upon blueprint.

The whole story was there.

At some point in the previous twenty years, a faction of the High Council of Hauga had tired of waiting for the light.

The Axis forces had shown no sign of leaving. In fact, had entrenched their occupation and enforced a total blockade of the planet, taking out beans and grain for their home bases, and anything else they could strip from the land. And when the first signs of rare-galaxy minerals were unearthed, the High Council knew they would never leave. Hauga was simply too valuable to give up.

A zealous but dominant faction of the monks hatched a plan and did a deal. A plan which evolved over the years and went off course; and a deal which betrayed their own people.

"Look," said Alard, zooming in on construction plans. "This is the palace on Hauga. Been there a century or so, right? But then they added a hidden, underground research facility. Fifteen years ago."

A connecting line snaked to a folder with a memorandum of agreement between the commander of the Axis occupying force and the High Council.

"Axis knew nothing about it, but the monks needed to keep the lights and power on, in order to continue working. So they did a deal – the palace got its creature comforts, and the High Council agreed to keep the population in line with the standard, 'Trust us, wait for the light' bullshit. And of course, nothing ever changed and wasn't supposed to. The High Council was buying time."

"Explains why the locals seem to hate them so much. Buying time for what, though?"

Alard touched another circle and more connecting lines appeared. "Looks like they were trying to build a bomb, under the palace. See, these are payload calculations. But they couldn't figure out delivery or targeting. And then some fucker had a much nastier idea. Save the planet, get rid of the Axis completely. Honestly, these religious types. Made perfect sense to them, they get to live forever in paradise or somesuch. Everyone else can go fuck themselves. Their faithful flock included."

Dix saw the next connection and touched a circle on the screen. More folders unspooled. Research notes, lab reports, equipment invoices, life-support assessments, ground scans, aerial visuals, floorplans. On a series of landscape images, Dix recognised the dark terrain and the shadows thrown by the canyon walls.

'That's Vitlok," he said. "They built a second facility on an uninhabited planet. Hid it away, built another lab." The dates matched – ten years previously, just before the full Axis blockade took effect.

A cascade of personnel files tumbled out of another folder. Thirty monks appointed to the Vitlok outpost – monks with either bio-research or combat skills, but Haugan monks of the High Council nonetheless.

The fathers.

Dix and the others had counted twenty-seven bodies on Vitlok, in total. A natural death or two, or a re-posting, and that added up as well.

Connecting lines on the screen expanded a final set of circle-dumps, all with the same LB prefix.

"I'm not sure I want to know," said Alard, and Dix knew what he meant, but touched the info-folders open anyway.

The earliest images were of a baby in a white cot in a sterile room. After that there were more pictures as the child, the boy, grew older – Dix recognised some of the backdrops as the main hall in the monks' HQ on Vitlok. And, of course, he recognised –

"Is that the kid? Sol?" Vaskez had appeared at their shoulders, woken by their conversation and the flickering of the screen.

"Lightburst," said Alard. "That really is what they called him." He shook his head in disbelief, while Dix caught Vaskez up with what they had discovered.

She flicked through some of the papers and followed the trail on the screen. "I don't get it," she said. "What did they do?"

Alard was busy digging into pages of analysis – readings, graphs, overlays, theses, and conclusions – but Dix already had answers to the first part.

"They took a kid, an orphan, a few months old. Plenty of those available on Hauga, especially if you're a caring, religious order." He snorted at that. "Took a few kids, as it happens. They've always done it, going back decades, it's how they replenish their ranks. Make sure they've got the next generation trained up."

"The boy's a monk?" said Vaskez.

"Technically I suppose, yes. But that's not what they wanted this batch for."

"Batch?"

"They had seven kids – babies – and spirited them away nine years ago."

"To the shithole planet? I mean, the even more shithole planet than this one?" Vaskez corrected herself.

"Vitlok, right, where they had a state-of-the-art biochem lab. And then they started experiments. To complement those they'd already been doing in their underground palace-lab on Hauga."

"Experiments? On kids?" Even Vaskez looked shocked. "What sort of experiments?"

This was where Dix ran out of answers, and he nudged Alard, who was still running his finger along read-outs. "Al?"

Alard looked up from the screen and drew his fingers through his hair, shook his head as if clearing it. "Not a doctor, obviously. Biotech geneticist, whatever the fuck these shithead science-monks were. But from what I can tell, they've been messing around with mirror bacteria and genetic coding. Editing, splicing, adding, refining. Didn't always work. In fact, almost never worked – hence subjects A to F."

Alard laid out an overlapping series of images – six nameless children, all under a year old – each stamped with the word 'Unviable.'

Dix blinked at the unforgivable word.

"But then they got it right," said Alard. "Luck or final refinement, I don't know. Subject G remained stable and continued to do so. At some point, they gave him a name."

A final image appeared on the screen, under the title, 'Lightburst.' It was the boy currently sleeping in the crook of a smuggler's arm, just a few feet away.

"Not much of a name," said Dix.

"Doesn't pay to get too attached to your lab rat,"

said Alard. "And it seems to be more of a project name, rather than personal."

He pointed to a circle on the screen with a sun motif and the title, 'The Book of Light.' As he touched it, the connecting lines from all the buried, internal folders converged and lit the sun. The rays pulsed and shone.

"The instructions are in here," he said. "For the High Council, back on Hauga. Once they had taken receipt of Lightburst. It's what they've been waiting for, for the last ten years."

"Instructions? Like orders, you mean?"

"No. Well, kind of. Surgical notes for bone-marrow biopsies, spinal taps, serum tests. Protocols for sequence analysis. Guidance for nano-implant extractions. All sorts of nasty medical shit that you can do to a person. The sort of nasty shit that you might not survive."

Vaskez looked at him, uncomprehendingly.

"Don't you get it?" said Alard.

"Explain it to us like we're hard-ass troopers, not freaky science-nerd mutants," said Vaskez.

"The High Council have a big bomb. They've always had a big bomb, that they built under the palace on Hauga. But it's not big enough to get rid of the Axis. Not on its own. So they grew another weapon on a planet far, far away, and filled it full of horrible stuff that would evade immune systems and cause lethal infections. Nurtured it, looked after it, in their own twisted way, and then when it was finally mature and stable enough to transport, they arranged to bring the two together. Some final, invasive tweaks and extractions, mix it all up with a big old pile of explosives, and boom. Inhabitants of all stripes cleared out, once the infections have ripped their way through. The planet itself will be fine, after a few thousand years, though you still probably wouldn't want to drink the water."

"Kid's a dirty bio-bomb?" Vaskez sounded almost impressed at the scale of the horror. "A carrier?"

"The cleansing fire. Light brings freedom," said Dix, remembering things the abbot on Vitlok had said, that Sol had repeated. Phrases he couldn't possibly have known referred to him, or to his purpose.

At least, Dix hoped Sol didn't know. The alternative was even worse.

"You got it." said Alard. "The High Council doesn't give a shit. 'It is written and it will be,' all that nonsense. It's collective suicide for them − though you wouldn't bet against them having a secret getaway plan, another little bolthole like Vitlok. But for everyone else on Hauga, Sol and the inhabitants included, it's a big middle finger. Face it, if the monks get their hands on the kid they're going to − oh, what's the technical term?"

Alard looked across at the sleeping child, before he adapted the answer to his own rhetorical question. "They're really going to fudge sheep up," he said. "The mad fuckers."

Chapter 22

THEY MOVED after darkness had fallen, scurrying from the tunnel entrance, across the forecourt, to the relative safety of the overgrown fence. From there, they could hear the passing whine of vehicles and the distant mutter of patrolling guards.

Once through the fence, they knew the ditch would give them cover, but at some point they were going to have to make a break across open land for the woods beyond. At least in there, they would have an advantage – Alard – in case of pursuit. They had weapons now, but avoiding attention was the best strategy by far, if they wanted to make it back to the farm.

And there was no question that that was what they were going to do. They all agreed. Sol was coming with them, and they were all going to get off this planet.

Alard and Drake went first, pushing through the brambles and clearing the fence. Dix listened for the low whistle and then he and Vaskez followed, with Sol in between them, and then all five of them crouched low in the drainage ditch.

The nearest guards were several hundred feet away to their left, with the town checkpoint beyond. Coming in from the right was an access road, which curved away out of sight, obscuring any advance view of oncoming, town-bound vehicles.

"Can't see anything," whispered Vaskez, risking a popped head above the top of the ditch.

"I've got this," said Alard, both hands on the ground.

They all fell silent, trusting entirely that the geopath had their backs. And after a minute or two – time that hung heavy in the night air – when Alard signalled it was safe to move, they climbed out of the ditch at pace and didn't look back. Across the access road and then a wider highway, empty of traffic, keeping where they could to the shadows thrown by road signs and abandoned vehicles.

In the woods, they moved into the trees far enough to be hidden from the tangle of roads and the stationed guards. They gave it a few minutes and crouched down again, waiting for a shout, a searchlight, the sound of running troops, but none came and Dix relaxed. A little anyway.

Alard took point, Vaskez the rear, and they moved in close single file through the dark woodland. After a while, as their eyes adjusted, they could move faster, though still not quick enough for Dix's liking.

Alard could probably have sprinted through the night, however close the trees and uneven the ground. Whatever he thought about his skill, his mutation, he seemed to have an almost supernatural affinity with his surroundings. It was everyone else that was slowing *him* down, but he kept a steady pace they could all follow, flagging up detours and obstacles as they approached them.

Some hours later, it was hard to know how many, Alard called a halt.

"Recognise where we are?" he said.

Dix looked up at the dark tree canopy, and around to all sides. He could barely see more than five yards in front of him. "Obviously not."

"The road and house are through there." Alard pointed. "Where, you know…"

Where Vaskez had gutted two Axis guards, and they got two women killed, or worse. Yes, Dix knew.

"So?"

"It's worth another look," said Alard. "I'm not sensing anyone there."

"Look for what? We need to keep moving."

"Food, for a start. We've barely had anything to eat today. The kid must be starving. I know I am."

"The house is right on the road."

"I know, but nothing has been up or down since we've been in the forest. I'd have heard them. And we could do with a break."

It wasn't the worst idea. Sol hadn't complained once – had barely spoken – but he had to be tired and hungry. They were down to scraps and crumbs in the rucksack Ash had given them.

They emerged from the forest, with the row of abandoned cottages before them. A sharp moon threw shards of light around the edges, playing across the road. The broken windows and boarded doorways appeared as dark gaps. Thirty-six hours since they'd last been here? Seemed longer, and it was as forlorn as it had been in daylight.

The jeep was still there, though it had been moved a few yards to the side of the road. Of the two men Vaskez had killed, there was no sign. The dead pig from the front garden had gone too, probably butchered by now and on an Axis guards' barbecue.

The two women were no longer there, of course. Dix was relieved in a way, not to be finding bodies, but fearing that their fate had been settled the minute Vaskez had stepped out of the trees the first time.

The other body was still there – the man on the road by the jeep, already dead when things had gone down. The older woman's husband? Killed because he, too, got involved? A dark stain was visible on the road, but – like the jeep – the body itself had been moved.

They didn't see it until they were almost upon it – pinned to the front door of the cottage, kitchen knives hammered through the corpse's shoulders. The same red 'X' as on the other front doors now sprayed across this one, too. Whoever did it hadn't even adjusted for the body – just painted two diagonals across the wood-work, over thigh, stomach and upper arm. A final 'Fuck

You' from the Axis guards, who had found their slain fellow soldiers and carted off the women to their fate.

Sol gasped, and Dix wished more than anything that the boy hadn't seen that.

"The forces of darkness," he said. For once, that didn't seem over-exaggerated.

"It's all right, kid," said Drake, steering him away from the sight. "How about me and you go next door, see what we can find?"

Alard took up a position by the side of the road and crouched down – "I'm your early warning system," he said. "Be quick."

Dix and Vaskez took the man down from the door and wrapped him in a rug they found inside the house. They dug a shallow grave in the garden, where he'd grown crops and tended the family pig. Figured they owed him that, at least.

"Why d'ya think they left the jeep?" said Vaskez.

Dix wandered over for a look. "Flat tyre," he said, pointing at the rear. "Maybe the first guys shot it out by mistake when they were having their fun. They weren't the brightest sparks, and they'd been drinking. Next guys started it up, moved it, and then realised? Thought they'd come back for it later. It's not like anyone's going to steal it."

"Is that right?' said Alard, standing up and joining them. "Because there's a spare at the back and even I know how to change a wheel."

Drake and Sol returned emptyhanded from going through the other cottages. A quick look inside the family cottage – trashed and stripped by the guards – turned up nothing more than a handful of dry crackers in a top-shelf glass jar, which Drake gave to Sol.

"I don't know," said Dix. "We're trying to avoid Axis attention. Taking one of their jeeps seems like the opposite of that." He looked up and down the road. "We've been here too long already."

"I'm with Al," said Vaskez, who was already wrestling with the spare tyre. "This'll only take a few minutes."

"Think about it," said Alard. "It's two days on foot back to the farm, and we've got no food, apart from squirrel surprise, if we can catch any. It's what – forty, fifty miles? That's only two hours on the road in this, tops – nice and careful through the night. Farmhouse full of food when we get there."

"You say food…" said Drake. "I can still taste that stew, and not in a good way."

"Point stands," said Alard. "Quicker we get there, the better all round, I'd say."

"Tyre's on," said Vaskez, dusting her hands.

"Safer in the woods and mountains," said Dix. "What about patrols? Place is on high alert – every scum-sucker on the planet will be looking for us."

"Well, not us, exactly," said Alard. "At worst, they think it's two outlaw locals – you and Drake – involved in the mess at the bar. They'll be tearing the town apart, looking for you two. They don't know about the rest of us, or that we've fled for the sticks. And if they're on the hunt for the mystery weapon as well, they sure as hell don't know what they're looking for." He nodded at Sol, the very picture of a nine-year-old child and not the key to a biological nightmare. "I reckon we've still got the edge here. Just. If we get going now."

This was another of those 'listen to the sarge' moments for Dix. If you're not sure, and you don't have a good reason not to be sure, keep moving. That had always been the sarge's mantra. It was safer than prevaricating in an exposed position. And maybe they could mitigate the danger.

"How are you at night-driving, without lights?" Dix asked Vaskez.

"You mean there's another way?"

"And Al, you're up top, too. Early warning, right? And try to look like mean Axis guards, the pair of you."

"No one's going to think Al's a vicious mercenary," said Vaskez. "Look at him."

"Whereas you…"

"Have all the necessary attributes," said Vaskez, finishing his sentence and brandishing her rifle.

"Please try not to shoot anyone, if you don't have to," said Dix. "I realise it's a big ask."

They found blankets in the house, and Dix, Drake and Sol tucked themselves underneath and out of sight in the back of the jeep.

"Are we still camping?" said Sol, as he snuggled down in the floor well, with the empty canvas rucksack under his head.

"You got it, kid," said Drake, stretching out as best he could.

"It's not very comfortable."

"That's camping for you. Don't ever let anyone tell you otherwise. Now, hotels, that's a different story. There's this five-star place on Drexol with a low-gravity massage parlour, where the massage therapists have got three – "

"That's enough, Drake. Kid doesn't need to know about your disgusting hobbies." Vaskez looked back to check her cargo. "Right, let's roll."

Chapter 23

Dix tensed against the bumps in the back of the jeep. This was the second time in the last few days that he'd been bounced around in the back of an army vehicle. The last time he'd been on his way to interrogation and then transportation to a prison hulk. This time, the outlook was only slightly rosier.

Vaskez was taking the road surprisingly slowly, partly out of necessity, given the low visibility, especially while they were still shadowing the forest edge. Dix heard Alard call for a halt every ten minutes or so, as the geopath got down and checked the way ahead – and behind – for pursuers or patrols.

They only had one close call. A slap on Dix's shoulder from Alard, a hurried, "Keep down and quiet!" and then a series of sharp jolts as Vaskez took the jeep off-road and into the shadows. A few minutes later, a truck roared past, lights blazing. They let it disappear off, heading for town, and stayed hidden a while longer until Alard gave the all-clear. Vaskez bumped the jeep back up onto the road and the journey continued.

At some point, Alard reached back and lifted the blankets off them. Stars spread across an ink-black sky, and the road stretched ahead through wide, open countryside. As Dix's eyes adjusted, he recognised where they were.

"Heading into the valley," confirmed Alard. "There's nothing out here, and even if there is, we'll see it coming from miles away. Farm can't be too far."

They all sat up and stretched, as Vaskez picked up speed on the straight road under the starlight. "There," she said, eventually, and slowed the jeep, pulling in at the side of the road.

There was a dark smudge a long way in the distance that Dix thought must be the farm. A lighter surface heading to it from the road itself was the stone track along which they had manoeuvred the Star-Jumper using the pilot-pushers.

No lights from the farm, though Dix didn't think that was unusual. No power out here, and no flicker of fire or lanterns. The family must be long in bed.

"We're not driving further in?" said Drake.

Dix shook his head, and he could tell that Vaskez agreed. It's why she'd stopped in the first place. He hadn't even needed to suggest it.

"Don't want any surprises, do we?" he said. "Let's keep it nice and quiet, until we know that Ash doesn't have visitors. Guards could be there waiting, for all we know."

They took everything from the jeep, and Dix led them on a wide circuit towards the farm – approaching not from the access track but from side on, through open countryside.

"Careful," whispered Alard, as they climbed out of a sunken depression into a paddock. There were shadowy shapes ahead of them that looked like defensive earth mounds – until Dix crept closer and saw they were resting cattle, slumped on their sides.

He picked his way through, unnerved by their sheer bulk and immediacy – he'd encountered bigger beasts than this before, such as the whale sharks of Calisto, but they'd always been on the end of a harpoon and winch. How people could live with these things roaming free, sharing space, he'd never know.

Beyond the cattle was a stock fence, with the gable end of the farmhouse now in front of them. Everything was still and quiet.

They huddled at the gable wall, the only window on this side located high above them. Dix signalled – Drake and the boy to stay, the other three of them around to the front door. Vaskez and Alard either side, Dix to enter.

At this point – the silence enveloping, no outward sign of Axis guards – Dix was more concerned about startling a sleeping Ash and getting a shovel in the face or worse.

He lifted the latch and pushed at the door, and it

swung open. Took a swift look inside, withdrew, and then signalled for all three of them to enter. They went in, weapons raised.

There was no one in the downstairs room that served as kitchen and living space; maybe not surprising, it was the middle of the night.

Dix took the stairs, covered by Vaskez, to an upper floor they had not seen before. The rooms here were empty, too. Bedrooms, one for Ash and his wife, the other for their two girls. Dix pushed open the window in the far room and whistled down to Drake.

"No one home," he said. "Come on in."

"What do we think?" said Vaskez, as they gathered downstairs in the gloom. "Axis paid them a visit?"

Alard looked for candles and matches, while Drake went through the cupboards searching for food. There was some hard bread and more of the dried meat Ash had given them, and rows of glass jars with pickled vegetables. Under the counter, in racks, were trays of root vegetables, potatoes and onions.

"Fire's cold," said Dix, putting his hands on the hearth. "No smell of smoke. That wasn't lit yesterday."

He looked around at the room – at the clean, stacked plates, the ordered cupboards, the bare dining table in the middle where they'd all shared a meal not so long ago. "They didn't leave in a hurry," he said. "Not interrupted, anyway. No signs of a struggle. Wherever they went, they tidied up first. Even swept the fireplace."

Vaskez took in what he said and disappeared

upstairs again. When she came down, she shook her head. "No clothes, no personal items," she said. "Beds are made – I didn't notice before. They've packed and gone."

"Doesn't make any sense. Where would they go?"

They pulled up chairs at the table and shared out some of the food. Drake ladled out water from a covered barrel.

Five, six days max, Ash had said. That's when he'd see them back here, after dropping the kid, mission completed. Using the jeep on the way back, they'd done it in four, so they were early.

But why would Ash have taken off with his family, knowing that they were due any time now? Unless he also knew that Axis guards were on their way? That his cover had been blown? Which meant maybe theirs had, too? And here they were, sitting around a dining table, waiting to be picked off.

Dix looked up from his hunk of stale bread and looked around the room again, trying to put himself in Ash's shoes. Ash was an agent of the Federation, living on the edge in hostile territory. He was in deep, with a family as cover, but he must have had a back-up plan. A getaway, if things ever went south. A plan to save his family. A plan it looked like he'd enacted.

Drake was now on his knees at the fireplace, trying to coax flames from damp kindling. "Soon get this place warm for you, kid," he said.

Dix's eyes ranged across the chimney breast, where a line was strung from side to side. Ash's wife had hung dried herbs from there in bunches. She'd used some in the soup she had served.

In between hung a dangling cord, strung with something else – Dix couldn't make it out, until Drake's fire caught and threw a glow upwards. Then he could see what it was – what *they* were. Two chip-tags, hanging together. The ones Dix had carried ever since that day on the mining planet – one taken from the sarge's body, the other given to him by Milo Kantor.

And Dix knew right there, right then, what Ash's plan had been.

"Oh shit," he said. "Barn!"

He ran out of the door without explanation, with Vaskez close behind him. Drake and Alard looked puzzled, but followed them across the courtyard.

Dix strained at the large barn doors, and the others joined in, pushing them around against the side. Panting with the exertion, they stood there in a line, looking into the barn.

"Uncle Drake?" said Sol. "Where's your spaceship gone?"

Chapter 24

Drake was incandescent. He covered Sol's ears and let loose a string of highly inventive profanities largely avoiding the f-word.

"We're totally fudged," said Alard, and Dix thought that just about covered it.

"He never had any intention of waiting," said Vaskez, bitterly. That was a good call, too, though they'd probably never know. "Said the job was done, got the codes from Galloway, and away he went." She kicked the barn door in frustration. "Absolute scum-sucking toe-rag."

Was that how it had gone down? Dix thought back. Had there been any indication that Ash was out to shaft them? If there had been, they'd missed it. He'd seemed genuine.

Or was it just a golden opportunity, too good to miss, for a man who'd been stationed clandestinely in harsh conditions on a horrible planet for seven years?

He'd talked a good talk about service to the Federation – about duty – but then one night a means of escape had literally landed in his backyard. All Ash had needed to do – a man whose job was lying – was tell one lie to Galloway and he'd be able to take his family away from ever-present danger.

Under the circumstances, Dix wondered if he might have been tempted to do the same? But deep down, he knew he wouldn't. Leave troops under fire in the field? Abandon people on the same side as him? That wasn't in Dix's make-up.

"Could he fly it, though?" said Alard, still grasping at straws. Dix half-expected him to start clawing at the hay bales, see if Ash had somehow hidden the ship from them. "Could anyone, except you?" meaning Drake.

"He could have got it back out on the pilot-pushers," said Drake. "You've seen how that works, and he knew his way around them. With comms help and the codes, he could get it in the air again. With an auto flightpath enabled, sure – he could fly it."

"I thought it was supposed to be hard?" said Alard. "Like you're some hot-shot pilot that we had to have to get us here?"

"It's hard if you want to fly in undetected," snapped Drake. "It's hard if you don't want to crash and burn while being scanned and tracked and shot at."

"I'm just saying. He said he was a Fed agent. Not a pilot."

"The clue's in the job title," said Dix. "Secret agent. Given to hiding things. Who knows what sort of training he had?"

"What does it matter, anyway?" said Drake. "Bastard's not here, and my lovely Star is gone." It was his turn to kick the door now. "She's been with me for fifteen years. Everything I own is on that ship." Another kick. "My gear, access to my funds. My weapons!"

"Our way out of here." Another hefty kick to the barn door by Vaskez.

Dix took control, before emotions spiralled further. They closed the barn doors, moved back to the farmhouse, and took stock. Dix made sure they all had something to eat and drink, and found a couple of blankets for Sol and tucked him up in front of the fire. It had been a long night so far for all of them, and the kid was out on his feet.

There were still a few hours until daylight. They had shelter, food and, for now, relative safety. So, what did they know? Start with Ash.

"He must have got the codes from Galloway, to be able to take the ship?"

"We know," said Vaskez. "Your point?"

"Which meant he either lied to Galloway about the job being done – and she didn't ask too many questions, or even want to confirm it with one of us? Or – him and Galloway had already cooked this up between them? Once we were off on our little delivery run, he was free to leave with his family?"

Vaskez was silent, though she drummed her fingers on the dining table while she thought it through.

"We weren't ever supposed to leave," she said, finally.

"That can't be right," said Drake. "We had a deal!"

"We had a deal with a black-ops spook," said Alard. "The sort of people who are famous for their trustworthiness and integrity. And then when we got here, we had another deal with an undercover agent, whose skillset is hiding inconvenient truths from people. Dix is right, I think we've been played."

Drake looked like he was about to pop with indignation again. "But that's just so – wrong. You can't run an operation – a deal – like that. You've got to have *some* trust."

Dix could hear the disbelief in his voice. It came to something when a black-market smuggler complained about a lack of trust between people. But a deal was a deal to a smuggler – you had to deliver or you'd be out of business, or worse.

It was the same in the army. You had to trust that your mates, your unit, and even your superiors had your back, or else it all fell apart. And if it fell apart, you could die. Right now, Dix realised that he trusted the three other people in the room, however flawed, more than the word of a Federation army major. If Galloway *was* a major. Or even Federation army.

Vaskez was rapidly coming to the same conclusion, and was as furious as Drake, though there was something else in her tone, too – the slow dawning of institutional betrayal. Unlike the others, Vaskez had volunteered to be here – for her own reasons – and had still been hung out to dry. That had to hurt.

"There's no help coming," she said. "We're on our own. Even if Galloway didn't know what Ash was going to do, she didn't stop him. She let him sail on out – helped him, even – and left us stranded. She must know that's what she's done. It's not a mistake."

But why? That was the only outstanding question for Dix.

As far as the Federation was concerned, no one knew if their mission had been a success or not. Not Ash, and not Galloway – though Ash might have told her that all had gone to plan. But she hadn't asked for evidence that the kid and the book had been handed over. There had been no oversight. Ash, her man on the ground, had stayed put, when he could have easily accompanied them and made sure the exchange happened.

If it was so hugely important for Galloway to get the Haugans their mystery weapon – well, once her handpicked team was on the planet and in play, she hadn't made much of an effort to see the mission through from her end.

None of that made sense. And it might never. It went back to the 'trust' thing. Perhaps, in the end, they had to take Major Galloway at her word.

Vaskez aside – and who knew what demons drove her – the three of them, Dix, Alard and Drake, had been up to their necks in trouble and had grasped at her mission as a way to save themselves. Dix's attributes for such a mission? Because he was "available," she'd said. "Expendable couriers" she'd called them.

She'd told them there was a window of opportunity to get a weapon to Hauga. She didn't know what it was or how it worked. "Let's get it to Hauga and see what happens," she had said, before waving them off.

Maybe that was all it ever was? A sudden opportunity, a chance, a gamble?

Probably, Galloway had all sorts of secret irons in the fire – ops, missions, assignments, tasks, plans, both short- and long-term? That was how spooks operated. Some plans would work, some wouldn't. Some operatives would be protected – Ash had spent seven years on Hauga, reporting back. And others were expendable.

Galloway heard rumours about a weapon of mass destruction, saw the chance to do a quick bit of mischief-making in a sector the Federation was interested in, and cast around for a crew.

And what do we have here? A busted trooper, a runaway pathfinder, and a captive smuggler-pilot – plus a hard-ass special operative, hard to command but eager to serve. They just fell into her lap, and she rolled the dice with them. Great if it worked, not a disaster if it didn't. No connections, no blowback – whether they completed the job or not.

Dix had thought before that it was all a game to people like Galloway. Now he was sure of it.

"So, we're on our own," said Alard. "Ideas?"

"Find Ash and Galloway, kill them both," said Vaskez.

"It's good to have goals," said Alard, "but I'm thinking more short-term. Like, avoiding being killed ourselves. It's only a matter of time before we're tracked down."

"No one knows we're here," said Dix. "And Ash managed to stay out of trouble for years."

"I am *not* living here," said Drake. He shuddered as he looked around.

"Not forever," said Dix. "But while we figure out a way to get off this planet."

"We need transport," said Vaskez. "The flying kind. There's a spaceport, right? We're going to have to try and steal something. Drake, you can fly anything?"

"Within reason. Won't know until I try."

"Let me get this right." Alard was counting off on his fingers. "We're going to hide away on Bare-Ass Farm and eat nettles, while Vaskez sneaks into a spaceport guarded by Axis psychos and steals a spaceship that Drake might or might not be able to fly?"

"Sounds like a plan!" Vaskez had cheered up no end at the thought of action.

"Yeah, well, I don't share your confidence. We should leave now while we can."

"And go where? And do what?" said Dix. "I've got a better idea."

They all looked at him. "You keep saying that," said Vaskez. "But, I'll be honest, all your ideas have been garbage so far. Let's hear it."

Dix was still formulating the full plan in his mind, but he kept that to himself. One thing at a time. And if it didn't work, no harm done, and they could go instead with Vaskez's suicidal assault on a heavily armed Axis spaceport. Or run for the hills, like Alard wanted to do.

"Ash said he had comms gear," said Dix. "Remember? Hidden somewhere on the farm. It's how Galloway contacted him."

"That's right!" said Alard. "An outbuilding? He must have used it to speak to Galloway to get the codes."

Drake's eyes widened with hope, before narrowing again. "What good will it do us? We can't broadcast an emergency call, we'll bring the whole Axis force down upon us the minute they see where the signal's coming from. We need a bio-marker to place a person-to-person, and we don't have Galloway's – and she's ditched us anyway. All my contacts are on Star, and Ash has got those now. Who are we going to call?"

Dix got up from the table and moved towards the fireplace, stepping over the sleeping Sol. He untied the chip-tags from the hanging string, and dangled them in front of the team.

"I know someone," he said. "Someone who might be able to help."

Chapter 25

THEY CAUGHT A FEW HOURS' sleep until dawn, when it was light enough to start looking properly for Ash's hidden comms gear.

Alard had continued to grouse about their situation. He didn't want to stay at the farm a moment longer than they had to.

"Too much space to cover," he said, by way of explanation, meaning the wide, open valley. "It's hard to know what's out there. What's coming."

"You'll figure it out," Dix had said. "We trust you, just buy us some time."

That didn't seem to calm him down; Alard grumbled indistinctly, wiping sweat from his brow.

Having scoured the barn, they moved on to the few other buildings within the farm's perimeter – grain store, chicken shed, tool lock-up – and after half an hour remained empty-handed.

"Took it with him?"

"Maybe." Although Dix thought not. If it was this well-hidden, he'd probably just left it. It's not like he'd need it on Drake's Star-Jumper.

"Where haven't we looked? There isn't anywhere else, only the outhouse." Alard meant the long-drop toilet in a shed behind the farmhouse. They'd all had cause to use it, and all had come out muttering.

Outbuilding. Outhouse.

It *was* the one place Axis guards probably wouldn't look, if they were turning over the farm for illicit tech.

"You've got to be kidding?" said Alard.

But Dix guessed right, having braved the smell for a closer look inside the shed.

A loose board shifted slightly underfoot as he stood contemplating the raised seat over the hole. He held his breath, leaned down and prised it loose. Once it was up, two more came away easily, and there in a cavity beneath the floor was a heavy, square box wrapped in an oiled, canvas bag.

A field-use comms-cube, nuke-chipped for power, satellite-enabled and with enough piggyback and cloaking capability to re-route and hide incoming and outgoing calls and messages – at least, if used sparingly. This was serious tech. If Axis guards had ever found it, Ash would have been killed on the spot – his family, too, no doubt.

"And I went to all that trouble with Star, retrofitting my weapons cache," said Drake. "Should have just hidden them all in the bog."

They unpacked the cube on the dining table and

Dix, with crossed fingers, hit the power button. As it booted up, he turned the chip-tags over in his hand.

You could call anyone, if you had their personal bio-marker, and that information was embedded on most chip-tags. It was always on military tags, along with every other record that a trooper needed – or that the Federation required to identify its personnel.

Civilian tags were different. You could pick and choose what you put on there. Some were simple calling-cards; others might contain full resumés or biographical information. Dix thought Milo Kantor's chip-tag – the one he'd been given in the prison cell – would be somewhere between the two.

But what he was counting on was the bio-marker – the doodah that enabled person-to-person contact – because what was a black-market trader doing, handing out chip-tags, unless he wanted people to contact him? Milo Kantor was in the business of taking calls and doing deals. And Dix hoped he'd bite.

"You met this guy in a cell?" said Alard. "One ear, arrested for arms dealing. Sounds legit."

"It was more like one and a half ears, and it's the only shot we have," said Dix.

"And why would he help us?"

"I don't know that he will. But I'm hoping information is as valuable to him as cargo."

"What information?"

Dix had given this some thought. What would a dodgy black-market trader be interested in? And he thought he had the answer.

"I'm thinking, tell him about Vitlok," said Dix. "There's a ton of abandoned equipment and weapons on that planet, just waiting for someone to go and help themselves."

"That isn't a totally stupid idea," said Alard. "One of your better ones, I'd say." He looked around for support, but didn't get it from all quarters.

"We're doing business with black-market snakes now, are we? Didn't he arm the other side in your last little skirmish?" Vaskez looked disgusted. Dix could see it was hard for her to accept the new reality – that they were cast out from Federation protection and reliant upon the kindness of criminals.

"We're in the business of not dying," said Alard. "Call the sucker up."

Dix slotted Milo Kantor's chip-tag into the cube, and the machine whirred while the various quantum entanglements and trans-system handshakes did their thing.

"What's the play?" said Vaskez, while they waited to see if anyone was home *chez* Kantor. If he was still tucked up in a cell somewhere, they could be out of luck.

"Transport out of here," said Dix. "If he can't help us himself, he must know a guy who knows a guy. Right, Drake?"

"I don't know why you're asking me, I'm strictly small-time. And I never touch arms. Well, never sell them anyway. Attracts entirely the wrong sort of attention, and I'm rather attached to my ears."

"So, we fly out of here? Then what? Go where? Because somehow, I think our army careers are over."

"Still working on that one," said Dix.

Vaskez sucked in a breath. "Seems to me," she said, "that you're making this up as you go along."

"It's called 'flexible response' in the manuals."

Vaskez wasn't mollified. "What about the kid? We can't leave him with Ash and family anymore – that was your plan, right? And things have changed. The kid's dangerous. I mean, seriously dangerous. Could-go-bang-at-any-minute dangerous, and you want to tuck him up next to us in a getaway ship?"

"That's not exactly right," said Alard. "He's got nasty shit in him, sure, but it's been carefully constructed. I mean, those monks were evil, but they weren't mad. It's all inert until extracted, mixed and blown up."

"Extracted? They were going to operate? Cut the kid open?"

"Far as I can tell? I did say they were evil. Point is, the notes said he was 'stable for transport,' like he was an object, poor kid. Primed, but not fully armed, if you like. We can take him with us."

"What if you're wrong, doctor?" Vaskez gave the last word a dismissive spin.

"Look, I'm doing my best here," said Alard. "If I'm wrong, then we all die. Horribly, I might add. But we probably do if we stay here as well, so what's the alternative? Don't tell me you want to leave the kid behind?"

Vaskez looked at the sleeping child by the fire. Caught Drake's eye, who was giving her a look and shaking his head.

"No," she said, reluctantly. "Fuck's sake, all this hassle, this is why I don't have kids."

Drake laughed. "Sure, that's the reason. You don't have kids because you're a terrifying, bad-ass soldier with an attitude problem."

Vaskez was nothing if not predictable. Instead of a glare and an objection, that got a high-five with Drake and a "Hell, yeah I am!" Then she turned serious again. "Fine, the kid comes, too. This friend of yours better come through, Dix."

"I wouldn't say friend, exactly."

The comms cube crackled. "Then what would you say, sport?" said a voice. "Who is this, interrupting my spa-time? It had better be good."

After a brief pause, the vid-screen resolved itself, to show a bare-chested man in a robe sitting in a lavishly tiled steam room. There was a chink of glasses in the background and a stifled laugh. The man peered forward, looking into a hand-held, checking out who had called him.

"Kantor?" said Dix. "Milo Kantor? It's – "

"Dix!" said the man, in delight. "Trooper Dix from Calisto, as I live and breathe. Never forget a face. And you're still alive! Now, don't tell me – striking a superior officer, disobeying an order in the field, wasn't it? How did you get away with that?"

"It's a long story," said Dix. "And you're no longer

in prison, unless they've changed since I was last in a cell?"

"Negotiations were ultimately successful, Dix, what can I say? Kept the rest of the ear, too. Just a big misunderstanding. Now then, sport, what can I do for you? I've got a fresh consignment of Paxo battle-spice, if that's your thing? Keeps you awake and alert for a week, just the thing for you trench-fighters they tell me."

"Hurry it up, Dix," growled Vaskez, tapping her wrist. "Every second counts, remember?"

"And who are your charming companions?" said Kantor, catching sight of Vaskez and Drake, leaning in behind Dix. "Goodness me, quite the units, aren't they? No point me throwing in some Bulko protein powder is there, although it is on offer if you're interested?"

"Kantor, listen," said Dix. "We haven't got much time. This line won't be secure for long. We need emergency transport out of here, asap."

"And where is here?"

"Hauga, it's a planet in the – "

"Hauga? Oh, you don't want to go there, sport, not a nice place at all. Crawling with Axis. Very nasty rules and regs, no place for a law-abiding trooper like yourself." Kantor smiled at his little joke.

"Tell us something we don't know," hissed Dix. "We're stuck here and need out. Can you help us or not?"

"Who's we? How many?"

"Five people." Dix kept it vague. "Immediate extraction. Long story. Very short on time."

"Interesting," said Kantor. "Also, extremely dangerous. You know the planet's blockaded? No official way in or out? That's not an easy job. And I'm guessing you're off-piste, shall we say? Not on official Federation business, or you wouldn't be calling me?"

"Can you do it or not, trader man?" said Vaskez, leaning into the screen. "Because time's a-ticking and if you can't, we have to run."

"Ooh, I like her," said Kantor. "Nice and direct. As it happens, I know a guy who can put a little extraction package together for you."

Of course he did.

"But it won't be cheap. Especially as, apparently, we're not 'friends exactly.'" Kantor had a steelier tone now he was in trader mode. "And last time I checked, Fed soldiers didn't get paid a whole lot. So, what have you got for me, Trooper Dix from Calisto?"

Dix looked at the others. It all hinged on this.

"What would you say," he said, "if I knew where you could lay your hands on a large amount of weaponry, plus tech gear from a fully equipped, state-of-the-art bio-med lab, and the coordinates for a secret planetary stronghold?" Dix looked around the room. "I could even throw in some jars of homemade pickled vegetables."

Kantor leaned forward. "I'm listening."

Chapter 26

The deal was done, the arrangements made. Now all they had to do was wait.

It was mid-morning and Kantor had promised wheels-down on Hauga in eight hours, which was plenty of time to sit in a farmhouse awaiting a visit with extreme prejudice by Axis forces.

"Who have no reason to patrol out this far," pointed out Dix.

"Who are nasty buggers who like to terrorise isolated properties," countered Alard, still visibly nervous.

That was a fair point, and Dix and Vaskez prepped for possible contact, starting with a weapons check.

Their total arsenal stood at three assault rifles and a handgun, taken from the Axis guards at the house; the two hunting knives Vaskez carried; plus an assortment of other knives and sharp farming implements in Ash's barn. Dix recognised the long handle and wicked, curving blade of a scythe, as Vaskez practiced slashing it around.

"I've no idea what any of these other things do," she said. "But if you feed a goon in this end" – pointing at a circular metal drum with jagged teeth and a crank handle – "I think you get minced goon out of the other."

"He's not going to agree to be fed in though, is he?"

"No, good point, I'd have to kill him first. With this?" Vaskez hefted a four-foot-long wooden frame embedded with six-inch spikes above her head, testing it for weight. Dix actually could see her going into battle brandishing that – it was very her – but hoped it wouldn't come to it.

"Al, you want to shift the jeep, hide it in the barn?" said Dix. He'd remembered it was still parked by the side of the road, a few hundred yards from the farm. No point advertising their presence. "And maybe check the road, see what you can – ?"

He still didn't know what the right word was, for the geopath's abilities. See? Hear? Feel? All of those?

Vaskez sent Alard on his way with an undulating 'woooo' noise and fluttering fingers, and Alard gave her a companionable finger in return.

No doubt about it, they were a pretty tight crew now.

Dix headed back to the farmhouse, thinking about closing the shutters on the lower windows and checking vantage points from upstairs, just in case. He didn't love the idea of having to defend the house with such limited means.

Drake came out to meet him. "Kid's asking questions," he said. "I don't know what to tell him. Maybe you can talk to him?"

Sol was inside, in front of the fire, tossing his softball from hand to hand. He was getting better at it though, truthfully, was starting from a very low base. You still wouldn't put him on your team.

"Dix," he said, "we're not going to see the fathers after all, are we?"

Might be useless at catch, but the kid certainly had a way of getting to the point.

"No," said Dix, sitting with him, cross-legged on the floor. "I'm sorry we've had to keep moving like this. I know it's been hard, but this place is – dangerous."

He picked his words carefully. Dix was sure that Sol knew nothing of what was in the damn book – the papers and records, the story of a stolen life. It really ought to stay that way. How much could a young boy be expected to understand? Especially one from whom the truth had always been hidden.

"The forces of darkness?" said Sol. "The ones who came before?"

"Something like that," said Dix. "Bad men who want to catch us."

"But why, Dix? Can't the fathers help us?"

How could he explain that there were bad men on both sides? Dix wasn't sure he could. Not in a way that Sol might understand.

"I'm sorry, but we can't rely on the fathers to help us," he said. "We have to leave this place. All of us. It's the only way to keep you safe."

Sol pondered this for a moment. "I'm coming with you?" he said. "You, and Al, and Uncle Drake and Auntie Vaskez?"

"That's right, kid. Is that OK with you?"

Not that he had a choice, but it seemed important to ask – to give the boy some agency. This kid, who they'd plucked from one hostile planet and brought to another, deserved better.

Sol paused again, then said, "You read *The Book of Light*, didn't you, Dix?" It was a straight question, not an accusation. Dix supposed he'd seen them poring over the documents in the tunnel. It was still in its leather satchel, hanging from a chair by the dining table.

"I did. The father in town – the one I went to see – he gave me a key." Which was truth-adjacent, but the best that Dix could do on the fly.

"Then you've seen it!" Sol clapped his hands, as though that settled it. "It is written and it will be, Dix. That's what the fathers always say. If I'm coming with you, it must be written. Isn't that right?"

Dix glanced sideways at Drake, who shrugged. And Dix – grateful for the naïve acceptance of an unworldly nine-year-old boy – told the lie that might just save his life.

"Sure kid," he said. "You know it." He reached for the satchel and patted it. "It is written."

Dix hated himself for even saying the words, but they seemed to satisfy Sol, who went back to his ball, bouncing it against one of the walls.

Alard drove the jeep up to the farm and they put it in the barn, hiding it in one of the empty animal pens at the rear. Ash had let them all out before he'd scarpered – they'd come across the cattle on their way in, and there were chickens scratching in the dirt all around the buildings.

"Nothing doing out there," said Alard.

"Let's hope it stays that way."

"How long do you reckon?"

Dix came out of the barn and squinted at the sun. "Few more hours yet. Three maybe?"

"Fine, I'll go back to the road, keep watch. I still don't think we should be waiting here at the farm. I don't like it."

"I know, you've made your point. But it's my call. We prepare, and we wait."

Alard shrugged and left, and Dix was left with his call, hoping he'd made the right one. He'd never thought about leadership much before – the decisions his officers, or even the sarge, had had to take in the field from day to day. Truthfully? Being responsible for other people's lives sucked, but he seemed to be in charge whether he liked it or not.

Dix was still in the farmhouse, filling rucksacks with food and produce, when Alard thundered in a while later, shouting, "We've got company! Four, five miles out."

"What are we looking at?"

"Can't tell, exactly. It's not vehicles. Not on foot either. Steady, rhythmic. Horses, maybe?"

Hauga was nothing if not full of surprises. "Friendly horses?"

"Haven't you noticed, Dix? Nothing friendly about this planet. Whoever they are, going on progress, we've got about forty minutes until we find out."

Action stations then.

The farmhouse was easier to defend, but it was small and there was nowhere to go if cornered. The barn was better – a lot more places to hide and move, with different vantage points, and a couple of rear exits to bust out from if necessary. That's where they'd stash the boy.

"You go with Drake and Alard, all right?" said Dix. "Quiet as a mouse."

"Is it another game?" said Sol.

"It's called hide and seek, kid. It's a great game. You're going to be doing the hiding, and you don't come out until I say so, OK?"

"All right, Dix." The boy skipped off with Drake, who took the satchel and book with him, too. "They'll have to come through me," he said as he left – not the first time the big man had stepped up. Impressive, for someone with no Federation skin in the game. Someone who might have skipped out on them at any time, given that Dix didn't doubt for one minute that Drake – the resourceful smuggler he was – couldn't have made a go of it, even on Hauga. But he hadn't.

He'd stayed, and would now stand as last line of defence, if it came to that.

Dix gave Alard a rifle, the handgun, and a rueful look. The geopath had been right, it was always going to come to this. Maybe they should have left after all, hidden out in the country somewhere? But he'd made the call, and here they were. "Don't look so worried," said Dix. "What's the worst that could happen?"

They looked each other in the eye for an instant, and then both laughed. "Fuck it," said Alard, as he turned to leave. "Just as we were having such a lovely time."

There were still a few tricks Dix reckoned they could play. Use the farmhouse as a decoy, for a start. Put the fire out, leave some food and plates on the table, door open – make it look like they had left in a hurry. Dix scuffed his feet up and down the ground between the house and stone track that led out to the road, hoping to add some texture to the deceit.

Vaskez came out of the barn carrying a coil of rope and a bucket, and dragging the farming implement she had found. The long, flat, spiked board left grooves in the dirt as she passed Dix.

"I'll take the house," she said. "Upstairs window gives us some height over the courtyard." She saw Dix's quizzical look at the gear. "Little surprise if they get too nosey." Then she patted her rifle. "Bigger surprise if they really piss me off."

That left Dix to find a hidden, flanking position outside house and barn. He took up a post behind two wooden water butts at the edge of the courtyard, dragging over a couple of lengths of corrugated iron, and placing them as if they'd been stacked and abandoned. That would have to do.

So, possibilities?

Were they going to get out of this without a fight? Unlikely.

How long until Kantor's ship touched down? Unknown. Could be within the hour, could be never.

On the face of things, Dix didn't like their odds. Then again, he'd beaten the odds before. It was only dumb luck he wasn't serving out a death sentence in chains on Arcana Minor.

There was a loud whistle for attention – Alard, outside the barn, on his knees, hands on the ground. "Incoming!" he shouted, before getting to his feet, heading inside and pulling the huge door behind him. Vaskez signalled from the house doorway and retreated inside, and Dix crouched down, out of sight behind the barrels.

They were set; they could do no more.

Several long minutes later, the sound of hooves on stone track got louder and closer. It was still and quiet in the yard, and no sign of life in house or barn – wherever the others were, Dix hoped they would stay well hidden. Their best chance lay in avoidance, not contact.

The horses were in the courtyard now and had come to a halt. Dix risked a slow, cautious peep around a corner of his shelter.

The riders – six of them – had their backs to him, twenty feet away, farmhouse to their left, barn in front of them. They dismounted, their robes flapping around their knees. Dix saw rifles slung on backs, and knife-sheaths strapped to calves as they stretched their legs. They dropped their hoods in turn, revealing close-shaven heads, and drank from water bottles, while the horses shifted their feet in the dirt.

Monks. Not Axis guards.

That was unexpected, but what did it mean?

Dix shuffled forward on his belly, looking for a better vantage point, needing to see how it played out before committing himself. Crossed his fingers that Vaskez was doing the same. Last thing they needed now was for her to go batshit assault commando. Not until they knew more about the threat.

Ignoring the house, four of the monks approached the barn and pulled the doors wide open. Dix could see beyond them into the gaping space – the piled hay bales, the farm machinery, the wooden stalls, the steps to the upper level. No sign of Drake, Alard and Sol.

The two remaining monks conferred. "It's gone," said one, his flat voice echoing across the courtyard.

Had they been hoping to find a spaceship there? Dix knew that feeling.

"Too late," said the other. He sounded anguished. "We're too late."

"Patience, father," said the first monk. He turned to look around the courtyard and Dix saw his face and knew who it was – the younger monk from the bar in town. The muscle, Dix had thought at the time. And in charge here, it seemed.

He walked over to the farmhouse and peered through a window, noticed the half-open door. He turned and looked intently at the ground, stooping to examine the scuffed trail that Dix had tried to lay. And then he walked slowly towards the barn, seemingly following another trail that led towards the closed doors and disappeared inside.

Tracks, Dix realised. Faint but visible – tyre tracks from the jeep. And footprints, here and there – two larger sets, one smaller.

The monk straightened up and addressed the others. "They're still here," he said. "There's nowhere else for them to go. Be careful. But find the boy and kill the rest."

Chapter 27

At a silent signal from the young monk, two of the fathers peeled off towards the first of the outbuildings beyond the barn. Two more headed for the barn, and the leader motioned for the remaining one to follow him to the house.

"Kill the rest" was unambiguous. Dix had seen steel and intransigence in the older monk's demeanour at the meet. No surprise the younger one was cut from the same cloth, tailored by the same asshole. Seemed they weren't getting out of here without a fight, after all.

They had one advantage – the monks didn't know who or how many they were, or what they were capable of. Likely didn't know they were trained soldiers, if the older monk's attitude in the bar had been any guide – dismissive of them as mere hired-hand smugglers.

That gave them an initial edge. Vaskez could take care of herself. Drake, Alard and Sol should be buried deep in the barn; it would take time to unearth them.

That left the other two to Dix – and taking away two from six would at least make the odds even. It wasn't much of a plan, but it was a start.

Dix snake-crawled out, away from farmhouse and barn, and once he was out of direct sight, he set off on a crouching run to the farm's perimeter fence. He hugged it until he reached the back of the chicken shed, where he listened for a moment.

Low voices on the other side – Dix heard, "I'll start over there" – and then the creak of a door opening. Single footsteps on the boards as someone entered the shed.

Dix inched down the side and risked a look around. One monk was walking away, intent on the other buildings; one was inside the shed.

Two shots, he could take them both out. But the noise would alert the others and give away what little advantage they currently had.

Old-school then.

The distant monk disappeared inside the tool store, as Dix stood to the side of the chicken shed threshold, rifle butt raised. As the other monk emerged, Dix struck with a heavy, brutal crack to the head. The monk went down in a heap, and Dix struck again before he could so much as moan, smashing into his temple and the side of his face. Bunching the stunned monk's robes around his neck – eyes white, bloodied head lolling – Dix dragged him inside the shed, closed the door on him, and darted back to the cover of the perimeter fence.

He made up ground towards the tool store, approaching from its rear, and through slats in the fence saw the other monk standing out in the open.

The monk called, "Father?" and, when there was no response, the monk tensed, in two minds, before walking slowly away, towards the closed door of the chicken shed.

Dix, now behind the outhouse, crept around its far side, unlatched the door, and stepped back again, hidden, before giving a couple of sharp bangs on the wooden boards with his rifle butt. At the noise, the monk whirled around. Dix shrank back against the side of the outhouse and waited.

Footsteps approached. There was a double click as the door latch rose and fell, and the door was slowly pulled open towards the side where Dix was hiding, giving him cover. He saw the monk's side and back as he entered, and heard another tentative, "Father?"

Two quick steps in, Dix could see the monk was distracted by the smell – one hand to his mouth and nose – as he clubbed him from behind. The monk moved at the last moment and the blow glanced off his ear. He half-turned, with a roar of pain, and stumbled against the raised sides and seat of the long-drop toilet. Dix hit him again and then grabbed the monk by hair and robe, upending him.

He went head first into the hole, a panicked shout muffled by the narrow confines of the dug-out latrine – shoulders pinned, feet scrabbling for purchase. Dix grabbed his legs and shoved him in, tighter, up to his thighs, and the shout became a choked gurgle.

Shit way to go, but Dix hadn't chosen this fight or its stakes.

He moved quickly to the back of the nearby barn, where a rough, wooden hatch was propped open. Straws of hay lay on the ground, pulled through when someone had exited this way. Sol? The others? Dix scanned the ground and fields behind him, but there was no sign of anyone.

Inside, though, he could hear voices – two more monks, still searching, dividing up zones. Dix thought about using the hatch, but the barn monks had come in from the front. Doing so, too, would bring him in on them from their rear, which – as a tactic – was working out nicely for him so far.

He crept along the long side of the barn and crouched at the corner, with a view into the courtyard. The six horses were still in place, grouped together, standing patiently. The farmhouse was away to his right, the door fully open and just one monk visible, hunkered down under the ground-floor window.

Bangs and cracks echoed across the courtyard – not shots, but impact sounds – and a moment later a robed body slumped backwards out of the door, blocking the entrance. The horses were momentarily startled and twitched their heads from side to side.

Even from across the yard, by the barn, Dix could see the wooden frame of the farming implement lying flush on top of the monk's body, from stomach to forehead, which meant the metal spikes were deeply, and probably terminally, embedded.

Vaskez, doing her thing. Looked like she'd had an opportunity to use her new toy after all.

The monk under the window turned at the noise and disappeared smartly around the back of the farmhouse. Dix left Vaskez to it. Knowing her, she wouldn't welcome any help. Anyway, he needed to find out what was going on inside the barn.

He lingered at the wide, open doors and then ducked inside and took cover by the mystery monk-mincer farming machine. Vaskez would have happily used this as well, except it was too heavy to move.

Still no sign of Drake or Alard, which was all to the good. Meant the two monks in here hadn't run them to ground yet − and the monks themselves hadn't shown at Dix's and Vaskez's interventions, which meant they didn't realise their number was now down to three. The odds were looking better by the minute.

Down at the far end, in the gloom, Dix could see a figure carefully opening the doors of the empty animal stalls and sweeping with a rifle. That was one of the monks, there.

The second then gave himself away, though not by choice − a body tumbled from the barn's upper level, robes swirling, crashing head first onto the ground in front of Dix's hiding place. There was the slightest of shouts as he fell − surprise, more than anything − and then a crack of bone, a hollow thud, and silence.

A face peered out from the upper level − it was

Drake – who clocked Dix below, gave him a thumbs-up and then withdrew from sight.

That noise brought the other monk rushing out from the stalls towards the barn entrance. He saw the body on the floor, looked back and up, assessing the upper gallery, and made for the ladder.

Dix would have sprinted from his hiding place and caught him silently from behind, but things were happening quickly now. There was the sound of a single shot, and then another, from somewhere outside. The monk turned, at the bottom of the ladder, and shouted out – "Father! In here!"

That was the element of surprise gone. Vaskez must have got tired of playing with her boobytraps. Ah well, good while it lasted.

Dix stood up. The monk by the ladder did a double-take and reached to his side for a hand-gun. And Dix plugged him with a rifle shot, right between the eyes.

Drake's head reappeared, tentatively.

"All right?" said Dix. "Sol?"

"Tucked away safely up here," said Drake. "Bloody monks, eh? Tenacious, aren't they? What's your count?"

"Two out back, two in here, one by the house, all – incapacitated." He had been going to say 'dead,' but he didn't know for sure about the first one he'd taken out, and more than that, he didn't think Sol needed to hear what they'd had to do to the fathers. Not yet, anyway. "The last one, Vaskez is on it by the sound of things."

"Nice," said Drake, and started down the ladder, shouting up to Sol to stay put for just a moment longer.

"Where's Alard?" said Dix.

The big man frowned, then spat. "Disappeared," he said, finally. "He was supposed to be covering the ladder from over that side, but as soon as these two started poking around, he was off. I saw him. Just upped and went, away down the back."

That explained the hatch at the rear of the barn.

"Coward," said Drake. "Once a run-boy, always a run-boy. He's been bitching about staying at this place for hours, you heard him."

"That can't be right. He wouldn't."

"Where is he then? I had to improvise." Drake nudged one of the fallen bodies with his foot. "And if you hadn't been here, it all might have gone down differently."

"One thing at a time," said Dix. "Here, help me clear these bodies, then let's get Sol down. He doesn't need to see this."

They carried the two bodies, shoulders and feet, into one of the nearby stalls, and called to Sol, whose face peeped out at the top of the ladder.

"Come on, mate," said Dix. "You can come down now."

"Have the bad men gone?"

Dix looked at the blood stains on the ground at the foot of the ladder and grimaced. Dragged his foot through the straw and dust to try and cover them up.

With any luck, Sol never needed to know what exactly had happened here.

"Yes, mate. Your Auntie Vaskez has been having stern words with them again." There was a loud, if indistinct, shout from outside in the courtyard. "That'll be her now," said Dix, "right as rain."

He shouldered his weapon and stepped out of the barn, with Sol and Drake behind him.

It was Vaskez all right, but she was on the ground, half-sitting, facing the barn. Drag marks from the house, and streaks of blood, indicated how she'd got there, hauled by the man standing behind her, who still had one hand at the scruff of her neck. She was bleeding badly from a head wound, while a dark stain spread from knee to ankle on one leg.

The young monk from the bar recognised Dix immediately, and jerked Vaskez's head. She groaned, but looked up and flashed her eyes at Dix.

The monk knelt slowly to his calf and pulled a knife, then straightened up and held it at Vaskez's neck.

"Stop there," said the monk. "Weapons on the floor. Give me the boy."

Dix looked round, and Drake pulled Sol behind him, protectively. The kid had the satchel with the book in it around his neck, the strap so long on him that it was resting against his knees.

"Weapons, now!" said the monk, yanking Vaskez's clothing again, so her head snapped back.

"All right," said Dix. "Take it easy." He showed the monk his rifle and placed it slowly on the ground, kicking it away at the monk's command. Drake did the same, all the while keeping Sol behind him with one arm.

"And the boy. Send him to me."

Vaskez stirred beneath him. Her voice was still clear, though she must have been in considerable pain. "Tell him to go fuck himself," she said. "I'd get up and tell him to his face, but the shithead put a bullet in my knee."

The monk hit her in the head with the hilt of his knife and her eyes glazed over.

"You will deliver the boy and the book," said the monk. "Or I will kill her." He pointed at Drake. "You, take him to one of the horses, now."

Sol wriggled out of Drake's grip and stood by his side, and the monk saw him clearly for the first time.

"Lightburst!" he said. "Come here, son."

The boy looked at the monk and Vaskez, and then back at Dix and Drake, as if searching for answers.

"Father?" he said.

"What is it, son?"

"You're hurting Auntie."

The monk shook his head dismissively. "These people are not important, Lightburst. Your future is with us. You must come now."

The boy hesitated, grasping the satchel strap tighter. "Is it written, Father?"

"Everything is written, son. It is always so. It will be. Come." He gestured with his knife.

Dix could see Sol wavering. The monk's robe was

authority. The robe was belonging. The robe was family. However twisted it was, Dix could understand that.

"It's wrong," said Dix. "What you're doing with the boy. What you're going to do. Immoral."

Insane. Deluded. Genocidal. There were plenty of other words Dix could have picked.

"Your opinion is of no consequence. It is written and it will be," said the monk.

"It is bullshit and you can fuck off," said Vaskez, stirring beneath him.

He hit her again, and Sol cried out.

"Quiet, boy!" said the monk. "You belong with us. Not these – unbelievers." He spat out the word.

Sol looked imploringly at Dix. "You read the book, Dix?" he said. "I have to come with you? The book said, didn't it?"

"Enough!" roared the monk. "There is no time. Give him to me now or she dies."

The horses bridled at the sudden noise, making a high-pitched whinny.

"I don't understand," said Sol to Dix. "How can different things be written? Why is he hurting her?"

"Because he's a bad man, Sol."

"But he's a father."

Dix had no answer to that.

Vaskez looked up once more. There was resolution in her voice. "Pick up the guns, shoot this fucker," she said. "Get the boy away."

The monk lent over and jabbed the knife in

Vaskez's other leg, in the fleshy part of her calf, and twisted it. She screamed.

"You will all die," said the monk. "There are more coming. Less forgiving than me. I just want the boy."

He twisted the knife again, and Vaskez screamed once more.

Sol dashed forward, the satchel flapping around his legs. "Auntie!"

The horses whinnied again.

"Come, Lightburst!" shouted the monk, dropping Vaskez heavily to the ground and reaching out a hand.

Alard stepped out from between the horses, handgun raised. He took four quick strides and was behind the monk before he even heard the footsteps. With Sol still a few paces away, Alard put the gun to the back of the monk's head and pulled the trigger.

In the silence afterwards, Alard wiped a fine spray of blood from his arm, as Sol reached Vaskez and hugged her around the neck. Dix came up behind him and gently extricated him, shielding him from the sight of the robed corpse with half his head missing. The boy shouldn't have had to see any of this – experience any of this.

"Where the fuck have you been?" said Drake, advancing on Alard with a raised fist.

"Easy, big man."

Drake towered over him, bunched Alard's shirt in his hand. "Fuck you, run-boy."

Alard bridled and shook Drake off. "That's what you think, still? After everything? Disappointing. Here, aren't I? Taking care of business. You're all welcome, by the way."

"Is Auntie Vaskez going to be all right?" said Sol, looking at her bloodied figure on the ground.

"Don't worry, Auntie V is just fine," growled Vaskez, lifting her head.

Auntie V looked a long way from being fine, but she was alive at least.

"We've got to go," said Alard, tucking his gun back in his waistband, and reaching down to help her. "Can you walk?"

Vaskez made a gurgling sound that could have been a laugh. "Course not," she said. "You two idiots will have to play nice and help me up."

"What's the deal, Al?" said Dix.

"Your man, Kantor, his ship's on its way. Heard it – well, felt it – from the barn. Went to check it out. Got back just in time to save all your sorry asses."

"Disturbance in the force, some shit like that?" said Drake. He raised his eyebrows at Alard. Dix knew that was about as much of an apology as Alard was going to get, and hoped it would be enough.

"You got it," said Alard, magnanimously. "But that's only the half of it. There's land traffic incoming – not horses, vehicles this time. Doubt they're friendly. We've got to hustle."

Axis, it had to be. The monk had said others were on their way.

They'd come out on top in one confrontation, but they had no time to prepare for another, and Axis guards were going to be far more heavily armed. And even less inclined to negotiate.

"We going to make it?" said Dix. "Have we got time?"

"Only one way to find out," said Alard. "Jeep's still in the barn."

Dix and Drake hoisted Vaskez by the shoulders, while Alard fetched the jeep. Vaskez flinched as they moved her, and bit back a groan when they put her in the back. "Just go," she said, through gritted teeth.

With Drake driving, and Alard riding shotgun, they roared out of the yard, down the track and into the valley. Alard pointed the way – back towards where Drake's Star had first dropped them. Dix scanned behind them, as the farm track receded into the distance. Leaned forward to Alard, in the passenger seat. "Nothing behind us," he said. "Maybe you heard wrong?"

"They're coming." Alard looked certain, grim, and put his hand behind him to reassure a moaning Vaskez, as Drake bashed the jeep over ruts and stones.

Up ahead, in a roar, a craft emerged from the clouds, circled once, and touched down. Maybe a mile away. Drake flashed a glance at Dix and grinned. Another Star-Jumper. The smuggler's ship of choice. "There's our ride!" he shouted, and gunned the engine, as everyone held on tight. Half a mile away now.

And there were the Axis guards, Dix realised. He could see rising clouds of dust from the valley behind, as vehicles converged in a rough wedge, arrowing towards them. Dix counted six – couldn't tell troop strength at this distance, but had to be at least a dozen of them, probably more. Too many to hold off.

As Drake bounced the jeep forward over the rough terrain, the pursuing vehicles made up some ground.

A couple of hundred feet ahead, the Star-Jumper's lower cargo ramp was down. Drake closed in, the jeep's tyres spitting stones out to the side. Dix could see the craft almost bobbling on the ground, straining against the firing thrusters.

The pilot was not going to wait around, and you could hardly blame them. It was a one-time deal, now or never.

Phht. Phht.

The first shots whistled past the jeep, and they all ducked instinctively. Drake – the biggest target – tucked his head into his shoulders and kept the jeep straight. Slowed down marginally to align the wheels with the oncoming ramp – Alard shouting, "Go! Go!"

A hundred feet away now.

There was a crack, and the jeep veered violently to one side, Drake struggling with the wheel to bring it back under control. "Tyre gone," he shouted, as the vehicle skidded out of alignment with the ramp. Bullet or stone? It didn't matter, result was the same. Drake's biceps bulged as he wrestled to regain the line.

Dix had a rifle, Alard a handgun, but there was no chance of them turning around in the jeep to return fire. It was as much as they could do to hold on, and avoid being thrown out by the jolting. In the back, Dix was almost lying on top of Vaskez and Sol to ground them.

Fifty feet, forty, thirty.

The jeep slowed again as Drake made his final approach to the waiting ramp. The vehicle lurched and banged as the flapping back wheel threatened to take them off course again. Drake shouted something unintelligible.

Dix raised his head and peered between Drake and Alard in the front seats. The ramp was there now, front wheels almost on, but surely too far over? Dix closed his eyes, as Drake jerked the wheel one last time.

They bounced up and on. Brakes squealed as the jeep slid onto metal decking. A jarring stop threw them all forward. Vaskez tumbled away from Dix's grip and hit the backs of the seats. There was an agonised shout. Dix's arms strained as he held onto Sol, a dead weight beneath him.

But they were inside, and the jeep had stopped moving.

There were metallic clangs as fire strafed the craft, which was already climbing vertically and then dipping and sheering. The pilot must have hit launch the second their wheels touched the ramp. Dix felt his stomach lurch.

Behind them, the ramp closed fully, and there was one final whump from an exterior explosion that rocked the craft.

The ship seemed to hang in time for a second – everyone, almost weightless, breath held. Then there was a huge roar, and a final acceleration that seemed almost vertical – like an elevator ascending.

Silence. A low hum, a steady drive. A ship under control and no longer under attack.

"Clearing Hauga now," said a crackly voice through the intercom. "Sorry about the bumps. Might be a few more, the locals seem a bit testy. Hyperspace in…" – a couple of clicking noises interrupted the pilot as he made his calculations – "let's see … one hour."

"Hauga, one star, do not recommend," said Drake, after a pregnant pause. "Last time I go on holiday anywhere with Dix."

Chapter 28

THEY LANDED ON A COLD MORNING, with their breath visible in the clear air as they stepped off the shuttle.

Vaskez was walking unaided, albeit with a limp, though the doc had said she'd regain full use of her knee if she listened to him and did her exercises. And Vaskez had said, "Does kicking Alard count?"

Sol was bouncing his ball on the dockside, though stopped as soon as he clocked the huge holding bays, transport elevators, servo-drones, bot-loaders and auto-shuttles. His eyes were wide, mouth open.

It was an overwhelming sight, to be fair, especially for a boy who'd had a sheltered upbringing. Even Dix had never seen a freight port this big before, going about its business – home produce out, off-world supplies in.

"Cool, eh, kid?" said Drake. "Fully automated."

And when Sol looked nonplussed, Drake just said,

"Robots," and did a jerky hand-and-head dance that made the kid laugh.

"What a dump," said Vaskez. "You said it was going to be nice."

"It's not all like this," said Dix, though in truth he wasn't sure what it was going to be like.

"Better not be. Been cooped up in that freighter for weeks. I need fresh air, proper food, and plenty of space to kick Alard, the doc said."

The escape from Hauga had been quick and intense; the journey since, slow and boring, though none of them had complained. Seeing as getting off the planet alive had been a close-run thing.

Milo Kantor's rescue pilot never told them his name. Just whipped them out of Hauga airspace quickly and without further trouble – decent flying, according to a grudging Drake.

The pilot had popped them out of hyperdrive a couple of hours later at a dark-flag moon-port – not on any chart Drake knew about – where he'd dropped them off at a ramshackle suite of buildings guarded by unsmiling men in black boots and tight shirts.

"All change here," the pilot had said. "You're too hot to handle any further. Milo will be in touch."

They had got Vaskez on a drip while they waited, in a windowless surgery overseen by an unshaven medic in a dirty white coat who smelled of last night's drinks.

"Is there another doctor on the base?" Dix had said.

"I am the other doctor," the man said, taking a

quick, medicinal suck from the med-bag nozzle before connecting it to Vaskez's drip. She slept – or passed out – but didn't look good. Pale, sweating. Heavy breaths. The doctor didn't look or sound much better.

Kantor had contacted Dix the next day, via the moon-port's comms room.

"Trooper Dix! Bit of a close call, my man tells me? Your Axis pals scratched his paintwork, so that's going to cost me extra." Kantor didn't look too cut up about that, and was clearly in a good mood.

"Did my info work out?" Dix had asked. "Vitlok? You found the gear?"

Kantor looked at him, benignly, hands spread. "What do you think, trooper? You're safe, aren't you? Quality accommodations and medical care?"

Dix had snorted. "We can't stay here. Vaskez needs proper medical attention. Surgery. She's in bad shape. And this place is a dump."

"Vaskez? Is that the charming one with the guns, muscles and tattoos? I liked her. You'll have to introduce me properly."

"Can you help us or not, Kantor?"

"Seems like I already have," the trader had said. "Your intel was good, and I did what I promised."

"Come on, man, you can't leave us here. I gave you a whole planet full of weapons and gear. I even threw in a last-minute Axis jeep."

"You did. And you a Federation trooper, Dix, very naughty. Who's to say what a man like myself, in the old import-export game, might do with all that lovely, state-of-the-art biotech equipment, not to mention the surveillance systems and high-calibre weaponry. Care to enlighten me as to how you knew about it? What it was all for? Why there were dead monks everywhere, that sort of thing?"

"Not really." Dix didn't have much, if any leverage, left. The knowledge of what the Haugan monks had been planning – had actually achieved – might turn into a final, get-out-of-jail card one day. But Kantor still didn't know about Sol – had just assumed five passengers were five adults – and Dix was going to keep it that way. At least for now.

"Thought not." Kantor flexed his fingers. "Playing it close to your chest, very wise. I'll make a trader of you yet, Trooper Dix. Tell you what, seeing as your tip paid off handsomely – very handsomely – I'm going to do you and your pals one more good turn. I'm feeling generous. Or call it paying it forward, you never know when I might need some Fed-trained muscle. Tell me what you need?"

So Dix had told him.

He'd been thinking about it for some time – even while holed up in the Haugan farmhouse, when it wasn't certain they would ever get off the planet. Kept it to himself, because – no point discussing something that might never happen. Plus, no one but him knew it was an option.

"A ship with a med-bay, surgical capabilities, that I can do," Kantor had said. "Although it rather depends on where you want to go? I'm guessing no one's got any paperwork? That narrows down your destinations."

When Dix told him, Kantor had just said, "Are you sure? Because that's a long trip, and once you're there, you're there, if you know what I mean? It's not exactly first choice for R&R. Bit quiet, so I'm told."

"Quiet is just fine."

Quiet is exactly what they needed. Quiet and remote, while Dix figured out what to do next.

Vaskez would doubtless be pissed off when she woke up, but at least she'd have a working knee and stitched wounds. Alard readily went along with it, if it meant putting considerable distance between himself and the Federation army. "I'm done with all of it," he'd said, and Dix could hardly blame him.

Drake? Surprisingly, just said, "Sure thing," and went off to play with Sol. Dix suspected that Drake would be all right, wherever they ended up. He was still furious about losing his ship, but – like Milo Kantor – was probably already working the angles, thinking about how to get back into business. After all, this was a reprieve for him.

For all of them, actually. Because there was no way back for Dix either – not to the life he'd had in the army, and probably not to Calisto, either. That's the first place they'd look.

Whatever the phantom Major Galloway had said or promised, Dix's life had been over the minute he had accepted her mission. Dix knew that you didn't ever escape a prison hulk. Not really. He'd just been lent some time.

Kantor had been as good as his word, and shuttled them out to meet a long-haul freighter where they had been given a couple of rooms, and the run of the gym and mess deck, with no questions asked. Vaskez had gone into surgery the same day, carried out by the resident medic, more used to dealing with crush injuries and the like, but competent enough. Smelled of aftershave and not because he'd been drinking it.

"And this concludes our business, Trooper Dix," Kantor had said, on a patched-in line from who-knewwhere. A book-lined office rather than a spa pool, this time; at least he had all his clothes on. "One day, I want to hear the whole story, but for now I think it's best we all go our separate ways. Chatter is that the Axis on Hauga are very unhappy. Bodies everywhere, apparently. Blaming the Fed for something or other and have started taking pot-shots at army vessels in disputed space. The Federation don't like that, as you can imagine, and are responding in kind. It's all getting a bit spicy. Don't suppose you know anything about it all? No? Ah well, it's been a pleasure, Trooper Dix from Calisto. Enjoy the journey, rather you than me."

They had endured rather than enjoyed the journey – three weeks in a working space freighter wasn't anyone's idea of a luxury cruise. Alard had been sick for the first week, but had gradually found his space legs, and now, finally, here they were. With Alard breathing in deeply and touching anything organic he could find, and Vaskez still complaining that the place was an absolute dump.

They hitched a ride from the port on a land-cruiser, and Sol pressed his face against the window as they left the dockside machinery behind and headed out through warehousing that stretched for miles.

Eventually, that petered out, replaced by the ring suburbs of the main city, which they skirted for another hour. And then they switched cruisers for a final run across vast steppes covered with plastic grow-tunnels, interspersed by regimented orchards and waving cereal fields.

The kid was transfixed. Endlessly asking Drake and Alard what things were, as they passed by in the cruiser. Saying "Look, Auntie!" about a hundred times as they bisected a massed herd of oversized gen-mod cows, maybe a couple of thousand strong, lolling either side of the highway. Vaskez pretended to be asleep and then, when Sol had turned back for the window, leaned forward and made a loud mooing noise in his ear. The kid squealed with alarm and then joy.

Not for the first time, Dix marvelled at Sol's good-natured adaptability. He sucked it all up, soaked it all in. Accepted everything. Never complained. He seemed to live in the moment, more than anyone Dix had ever met, and while Dix didn't want to give the Haugan monks any credit for Sol's messed-up upbringing, perhaps the whole 'It is written, it will be' business had given the kid a solid, unflappable outlook on life?

Or maybe the kid was just his own kind of person, after all. Like Alard, like all of them, in a way.

They got off the cruiser at the town terminal and trudged down the road, heading away from the centre. "East, right?" said Alard, leading the way. Dix had a rough location in mind, and figured he'd know it when he saw it.

The group fell into shape – Alard up top with Dix, Vaskez in the middle, Drake and Sol bringing up the rear. No one mentioned it, but they set their pace to Vaskez's limp – she grimaced as she tried to pick it up, scuffing her way down the suburban streets.

The rows of houses thinned out and, eventually, came in ones and twos – on larger plots surrounded by fields. And then, in the distance, there was just one, set well back from the road – a solid, two-storey, prairie house, with wooden shutters and a wraparound verandah.

Two children were playing in the yard, a boy and a girl, one at the top of a slide, rolling down stones and balls which the other was collecting in a bucket. Dix could hear them giggling as he put his hand on the gate.

They walked up the path, and the woman on the verandah looked up from her work – sorting vegetables into three crates placed in front of her.

She appraised them swiftly, eyes darting, and called to her kids. Dix would have done the same. What must they look like to her? Bruised, bandaged, limping.

Patchwork clothes. Slung rifles. One huge man, child in tow.

The kids were still playing, and the woman shouted again. "Gerrin' 'ere, you little boggers! Now!" She leaned behind her and picked up a shotgun. "And you boggin' lot, stop right there or we'll 'ave a little problem."

Alard looked at Dix, who nodded.

Yup, this was the place. That *had* to be the sarge's sister.

Chapter 29

THEY HELD a ceremony for the sarge around a fire in a paddock at the back of the property.

"Born in this house, he was," said the sarge's sister, Anuri. "We both were. But Kallax was never for 'im. Never a farmer. Knew when he left that he'd never come back. Gotta do his duty, he said, silly sod."

She took the sarge's chip-tag from Dix and placed it in a tin box, buried it in the ground. "Died saving his lads?"

Dix nodded. It's what he'd told her. Almost the truth – she didn't need to know what a waste it had been. That he might have lived if not for an incompetent officer.

"Just like 'im, always the boggin' hero." She said it kindly. "He loved his lads. Never said, but you could tell. Messages, photographs, you know?"

Dix had seen one pinned to a wall in the house. He

recognised himself in a group picture, taken somewhere on a training camp, couple of years before, he couldn't remember where. The sarge must have taken it and sent it home. "That's you, ain't it?" said Anuri. "One of his lads. Thank you for coming 'ere and tellin' me."

They placed a stone marker by the buried tin. Anuri's husband, a strong, quiet man with farmer's hands, had chiselled the inscription. The sarge's name was Jago.

Somehow, that didn't seem right to Dix. Not big enough for the man, not solid enough. He'd always be the sarge.

"And the boy?" said Anuri. "War orphan, you say?"

Another white lie that blurred the truth, but one told for the best reasons. The only survivor of a mission gone wrong, is how Dix had presented Sol. The sister had assumed that it was the sarge's mission – an official army op – and Dix hadn't corrected her. Jago had died and Sol needed protection, that was the story she believed.

Or perhaps she didn't care if it was true or not? Maybe Anuri looked at the strange boy with the trusting eyes – saw how he unfurled as he played with her two – saw he needed a family that wasn't three banged-up troopers and a hulking smuggler – and then talked in a low voice to her husband.

"He can stay," she said. "Maybe he'll be the farmer Jago never was." Dix mumbled his thanks, but Anuri wasn't finished. Nor was she entirely fooled. Of course not, she was the sarge's sister.

"You can stay, too," she said. "At least, while your friend recovers." She looked over at Vaskez who was hobbling away from the fire. "Not going back, I take it? To the army? Thought not. Just tell me, you're not bringing trouble to my house?"

"No one knows we're here," said Dix. Another white lie – hoping Milo Kantor didn't count. "No one can trace us." He was on firmer ground with that one – without their chip-tags, they had no identity for anyone to uncover. "Mission's over, but we're not going back. We can't go back."

Anuri looked at him for a while in the fading light. "Boggin' army took my brother," she said, finally. "Reckon we'll call it even."

Dix left Anuri and her husband staring into the flames and made his way back to the house. Sol had made friends already, careering around the paddock, chased by two strapping farm children. Alard, Drake and Vaskez were sitting on the verandah, giving the family – and Dix – some space. Wasn't their sarge, their brother.

"The kid can stay," said Dix. "It's for the best."

Drake started to say something, but thought better of it. Just nodded. "I'll miss the little guy," he said.

"He'll like it," said Alard. "He needs kids his own age – a place to grow up properly."

"You tell them about his little modifications?" said Vaskez. "All the crap inside him?"

"Obviously not, but I'm going to stick around for a while, make sure he's all right. And I've got a few ideas."

Dix still had the book – secure in the satchel, tucked under a bed in the farmhouse. And he knew a guy, Milo Kantor, who knew lots of other guys. There was information in *The Book of Light* about Hauga, and information they had gleaned about the Axis, that might interest a man like Kantor. Such as the discovery of rare-galaxy minerals on Hauga, for a start. A man like Kantor was always looking for new markets and outlets, where the rewards might outweigh the considerable risks.

In return, Dix hoped Kantor could rustle up a tame or disgraced, but eminently qualified, bio-medical scientist to take a look at Sol. Check him out, neutralise the bad stuff, give him the all-clear. Dix didn't even know if any of that was possible, but it had to be worth a try.

And if it was bad news, well – let the kid live a normal life here for as long as possible.

"You can all stay, too," said Dix. "For a while, at least."

"The countryside? Hell, no," said Vaskez. "Look at it."

The fire danced in the dying light, as the edges of the paddock dissolved into darkness. A few lights from the distant town could be seen, but otherwise it was dark and still – just the creak of rocking seats on the verandah and the chirrup of crickets, a hoot of an owl. Nothing like the horrors of Vitlok or Hauga.

Serene, beautiful, restful.

"Dump," said Vaskez. "Soon as I can walk properly, I'm out of here. Me and Drake have got a plan."

"Makes a change from relying on me," said Dix, grinning.

"Difference is," said Vaskez, "we've thought our plan through."

"That freighter port," said Drake. "There isn't one in the galaxy where someone isn't making a few credits on the side. There'll be a bar – there's always a bar – and I'm going to hang around and listen to the big mouths, spot me an opportunity."

"Back to smuggling?" said Dix. He was almost disappointed in the big man.

"Let's say, facilitating. With Auntie here as muscle." Drake fended off a half-hearted punch from Vaskez. "We only need a leg up, no offence" – another half-punch – "until we can earn enough for a ride out of here."

"It's a long way back. They don't call it the outer rim for nothing. Where will you go, anyway?"

"Wherever my Star went," said Drake. "Fucker doesn't get to steal my baby and just disappear. There'll be a trail, and Vaskez here is going to help me track her down."

"No more army for you then, Vaskez?" Dix had to ask.

She had volunteered. She was the only one of them who could potentially return. Not sure under what circumstances, or what story she would have to tell, but it was at least a possibility for her.

Vaskez was dismissive. "Remember, back when, I called this for the shit mission it was? Which I wouldn't mind – because that's just what the army's like, shit mission after shit mission. Except someone tied our hands behind our backs from the outset, lied their faces off, and then left us to die. Ash, Galloway, doesn't matter who. I say, fuck 'em. I gave them eight good years, and never got anywhere. Going to go freelance for a bit. Drake says there's money in it. Plus, the big guy here has something you don't have."

She looked at Drake fondly, and Dix looked in turn at the pair of them. A budding romance, surely not?

"A ship of his own, full of badass weapons," said Vaskez. "Just as soon as we can find it."

Of course, he might have known.

"Guess that only leaves you, Alard?"

"I'd like to point out the irony of you lot deciding to become deserters and outlaws, after giving me all that grief. I told you it sucked being a Fed soldier."

Vaskez jeered at him, though the statement hit harder with Dix.

He had tried to be a good soldier. He'd trained well and fought well, and covered his mates' backs. The only time he'd ever disobeyed an order had been to save his unit, and look where that had got him? Even so, the sarge would never have quit on the army – but the army had quit on the sarge, and on Dix. If that now made him a deserter, so be it.

"I'm staying," said Alard, when the back and forth with Vaskez had died down. "Can't take any more space rides, not for a long while. Besides, the husband says there's work for me on the farm, if I want it. Feet on the ground, hands in the soil – "

"Dung on the clothes, turnips for breakfast," crowed Vaskez.

Alard persevered. "Just be nice not to have to run for a while. Or be shot at. Use my skills for people who appreciate them."

"You gonna talk to the cabbages for him, Al?"

"Been doing that for the last few weeks, V." Alard winked at Dix. "Get more sense out of the worms than you, that's for sure."

The gentle bickering began again, but it no longer had an edge. There was an underlying tone between all of them now. Respect, certainly. Trust, for sure. Friendship, of a kind. Their pot-luck crew had turned into a tight unit. Maybe the army had given them something, after all?

Dix left them to it and went to find Sol, who was drinking from a glass at the kitchen table with the other two kids.

"It's milk, Dix," he said. "It's from a cow, but it's all right to drink. The cows don't mind."

You had to love that kid.

"I know," said Dix. "Cows are good like that. Mind if we have a talk?"

They walked outside into the night air and stood by the fire. Sol couldn't get enough of the flames, higher than any he'd ever seen, and threw a couple more sticks on, hopping from foot to foot as the sparks flew.

"Do you like it here?" said Dix.

"They've got horses!" said Sol. "You can ride them!" His eyes were wide at the very thought.

"Sounds great. So, you like it then?"

Sol considered the question, reverting to that equable way he had. Neutral face that gave no hint of what he was thinking as he worked through the variables.

"I think it's boggin' brilliant," he said finally, in a considered tone.

Great. Less than a day, kid was a local.

"Only, you could stay here," said Dix. "If you like. Ride the horses. Go to school, even."

"I could?" Sol thought about this, and then said something Dix didn't expect. "I'm not going home, am I?"

Dix's throat caught at that. Home? What kind of home had the kid ever had? That prison of a monastery on Vitlok, with self-serving monks who saw him as a weapon. But it was the only home he'd ever known, with the only family he'd ever had.

"No, Sol, you're not," said Dix.

"And I won't see the fathers again, will I?"

Not if Dix had anything to say about it. Not if they could make a life for him out here in the sticks, far from the politics of trade, expansion and power. Far from those who would do the boy harm. Far away from the bad men.

That wasn't a given, of course, even if Dix could keep him hidden here on Kallax. There was danger in the boy himself, whether or not anyone ever found him. Lightburst might still live up to his name. But this was a start, and Dix would do his best to keep the light contained.

"I think it's time you had a proper family," said Dix. "How does that sound?"

"If it's written, then it will be," said Sol. "Isn't that right, Dix?"

Dix thought about the easy answer, but the kid deserved to know the truth about the world, if he was going to live a normal life. Dix had had enough of *The Book of Light*. He was going to bury it deep in the paddock and forget about it, unless and until he found someone who could undo its damage.

"Nothing is written, kid," said Dix. "We all get to choose what we do with our lives. You can start today."

And Sol smiled, leaned down to pick up a stick, and threw it into the fire.

THE END

———

Want another Sci-Fi read? Why not grab a **free short story** introducing you to the 'Odyssey Earth' trilogy – a feelgood, character-led space opera with heart and humour.

Just scan the QR code to download the free short story.

Author's note: story background

Ideas for books come to me in all sorts of ways – the first germ of what became *Orphan Planet* was a disastrous camping trip one of my sons went on; *The Wrong Stop* came out of a lifetime spent travelling around Europe on trains, and wondering about the people I met on board. (I don't think any of them were aliens, but you never know.)

And sometimes a single thought is enough. Back in 2024, as I hurtled through the south of France overnight on a sleeper-train, a fully formed sentence popped into my head, unbidden.

'Their unit, OneSquad, had been fighting hard all day across difficult terrain.'

That's the first sentence of *Special Delivery*, though I didn't know it at the time. But as the train jolted, and my fellow passengers snored, and I failed to get to sleep, a full paragraph's worth of sentences followed – about a group of troopers having as uncomfortable a time as I was, though featuring considerably more mud, blood and explosives.

When the train finally stopped the next morning, I wrote the sentences down and then put them to one side, because I was in the south of France, it was sunny and warm, and there was a *café au lait* with my name on it. And the sentences stayed to one side, because the book I was actually writing then was *Third Loch From the Sun*, which had an altogether different vibe. No one gets blown up in the first few pages, put it like that.

Six months later, though, wondering what to write next, I dusted off my train-fugue sentences and still liked the look of them. But the story they told seemed to be much more hard-edged than I would usually write – a military Sci-Fi action adventure about space troopers on a secret mission. And if I don't know very much about the astrophysics of space travel, then I know even less about military matters, so I wondered how sensible it was to keep going.

Then I remembered, I'm a Sci-Fi writer. I can just make it all up.

The story took hold as it developed, and I became invested in the lives of these troopers and the others who were drawn into their world. They all cursed a whole lot more than I was expecting, so apologies if you've come straight from *Orphan Planet*, where (intentionally) the worst anyone says is 'bloody,' and even then, only very occasionally. But I didn't think it would be realistic to have soldiers treading carefully around their language – though I did have some fun with it when they first encountered Sol and tried not to swear so much.

The story is also darker and more gruesome at times than anything in any of my other books so far. And again, that seemed to fit the characters and their mission, though I did worry about putting some of you off. If you came for the feelgood banter and the lolz ("It's a Rex Burke, it'll be fine"), I appreciate you might not be so keen on the graphic fight scenes and the casual violence.

In the end, though, having read to the end, I hope you think that *Special Delivery* is a worthy addition to the roster. I'd say it still is recognizably a Rex Burke book – full of banter, laughs, scrapes and mysteries, with a healthy dollop of found-family vibes, and an upbeat ending. I think so anyway, but I guess you'll tell me if not?

The other thing to say about the book is that, like *Star Wars*, it's set in a galaxy far, far away. It's not necessarily in the future, all the characters are human, though it's never explicitly said, and obviously, they're all speaking English. Look, you never question it in *Star Wars*.

I like that set-up, because it gives an author *carte blanche* to make more stuff up without having to worry about real-world accuracy – though I did consult the supremely knowledgeable David Clegg (@davidcauthor.bsky.social) about military ranks, discipline and weaponry. He knows it all, and writes military Sci-Fi too, so you should check him out.

But – for my own amusement, and for yours too, I hope – I also added anachronistic and other popular culture references that wouldn't make any sense in that galaxy or universe. Why? Because it makes me laugh when I drop them throughout a book, and now I've told you, you can go back and look for the ones you've missed.

In no particular order, there are namechecks for a character in *Aliens*, and in the Demi Moore movie *A Few Good Men*. Vaskez (doh!) quotes a line from *Casablanca*, and Ash, the sleeper agent on Hauga, one from the Liam Neeson *Taken* movies. There are also throwaway lines and references to the Australian TV soap, *Neighbours*, and the classic Ferrero Rocher chocolate ads, and a whole planetary naming system taken from the IKEA furniture catalogue. I told you, it's fun, plus I can't help myself.

There's no meaning behind the names Dix and Drake, while Sol – instead of Lightburst – speaks for itself. But I did want to find a name that suited one character's unique capabilities, and alighted upon the Arabic word *al'ard*, which I am reliably informed by the internet means 'the Earth.'

So, that's the end of my special delivery – a different kind of book for me but one I hope you've still enjoyed. Will we go back and see how Dix, Sol and the rest are getting on? Drake, for one, wants to get his beloved Star-Jumper back, and Vaskez would happily kick Major Galloway's arse, so it's not like the story isn't continuing out there in that galaxy far, far away. Maybe I just need to take another long train ride…

Rex Burke, April 2025

About the Author

Rex Burke is a SciFi writer based in North Yorkshire, UK.

When he was young, he read every one of those yellow-jacketed Victor Gollancz hardbacks in his local library. That feeling of out-of-this-world amazement never left him – and keeps him company as he writes his own Sci-Fi adventures.

When he's not writing, he travels – one way or another, he'll get to the stars, even if it's just as stardust when his own story is done.

Find out more

To find out more, and grab a free short story, visit Rex's website – rexburke.com

www.ingramcontent.com/pod-product-compliance
Lightning Source LLC
Chambersburg PA
CBHW030540190726
48283CB00006B/1953